Dominic laughed. "I think I'm in love." He assessed her from the short-cut hair framing her angry brown face to the wool cape covering her blue gown, to her small-heeled slippers.

"I demand you restore me to the frigate, immediately!"

Bowing to the hellcat with a courtly grace, he gestured to the door. "If you will step inside, mademoiselle."

"Did you not hear me?" Clare stormed.

The grin that spread across Dominic's handsome face had warmed the hearts of females from Cuba to Spain, and the arms that scooped her up and tossed her back over his shoulder, like a silken sack of meal, were strong.

"Put me down!" She pounded his back with her fists.

He slapped her across her blue-gowned behind and swung around to face his quarter master. "Gaspar, see to it that the lady and I are not disturbed."

Then he carried the furious captive into his quarters and shut out the world with a kick of his booted foot.

Romances by **Beverly Jenkins**

CAPTURED
JEWEL
WILD SWEET LOVE
WINDS OF THE STORM
SOMETHING LIKE LOVE
A CHANCE AT LOVE
BEFORE THE DAWN
ALWAYS AND FOREVER
TAMING OF JESSE ROSE
THROUGH THE STORM
TOPAZ
INDIGO
VIVID
NIGHT SONG

CAPTURED

BEVERLY JENKINS

AVON

An Imprint of HarperCollinsPublishers

AVON BOOKS
An Imprint of HarperCollins*Publishers*
10 East 53rd Street
New York, New York 10022-5299

Copyright © 2009 by Beverly Jenkins
ISBN 978-0-06-154779-9
www.avonromance.com

First Avon Books paperback printing: October 2009

Avon Trademark Reg. U.S. Pat. Off. and in Other Countries, Marca Registrada, Hecho en U.S.A.
HarperCollins® is a registered trademark of HarperCollins Publishers.

Printed in the U.S.A.

10 9 8 7 6 5 4 3 2 1

For Schreba

On Thursday last arrived from the coast of Africa, the brig *Royal Charlotte* with a parcel of extremely fine, healthy, well limb'd Gold Coast slaves, men, women, boys and girls. They are to be seen on the vessel at Taylor's Wharf. Apply to Thomas Teckle Taylor, Samuel & William Vernon. . . .

Newport Gazette, June 6, 1763

CAPTURED

Prologue

Autumn 1774

It was beginning to rain, so Dominic LeVeq pushed the white stallion to a faster pace in order to cover the remaining half mile to his late father's estate on the outskirts of Paris. The rising wind lifted the hem of his greatcoat like a sail while the dark clouds gathering overhead mirrored his mood. The solicitors were supposed to read his father's will this afternoon, and if the rumors were true, Dominic's half brother Eduard would inherit everything. Dom didn't mind. He'd spent the past twenty years sailing the world at his father's side, and their shared adventure was far more dear to him than land and stone. What he did mind, and the reason for his dark mood, were the rumors of Eduard's dastardly plans for their father's three hundred workers on the island of Martinique.

He reached the sprawling stone castle just as thunder sounded and the skies opened up to release a pelting, cold downpour. Handing the stallion's reins to one of the stable boys, he hurried up the stone steps to the heavy front door.

Inside, he was met by the family's oldest retainer, the butler Martine Rousseau.

"Dominic!" he exclaimed, pulling the younger man into his aged arms. "Thank you for coming. Thank you." The relief in his voice was apparent.

"Thank you for sending the note down to the dock. How are you, Martine?"

The butler stepped back and viewed Dominic with deep affection before taking his wet cloak. "I'm getting old, but still here by the grace of God. It is good to see you."

"You as well. How did you know I was in port?"

"Cook saw your ship down on the wharf a few days ago when she was buying fish. When I learned the reading of the estate papers would be today, I sent the boy to find you with the hopes that you were still here."

"I'm glad you did."

The old, dark-skinned man shook his head sadly. "It was a terrible day for the House of LeVeq when your father passed away, but this day—this day . . ." He seemed unable to find the words to continue. "Your brother and Nancine are in the study. They will not be pleased that you are here."

"Then nothing has changed."

Martine smiled and patted him on the shoulder. "Go, represent your father's word. They certainly will not."

Dominic nodded grimly and set off for the study. His boots echoed loudly against the marble floors as he made his way through the silent, dimly lit halls. Were it not for Martine's summons, he would never have willingly entered the LeVeq ancestral home. He had no connection to the home established by the original duke during the fifteenth century, or to the ornately framed portraits of his descendants lining the walls. He was the bastard child of Antoine and his beloved mistress, Dominic's mother, Marie, a manumitted slave. Dominic had visited this place a few times in his youth, but his mother of course had not. The only reason Antoine's wife, Nancine, had allowed Dominic inside was that her husband wouldn't visit without him. When Marie died on Martinique under suspicious circumstances, Antoine turned his back on Nancine, Eduard, and France forever and took to the sea. His death in England last month from pneumonia had come as a shock. Dominic had been certain the old man would live forever. He hadn't attended the funeral because he knew Nancine would not have allowed his presence, so he and the other seamen who'd called Antoine LeVeq friend had honored his passing from afar.

When he opened the door to the study, one of the lawyers was reading the will aloud, but at Dominic's unannounced entrance he stopped and stared, as did the others seated about the elegant book-lined room. "I see you started without me," Dominic stated easily, closing the door behind him.

Eduard LeVeq shot to his feet. "What are you doing here?"

"It is good to see you, too, *mon frere*," Dominic

tossed back sarcastically, before turning cold eyes on his late father's wife. "Nancine," he voiced with cool politeness. He didn't expect her to acknowledge him. She didn't disappoint, so he answered Eduard's question, "I came to hear the will."

The two lawyers quickly looked to each other in what appeared to be panic before regaining their composure. Their reactions put Dominic on notice that something was indeed afoot.

Eduard, whose blond hair and brown eyes mimicked his mother, Nancine's, replied bitterly, "This has nothing to do with you. Leave us."

Dominic countered, "I am a son of the House of LeVeq, and whether our father left me everything or nothing, I have the right to be here." And he took a seat.

Eduard's lips tightened. He looked as if he might say more, but Dominic ignored him and turned to the lawyers. "Continue."

Neither man was familiar to Dominic. During Antoine LeVeq's lifetime, all legal matters had been handled by a cadre of London-based solicitors who were also friends, but Eduard and Nancine had probably terminated their services even before the soil settled over the old duke's grave.

The lawyer who'd been interrupted by Dom's entrance cleared his throat. "As I was saying, everything has been left to you, Eduard." He turned to Dominic and repeated pointedly, "Everything." Moving his focus back to the smug-faced Eduard, he added, "I have looked into the situation in the Indies as you requested, and the courts agree that because there is nothing in the will freeing the Blacks, they are now owned by you."

Dominic froze. "What Blacks?"

Eduard answered, "The ones in Martinique."

"Father freed them the day I was born."

Eduard's ice blue eyes glittered. "Not according to the courts, and as soon as these papers are sealed and filed, they belong to me."

Dominic shot the lawyers a deadly stare, and they looked so uncomfortable they wouldn't or couldn't meet his gaze.

Eduard continued smoothly, "As Father's only legitimate son, I inherit those Blacks, and although he may not have cared whether those cane fields produced a profit, I do. I will be dismissing the present overseers, who are obviously too soft, and replace them with ones who will work those Africans from sunup to death if they have to."

Dominic was on him in an instant and dragged him by his coat collar across the desk so there'd be no mistaking what he was about to say. "Go through with this heinous plan and I will do everything in my power to break you!"

Eduard sneered, "How? You're the bastard of a slave. You have no power."

Dominic flung him away. Fury raging within like a gale, he took in the wide-eyed lawyers and then Nancine, who offered him a nasty little smile.

To prevent himself from doing something that would dishonor his father's name, Dominic turned and exited the study without another word.

As he regained the foyer, Martine appeared, took

one look at Dominic's furious face, and asked with concern, "It is true then?"

Dominic nodded tightly.

Martine was from Martinique and had family members working in the LeVeq fields. "He is going to enslave my daughters? My grandchildren?"

"Only if he can sail to Martinique faster than I. Is the *Marie* still docked?" he asked, referring to Antoine's schooner.

"As far as I know, yes. You are going to stop this, *non*?"

"Oh yes, and if you would like to come along, you are welcome."

"When and where?" Age seemed to have slid away from Martine's face. He stood before Dominic with determination in his eyes and declared, "I will kill him myself before letting him enslave my grandchildren."

Dominic gave him the name of a tavern near the docks where the *Marie* was moored. "Meet me there in three days. I should have a crew in place by then."

Eduard suddenly appeared at the far end of the hall and barked, "What are you doing still here! Get out before I call the gendarmes!"

Dominic ignored him. "Three days, Martine."

"I'll be there."

Dominic strode back out in the rain.

Three days later, the *Marie* and a Spanish ship named the *Isabella* left France for the island of Martinique.

The voyage across the brooding Atlantic Ocean took weeks, giving Dominic ample time to weigh the ramifications of the actions he intended to set into motion. He knew in his heart that the rightness of his plan far outweighed any consequences Eduard or the legal authorities might demand in response. And besides, in order to mete out any punishment, they'd have to find him first. Oceans covered the world, and on every continent in between there were places to hide.

The two, three-hundred-ton vessels arrived at midday. After dropping anchor offshore, Dominic and crews from both ships were met on the beach by a group of workers and the LeVeq overseer, a fugitive slave from the American colonies named Washington Julian.

"Welcome home, Dominic, but I thought you weren't returning until autumn."

"Seeing my brother warranted a change in plans."

Julian asked warily, "What's happened?"

Dominic explained, and when he was done, Washington swore, "That bastard. These people have been free for decades."

"I know. Do you think you can get everyone gathered so I can relate Eduard's intentions?"

"Of course."

Less than an hour later, Dominic looked out over the assemblage of people he'd grown up among and told them of Eduard's terrible plan for their future.

Gasps of disbelief were heard. A woman cried out in fear. Men raised their voices in anger.

Dom sought to calm them. "My father would rise from the grave if he knew of Eduard's perfidy, so the ships are here to take away all who wish to leave here."

A murmur went through the crowd.

"But where will we go?" asked a woman named Anna Spelling. He knew her well. She'd been a friend of his mother, Marie. Beside Anna stood her young grandson, Richmond.

"East. And once we arrive, we'll have to start over. We'll have to clear fields, plant, build homes."

A murmur went through the crowd.

"It will not be easy, but it will not be slavery."

And with that, the decision was made.

It took two days of around-the-clock work to load the ships. Caged chickens, milk cows, and oxen shared space on the decks with axes, plows, and the machetes used for harvesting sugarcane, along with seed and many barrels of fresh water. Household items like crockery and cooking pots were taken aboard, along with the personal items of the families. Dominic, with the help of his crew, removed some of the more treasured furniture from the house his parents had resided in, particularly their bed and his father's weathered but stately desk, and added them to the other items in the *Marie*'s hold. Everyone worked with urgency because they had no idea if Eduard had already set sail from France to review his newly inherited Martinique property and slaves.

By the end of the second day they were finished loading all the two ships could carry safely, but

Dominic had one last thing to do. He knew his brother would be furious to find the place deserted and the workers gone, but to make sure it would not be easy to bring the vast sugarcane plantation back to life, he set fire to almost everything that remained. He hadn't the heart to torch his parents' home.

Now, standing on the deck of the *Marie*, Dominic LeVeq watched the flames glow bright against the night sky, then he and his people sailed east to sanctuary.

Chapter 1

April 1778
Atlantic Ocean

Clare Sullivan didn't care for sea voyages. Traveling by ship brought back memories of the slaver she'd been forced to endure after being kidnapped from her home during her seventh summer. Torn away from her family and the life she'd come to know, she found the fetid, suffocating journey terrifying. Now, at the age of thirty, she'd made several more journeys across that same Atlantic but as a servant to her mistress, Violet Sullivan. Violet and her thirty-year-old twin brother, Victor, were residents of Savannah, Georgia, and like a majority of their colonial neighbors, had ancestral ties to England. The journey they were on now had been taken to visit the gravesite of a distant Sullivan relative who'd died recently. With that accomplished they were heading home back to Savannah. Clare couldn't be happier even while she dreaded every nautical mile.

Clare tidied up the small compartment she and

her mistress were sharing below deck. She was certain this would be the last voyage for some time to come, though, and that pleased her as well. With the colonists fighting the crown for independence, the coastal blockades instituted by both sides in the conflict were making seafaring dangerous. The upstart American government had issued letters of marque to hundreds of rebel sea captains, sanctioning the boarding and confiscation of any British ship and its cargo caught in American territorial waters.

"Afternoon, Miss Clare."

In the open doorway stood the ship's purser, a young British seaman with pleasant enough features and a ready smile. "Afternoon, Mr. Purcell." Violet was above deck taking in fresh air on the arm of the captain.

"We'll be in Georgia in just a few more days, miss."

"That is good news, but I wish the time would pass more quickly," she replied.

"I do as well. My mum and dad live in Virginia, and I'm anxious to see how they've fared while I've been away."

They were sailing the traditional southern passage that led from England to the Azores, where they'd put in for supplies and fresh water, and were now sailing west to the coastal waters of Florida and Georgia. Their British-owned ship, manned by a merchant captain and his crew, was not the fastest vessel on the water, but it was formidable enough to make any privateers looting and pillaging on behalf of the rebel colonists think twice about attacking.

"Your family are loyalists then?"

He nodded. "My father said the crown would whip the rebels in a fortnight, but I guess he was wrong."

"I think many people underestimated them." Most importantly the crown, Clare knew. The rebel army had scored quite a few solid victories to date. Last October's defeat of the British army at Saratoga and the surrender of six thousand of its soldiers, also called regulars, stunned not only England but the rest of Europe as well.

"Will you be joining us for supper?" he asked.

She picked up the day gown Violet had carelessly tossed onto one of the chairs and hung it back in the small wardrobe where her simple clothes hung also. "That is up to Miss Sullivan."

"I hope you will. We rarely get to dine with women as lovely as you and Miss Sullivan."

At that moment, Violet entered on the arm of the tall, barrel-chested captain, a man named Davies. Violet, dressed as richly as if she were home in Savannah, took one look at Purcell and a longer, more pointed one at Clare before asking, "Is something the matter, Mr. Purcell?"

"No, ma'am. I was just asking if Miss Clare would be joining us at supper."

"Clare is not a miss, Mr. Purcell, she's a slave. We don't want her thinking above her station, now, do we?" she asked in her sugar-sweet, Savannah drawl.

Red-faced with embarrassment, he gave a quick

shake of his head and mumbled, "No, ma'am."

The smile she gave him was as frosty as the violet eyes for which she'd been named. "Good. Clare will be joining us, but as my servant, nothing more."

He nodded, careful to keep his eyes away from Clare's emotionless face.

The captain, his blue eyes a stark contrast to his snow white wig, cleared his throat. "I'm sure you have work to do, Purcell?"

Offering a hasty nod, the young purser exited.

Violet studied Clare for a silent beat longer before turning her attention to the captain. "Thank you for your excellent company, Captain Davies. The fresh air was bracing."

"My pleasure, Miss Sullivan. I'll see you and Mr. Sullivan at supper."

He bowed solicitously and was gone.

In the silence that followed, Violet undid the strings of her green satin bonnet and set it on a chair. "I believe that young Purcell is interested in you, dear Clare. Surely he knows that's impossible."

"I'm sure he does."

Violet's smile was smug. "All of that walking above decks has exhausted me. Fetch that folio of Mr. Shakespeare's from the trunk and read me a bit of *Romeo and Juliet* until I fall asleep."

Someone else might have pointed out to Violet that she had risen less than three hours earlier, and that one of those hours had been spent getting her properly dressed and applying her face paint, but Clare remained silent and retrieved the volume as instructed.

"I'll rise in time for supper of course," Violet said. "I wouldn't want to disappoint the captain. Have you seen my brother of late?"

"No."

"Probably holed up below gambling with the sailors."

Clare didn't respond.

"Come, help me out of this gown. I'm sure he'll find us in time for the meal."

Dressed in a beautiful, navy blue gown, Clare sat at the table and ate silently while Violet and her twin brother, Victor, made polite conversation with Captain Davies. In spite of her presence, Clare knew Violet would not tolerate her adding to the conversation, so she concentrated on her meal. The food was bland and boiled, making her long for home and the well-seasoned fare prepared by the Sullivans' indentured cook, Birgit.

"So, Clare," Victor asked, "what's your opinion on the rebels?"

She glanced up. Victor was a doctor by trade and a decent enough person, when he wasn't gambling. "I have no opinion, sir."

"Oh come now. I'm sure you've shared conversations with that seditious aunt of mine."

The seditious aunt in question was his aunt Theodora Sullivan, commonly known as Teddy. Teddy was a walking scandal, from her penchant for men's clothing and tobacco-filled pipes, to her unabashed support of General Washington and the rebel army. Violet dearly wanted to have Teddy exiled to a place where no one knew the Sullivan name; an asylum for the insane perhaps, but over the years Teddy had proven to be more than a match for her niece in both smarts and spirit.

But before Clare could respond, Purcell burst into the cabin. "A schooner, Captain! Closing fast."

"Their flag?"

"French."

Davies tossed down his napkin and rose to his feet. "If you all would excuse me. You might want to return to your cabins until we learn whether they are friend or foe."

Violet's eyes widened. "Foe? Are we in danger?"

"The French are allied with the rebels now and have issued many letters of marque," Davies explained.

"So the schooner could be manned by pirates?" Victor asked, sounding alarmed.

"We'll see. Please, go to your cabins. I'll send down word as soon as I'm able."

On the deck of the *Marie*, Dominic LeVeq eyed the frigate through his spyglass. "She's a good size, Gaspar."

Gaspar, the *Marie*'s quartermaster and Dominic's best friend, nodded. "Aye, and filled with gold if the rumors are true."

Dominic was dressed in a red jacket he'd taken off a British general. "I count at least sixty guns. Makes our thirty seem paltry at best."

"But we're faster."

"And far more handsome."

Gaspar laughed. "That we are."

"Shall we pay her court?"

"Aye."

Dominic shouted to his eighty-man crew, "Raise the flag! Let's show them who we really are!"

The men cheered as one. The French flag was hauled down, and the black standard with its pitchfork flanked by two sets of devil horns was run up in its stead.

Below decks on the frigate, as the sounds of the cannons boomed again and again, Clare prayed to all the gods and Ancestors she could remember for deliverance.

"I can't stand this!" Violet cried, hands over her ears.

Clare did not fault Violet's reaction. The battle had been raging for over an hour. Not knowing how the fight fared only added to their fears. A short while ago, at the request of the captain, Victor had hurriedly left them to lend what help he could to the injured. Davies had stationed an armed guard outside their cabin's door for protection, but Clare hoped the situation would not come to that.

The cannons were firing nonstop now, and Violet wailed over the thundering din, "Surely a pirate vessel is no match for a ship of this size!"

"If that is what it is!" They had no verification that the attackers were pirates, or how large the opposing attacking ship might be, but if the length of the battle was any indication, the frigate was engaged in a formidable fight.

Suddenly three deafening concussions rocked the ship so forcefully both women were thrown to the floor. As they struggled to right themselves, they could hear above them the raised voices of shouting men meld with the thunder of running feet. Muskets were being fired. Captain Davies could be heard roaring orders as a cacophony of competing noises filled the air.

Clare didn't need to be up on the deck to know what the sounds meant. She said ominously, "We've been boarded."

"My god! No!"

Although terrified by the ramifications, Clare vowed to keep her wits about her.

"I have to hide my jewels!"

Clare looked around for a suitable place when suddenly the noise ceased. A silence as eerie as the grave raised the hairs on the back of her neck.

A pounding on the door caused the women to jump fearfully.

Violet snapped at Clare, "I expect you to protect me with your life, you hear!"

Clare nodded curtly.

"Miss Sullivan! It's Mr. Purcell. The captain requests your presence."

Clare hurried over and threw off the bolt. Opening the door, she froze with alarm at the sight of the blood and gunpowder staining Purcell's weary face and uniform.

"You ladies have to come with me."

Clare glanced over at Violet, who asked in a shaky voice, "Where?"

"Please ma'am, no questions. Just come."

Neither woman wanted to leave the safety of the cabin, but apparently they had no choice.

Above decks they were assaulted by the smells of men, battle, and death. The way was littered with splintered masts, downed rigging, and injured men being tended to by the ship's doctor and a grim-faced Victor Sullivan. At the sight of his sister and Clare he stopped his ministrations, silently acknowledged their passing with a tight-lipped nod, and returned to his patient. Only then did Clare see the shabbily dressed armed man standing guard over him.

Purcell led them up another deck, bringing into view the attacking schooner bobbing next to the frigate. Grappling hooks stretched from its decks to the frigate's rails, as did wide planks of wood she assumed had been employed in the boarding. The sight of the schooner and the scores of dirty-faced men looking on was frightening enough, but the black flag flapping malevolently in the breeze, verifying that the men were indeed pirates, almost made her knees buckle. Swallowing her fear, she stiffened her spine and focused her attention back on deck, where a dozen or so ragtag pirates held muskets, swords, and knives on the defeated-looking British seamen.

Clare could see the fury on the face of Captain Davies. He was being questioned by a tall man wearing the red coat of the British Army. The garment was worn and grimy, but the face of its owner as he turned to view their approach was so darkly handsome and arresting it looked to have been sculpted by a god's own hand. His chin was covered by a beard that appeared weeks old and his eyes were black as night. Those same eyes brushed hers and widened with surprise. She watched him look her slowly up and down. Holding on to the edges of her cloak, she willed herself to remain still. It was her hope that if she did not call attention to herself, the ink black eyes would settle elsewhere, but it was not to be.

"Your name, mademoiselle?" he asked in French-inflected English. Around his neck he wore a length of black lace. Tied to each end was an ornate black pistol. The hue of his face showed him to be a son of Mother Africa, but the hair pulled back into a queue belonged to a mulatto.

Violet answered coldly, "That's none of your concern."

Eyes still on Clare, he asked, "Are you a slave?"

"I told you—"

The angry look he shot Violet silenced her instantly. Ignoring her now, he said to Davies, "If the mademoiselle has trunks, send someone to fetch them."

Clare felt sick.

"Now, look here," Davies countered. "This young woman is under my protection."

"So was the crown's gold," the pirate offered, "but you couldn't protect that, either."

Clare had no idea that the frigate was carrying gold but she watched as wooden strongboxes outfitted on poles were being transported by members of the pirate's crew over to the moored, three-masted schooner.

"Is that the lot of them?" the pirate captain called out to his men.

One crewman, a tall, shirtless man with a face the color of obsidian and the form of a Titan, replied, "Of the gold, aye. We'll start on the grain and guns momentarily."

His captain nodded approvingly, then turned back to Davies. "Please relay our thanks to the crown for the gold, and the rebels thank you for the guns."

"I'll see you hanged for this."

"I'm sure you think you might."

Clare hoped she'd been forgotten in the bantering, but her bad fortune held.

The pirate bowed. "After you, mademoiselle."

Fearful, she took a step back.

"*Non?*" he asked softly.

Terror took her voice. She could only nod.

"Either come or I will sink this ship. I don't allow slavers in my waters."

The quiet intensity resonating from his eyes and in his voice frightened her even more. She saw the Sullivans and the frigate's defeated seamen looking on with alarm.

"Please don't take me," she whispered desperately. "Please."

He appeared unmoved by her plea. "Decide."

Violet called angrily, "Go on, Clare. Think of the rest of us."

As always, Violet's only concern was Violet. Clare glanced Captain Davies's way, but he wouldn't or couldn't meet her eyes. She searched the faces of his men, praying someone would come to her aid. No one moved.

Victor spoke up quietly, "Clare, we're sorry, but we have no choice. The captain and I will alert the authorities. I promise."

The pirate waited.

"No!" and she hiked up her skirts to bolt, but before she could take a full step, an iron arm clamped onto her waist and she was swung back into the pirate captain's iron chest. As she looked up at him, time seemed to cease. She could feel every inch of herself flush against every hard inch of him. A strange unfamiliar heat coursed through her, mingling with her fear. He offered a soft smile and then abruptly tossed her over his broad, red-coated shoulder. Her kicking and screaming and twisting attempts to free herself were for naught. With an arm bolted against the back of her knees, he stepped up onto one of the wooden planks. Employing strides both confident and sure, he traversed the short distance between the vessels. Raging and fighting for what she assumed would be her very life, Clare was taken aboard.

As soon as he put her on her feet, she did her best to sock him. He grinned, grabbed her wrist, and forced her to walk.

"Get your hands off of me, you cretin!" Her outraged anger was poor defense against his powerful grip, but she was not surrendering meekly. "Release me!"

Paying her no mind and ignoring the wide eyes of

his crew, he forced her to follow him down a short flight of stairs and into the shadow-filled area below decks towards a large wooden door.

"No!" she screamed, and attempted to set her feet to keep from rendezvousing with whatever fate lay on the other side.

Gaspar, walking behind them, asked, "Are you sure you want to do this, Dominic? She's a feisty little cat."

Walking beside Gaspar was the blond-haired Scotsman James Early, who replied over her thunderous protests, "Might be more trouble than she's gonna be worth, Captain."

"Let me go!" Clare screamed, and began cursing them in all the languages that she knew.

At the sound of that, Dominic stopped and stared into her face with amazement. He looked to Gaspar. "She's cursing me in French!"

Gaspar's laugh filled the shadows. "That she is."

"*Cerdos!* Release me!"

"She just called us pigs, in Spanish," Early pointed out, staring as if she'd just transformed herself into King George.

The mesmerized Dominic laughed. "I think I'm in love." He assessed her from the short-cut hair framing the angry brown face to the heavy wool cape covering the costly blue gown, to the small heeled slippers of the same shade. The string of pearls accenting her throat appeared to be of great value as well.

Clare snarled, "I demand you restore me to the frigate, immediately!"

"*Merci, mes amies,*" he said to his men. "I'll handle it from here." He dismissed them with a nod of his handsome head, never taking his eyes off the blue-gowned prize. Bowing to the hellcat with a courtly grace, he gestured to the door. "If you will step inside, mademoiselle."

"Did you not hear me?" she stormed.

He straightened.

Gaspar, who'd hung around to see how this might play out, folded his arms over his massive chest and looked on in amusement.

"Take me back!"

The grin that spread across Dominic's legendary handsome face had warmed the hearts of females from Cuba to Spain, and the arms that scooped her up and tossed her back over his shoulder again, like a silken sack of meal, were strong.

"Put me down!" She pounded his back with her fists.

He slapped her across her blue-gowned behind. That drew more outraged curses, this time in Italian, but he ignored them and swung around to face his quartermaster. "Gaspar, see to it that the lady and I are not disturbed."

"Aye, sir. Good luck."

"LeVeqs don't need luck." He carried the furious captive into his quarters and shut out the world with a kick of his booted foot.

"Put me down!"

He complied, and she bounced on something soft and came to rest. Realizing it was a large bed, she scrambled off as if it were a lake of lava and angrily adjusted the petticoats on display beneath the open halves of her gown, then snatched her cloak closed. Thrusting out her chin, she declared, "If you're planning to debauch me, do it quickly so that I might return to the frigate."

"What makes you think I'm going to debauch you?" Intrigued by the novelty of her, his eyes roamed over her again. She was a beauty; a short angry one, but a beauty all the same.

"Isn't that what you pirates are known for?"

"We prefer the term *privateer*."

"As opposed to thieves and murderers?"

"I'd take offense if I didn't find you so fascinating. Your name, mademoiselle?"

"Does it matter?"

"Strangely enough it does, but never mind, I remember. They called you Clare. You are a slave?"

"I am."

"Well kept."

"Violet views me as a pet of sorts."

His brow raised. "A pet?"

"Yes. She dresses me up in the latest fashions and parades me around as if I were an exotic parrot that has been taught to read and mimic its betters. I play the harpsichord, speak four languages, know the latest dances and how to use my cutlery properly. She also thinks that when we travel to Europe, dressing me this way will make people believe I'm not a slave and thus prevent them from rescuing me and offering me freedom."

Dominic heard the icy bitterness in her tone, and that intrigued him as well. "Not a content slave."

"Name one who is, sir."

"Yet you wish to return to your mistress."

"Rather the devil I know than one I do not."

He responded with a short nod of understanding. "I've never met anyone like you."

"I've certainly never met anyone like you, so let me return to my mistress."

"I think not."

"And your reasoning?"

"You are far too—alluring, enchanting, intriguing. Pick one."

"I'm sure the women of your realm take that as a compliment, but I am less swayed."

"You're too beautiful to be a slave."

"And of no mind to be your doxy."

He smiled. "You're quick."

"I had excellent tutors."

He left her standing there for a moment while he went to the door and called for Gaspar, who soon appeared. "Her trunks?"

"Up on deck. There's just the one."

"Bring it if you would."

Fear grabbed her again. Did he plan for her to share his quarters? This was truly a nightmare. She prayed she'd wake up.

Gaspar returned a few moments later and placed the battered leather trunk holding her belongings on the carpet-covered floor. With a nod to his captain he departed.

"While you are on board you shall be my guest."

She looked around. The space was far more lavish and well kept than she might have assumed the quarters of a pirate captain would be. Velvet draperies the color of indigo covered the portholes and matched the coverings on the large four-poster bed. Beside the bed stood a small wardrobe with a mirror on top, and next to it a beautiful silk screen, embroidered with golden dragons and birds that appeared as if it might have come from Cathay. She assumed it concealed the chamber pot. Across the room was a well-polished mahogany table flanked by two beautifully carved chairs, and an old weathered desk, complete with neatly stacked charts, a receptacle for pens and inks, and an aged bronze sextant. "Are your guests allowed to come and go at their leisure?"

"Aye."

"Then I shall leave."

"No."

She sighed aloud. "What are you going to do with me?"

"Offer you freedom."

She stared. She had to admit he was the handsomest man she'd ever seen. What with his roguish beard, his penetrating gaze, and the ornate gold hoop in his lobe, no woman alive would be untouched by the powerful aura he exuded, but he was still a pirate, and everyone knew what they stood for. "And in exchange?"

He shrugged. "We'll start with a meal. Are you hungry?"

She was. The sea battle had interrupted dinner, and since then, there'd been precious little time to waste on such mundane pleasantries as a leisurely repast.

"So?" he asked, bringing her back to his question.

She nodded tersely. Starving herself would not be wise; she'd need her strength. "I will eat."

"Good," and he gave her a saucy wink as if her agreeing pleased him. "Let's see what Cook can surprise us with."

They were interrupted by a knock on the door. Gaspar's voice called from the other side. "We're under way, Captain."

"Aye," Dominic replied. "Head for home."

"And that is where?" Clare asked.

"An island where the wind blows fair and the air is sweet with freedom."

"You brag of freedom, yet you brought me here against my will."

In the doorway, Gaspar gave a tiny cough.

The determination blazing in her cool gaze gave Dominic pause, so much so that he bowed low. "Touché, *petite*." Straightening to his full height, he found himself even more fascinated by her. He knew she was afraid, but apparently not enough to be cowed. He wondered what her reaction would be were he to point out that her show of strength only added to her allure. Masking the thought, he turned to Gaspar. "The lady is hungry. See what Cook can find."

"Aye."

Upon Gaspar's exit, Dominic gestured her towards the table, then helped her with her chair. "Wine?" he asked as he withdrew a decanter from within a short sideboard.

"No, thank you," she replied quietly.

He poured some of the amber liquid into a jeweled silver goblet and took a sip.

In the lengthening silence, he leaned against the sideboard and watched her. Clare tried her best not to be affected by his unhurried attention but it was difficult. She'd never been alone with a man this way, especially not one as dangerous as he'd proven himself to be. The room had become so still, one could hear the creaking of the boat around them and the voices and footfalls of the men up on deck, but his presence was loud as cannon shot. She cast him a nervous glance. Upon meeting his eyes, she quickly looked away. A knock on the door announced Gaspar's return, and she inwardly sighed with relief.

They dined on bowls of turtle soup, stale bread, and slices of oranges. The dried apple she'd had as a midday meal back on the frigate had long since been forgotten by her stomach, so she ate far more heartily of the pirate's fare than she'd planned. She'd had turtle soup a few times in the past, but this version was far tastier and excellently seasoned. Looking up, she found him watching her, and her movements slowed in response to the return of her nervousness.

"This is much better than being debauched, don't you think?"

"I wouldn't know."

His amusement plain, he went back to his meal. "So tell me about yourself. What made your master educate you?"

"A wager between Violet's father and his sister Theodora. Theodora's position was that a slave given the advantage of education could be as genteel as its betters."

"Betters being the slave owners."

"Correct."

"Novel, that," he said with cool sarcasm.

"The Sullivan family and friends thought the experiment novel as well—appalling, but novel."

"And you?"

"I am happy to be learned, but it has only made the bonds of slavery chafe that much more. I've been given access to a world that I may not walk in legally."

He viewed her over his jewel-crusted goblet of wine. "How long have you been a captive?"

"I was seven when I was taken."

"Where were you born?"

"I don't know. I remember mountains and desert, and a war that killed my parents and others in the village. Afterwards, men in long white robes riding camels and horses took me and many of the other children on a long trek before turning us over to the enslavers. Teddy, that's Theodora Sullivan, believes I am from northern Africa, somewhere near the biblical Ethiopia."

Dominic thought that this Teddy might be correct. In his voyages he'd seen beautiful women from all over the world, but in his opinion, the Mother

Continent offered the most striking. In Africa, the women were of every hue, shape, and size. The ones bearing Clare's angular features were commonly found among the nomadic tribes and villages of the north and east. "Any children?"

"Two, but they've been sold."

He stilled. She showed no emotion. Like most captives, she hid her true self behind a mask. He knew it was a necessary tactic for survival, but being privy to this tiny portion of her life only intensified his desire to delve further into the mysteries of the woman who lay beneath. He also wanted to ask if she knew where her children were, but didn't, rather than add more pain to her loss.

And for Clare, it was pain. She let herself remember the day her babies were taken away, and the blade-sharp grief rose up to engulf her as it always did, and as always, she forced the emotions back down into the secret place she kept locked away. "Tell me about yourself," she asked, deftly changing the subject to move the focus of the conversation elsewhere.

"What would you like to know?"

She studied him over her cup of tea. "Your name? Where you are from?"

"Dominic LeVeq. Born on the island of Martinique."

"Why pirating?"

"I'm a second son. With no chance to inherit I have to feed myself."

"So you steal from others?"

The censure in her voice made him smile. "Only those who can afford it, or deserve it."

" 'Tis wrong."

He shrugged and said softly, "That depends, *petite* Clare."

The vibrant timbre of his voice made her feel caressed by someone who thought her precious. She'd never experienced such a feeling. He appeared to be a man who knew his way around women, so she cautioned herself to remember that, less she be lulled into believing herself anything other than his prey. "Surely there are legitimate avenues available to you?"

He shrugged again. "None that I wanted."

"Stealing is easier, you mean?"

"Is the world always so black and white for you?"

"Answering my question with a question is not an answer."

"You're proving to be a hard taskmaster."

"I'll take that as a compliment."

Merriment shone in his eyes. "I can see that this is going to be an interesting voyage home."

"Does your family approve of your way of life?"

"In truth, no. But then I don't approve of his life either, so we are even, he and I."

"This is your father?"

"My brother. My father died four years ago."

"You said you were a second son, so he inherited?"

"Everything, or so he claims."

"You doubt his claims."

"I do, but the will reads exactly as my brother's solicitors say it does. *Mon pere* left everything to *mon* fair *frere*."

"You sound bitter?"

He shrugged as if no words were necessary, then poured himself more wine.

Clare had to admit he was far more complex than she'd first imagined, but it didn't change her position. She had to find a way back to Savannah. Too much was at stake.

Chapter 2

With the meal now finished, Clare steeled herself for what might follow. Although he seemed at ease, leisurely sipping his wine, she fought to keep her anxiety under control. "And now?" she asked.

He set the goblet aside. "'Twill be dark soon. Would you like some air above deck before turning in?"

She shook her head.

"Bed then?"

She looked around the small room warily. "Where?"

"Here."

"Is there no other place?"

"With so large a crew, no."

"And where will you sleep?"

He studied her for a moment, touching her with his intense gaze. "Here."

"Can you not sleep elsewhere?"

"And miss the chance that you might debauch me in the middle of the night? No, and it is my bed, after all."

She rolled her eyes and got up from the table, mostly in an effort to distance herself from his unnerving pull on her senses. "A pallet on the floor will suffice. It's where I am accustomed to sleeping."

"Your mistress has no bed for you?"

"Violet has never had a bed for me."

"You've never slept in a bed?"

"No," she replied simply. "I've slept on a pallet on her bedroom floor since the day I was purchased."

Admittedly, Dominic had no idea what to say to such a surprising response. Of course he knew that captives were given few luxuries, but when had a bed become so dear? Her response also made him wonder what else this beautiful, intelligent woman had been denied besides her liberty. "A pallet it will be then, if that is what you prefer."

"I do. Thank you."

He silently evaluated what he could see of her lovely form peeking out from within the confines of her heavy wool cloak. " 'Tis a waste though, sweet Clare."

"The pallet?" she reminded him, refusing to let his teasing penetrate her resolve although it was difficult. A woman with less fortitude might have jumped at the chance to share his bed, but the hardships forced upon her by captivity had made her strong enough to know her own mind. That was not to say she was made of stone. Although she was still leery of him and unconvinced he'd remain so gallant, Captain Dominic LeVeq was a handsome man; too handsome for his own good maybe, yet there were far more important things in life than sharing the bed of one such as he.

So, she watched and waited as he walked over to one of the large chests beside the bed and withdrew some folded rugs. He set three of them atop each other, then added a sheet that she prayed was clean. He retrieved a fat pillow from his bed, slid it into a pillow slip from the chest, and laid it atop the makeshift pallet. "Will this do?" he asked, turning to gauge her reaction.

"Yes. Thank you."

Dominic tried to remember if he'd ever been this accommodating to a woman before. Most females he encountered were usually so besotted by his charms that they made a beeline for his bed. Not this one. "Are you certain this is what you desire?"

Clare was certain that velvet-edged voice had undoubtedly persuaded women to do his bidding from the day he was born, but she held fast. "What I desire is for you to take me to the nearest port so that I may return home. Short of that, I am certain I do not wish to share your bed."

He gave her a wry smile and rose to his full height. "Circumstances change."

She folded her arms and waited.

"Besides," he went on, eyeing her confidently. "When the time comes, you'll be willing enough."

"Before or after pigs fly?" she tossed back easily.

He bowed his head gallantly, "Believe what you will, but take it from a man who knows women."

"You do not know this woman."

"The pleasure we could share . . ."

"Your pleasure, my displeasure."

"Will you be this spirited in bed, I wonder?"

"Wonder until the seas boil, I've no intentions of providing the answer."

"I think the answer is yes, *petite* Clare."

The low heat resonating through his response made her senses ripple like a flag in the wind, but again she held fast. "I'm certain there are women who are flattered by your blarney, but I am not one of them, nor do I aspire to be. Why is that so difficult to fathom? Have you never been told, 'No thank you'?"

"Look at me. What do you think?"

She assessed his superior physique and dark handsome face and sighed. "I think this ship is not large enough to hold the inflated value you place upon yourself."

He grinned. "We are going to do well, *petite*."

"And I think you've had far too much wine."

He laughed at that. "I'll leave you now. Make yourself comfortable." Reminding himself not to underestimate her, Dominic retrieved his laced pistols and the one he kept hidden in a drawer of his desk. He glanced around his quarters for anything else she might employ as a weapon. Seeing nothing, he picked up the china and cutlery from their meal and exited.

When Clare heard the scratch of the key indicating he'd locked her in, she sighed with weary relief. The captain had proven to be a gentleman so far, but as she'd noted earlier, she doubted his largesse would last. With that in mind, she gazed around for anything he might have missed that she could use to defend herself. A quick search of the cabin turned up nothing. Beneath his bed, she found a white silk corset designed for someone far more buxom than she, but because it held no defensive value she tossed it back into the shadows and got to her feet, dusting off her hands. There was nothing in his armoire or hidden away in the drawers of the desk, either. Defeated, she focused on the pallet he'd fashioned.

It appeared adequate enough, but she doubted she'd sleep. She was too anxious. The day had been an awful one, and she wondered if she'd ever see Savannah again. More importantly, would she ever see her children again? In the colonies, Sunday was the only day most captives did not have to work, so with the master's permission, the Sabbath could be spent visiting family members in other places. For Clare, that family meant her ten-year-old daughter, Sarah, and twelve-year-old son, Benjamin. Eight years ago, they became the property of the Hamptons, loyalist planters in a neighboring county. By foot, the journey to the Hampton home was twelve miles there and back, but if Clare left the Sullivans' place early enough on Sunday morning, she could spend most of the day with Sarah and Ben before having to return. The idea of never seeing them again was something she didn't want to contemplate. They were her world. Finding a way to gain their liberty gave purpose to her life. She didn't believe that anyone should be made to spend the entire time on earth as property of someone else. No matter what it took, she was determined to see them free before she went to her grave.

Now, however, she was the unwilling captive of pirates on a ship heading to only the Ancestors knew where. Outside of convincing the captain to send her home, she had to escape. Her hope was that the opportunity would present itself soon. In the meantime, the only person she had to rely on was herself. With that in mind, she curled up on the pallet, tightened her cloak around herself, and waited to be delivered into the arms of Morpheus.

After leaving Clare in the cabin, Dominic took the dishes to the galley. He then spent time walking the ship, checking on the welfare of his crew, and letting them know how much he appreciated their fine conduct during the encounter with the frigate. He called up his thanks to the men in the riggings inspecting the sails, and gave a good word to others going about their duties keeping the *Marie* in good sailing shape. With no battles ahead or prey to focus upon, many were relaxing, playing cards or listening to the merry tunes of the ship's fiddler, a Frenchman named Pierre Tait.

Below decks now, Dominic spotted one of the powder monkeys, fifteen-year-old Richmond Spelling, the grandson of his mother's old friend Anna. The monkeys were responsible for loading the cannons.

"You handled your chores well today, Spelling." Richmond was one of the youngest of the crew.

In response to the praise, he smiled through the grime and powder covering his young face. "Thank you, sir."

"Anyone injured that you know of?"

"Not in my crew, sir. I hear Watkins got a bump on the head when he tripped over the rigging but Dr. Early would know better. How's the lady, sir?"

Dominic was caught off guard by the question. The crew knew of his reputation with the softer sex, but no one had ever asked questions about who might be sharing his cabin. Until now. "She's fine. Why do you ask?"

Looking uncomfortable, Richmond dropped his eyes. "No offense meant, sir. It's just we've never taken a woman as a prize before. I—I was worried about her."

"I see. She's faring well, and don't worry, she isn't a prize. For now, she's a guest."

Richmond seemed relieved. "Thank you, sir. I'll pass the word. I know that some of the crew had questions, too."

"Please do. Now, finish your duties and get some rest, you've earned it."

Richmond nodded, and Dominic went on his way.

As the *Marie*'s quartermaster, Gaspar had many duties, and one of the most important was divvying up the profits among the crew.

"How much gold was the frigate carrying?" Dominic asked Gaspar upon entering the small, shadow-filled room near the hold. The light sputtering from the candle stubs placed on the scarred worn table where Gaspar worked offered just enough illumination for him to see to the task. Also at the table were Dr. James Early and the ship's pilot and navigator, a Spaniard named Esteban da Silva.

Gaspar looked up from the gold coins he was stacking. "More than we expected. About ten thousand, wouldn't you say, James."

The doctor agreed, "Aye, by the weight of the strongboxes, it's ten easily."

Dominic was pleased. His men would be well paid for this voyage.

"Is the *petite* Clare bedded and well?" Gaspar asked while he continued to stack and count. Esteban was entering the numbers into the ship's tattered leather ledger.

"No."

"No?" the men crowed in unison.

Dominic knew they were about to flay him. "I've no need to bed unwilling women."

"*Dios!*" Esteban exclaimed, grinning in the half dark. "There is a woman on this earth able to resist the legendary charms of the House of LeVeq? Surely, you jest?"

Dominic replied levelly. "Apparently, or so she professes."

"I say give her a few more days and she'll be eating out of your hand," Gaspar said, prying open the next strongbox.

"I'm not so sure."

"Really?" Gaspar could not hide his surprise.

"She's a slave. Never even slept in a bed," he told them, still trying to wrap his mind around that fact.

"The life of a captive is not all cakes and tea," James reminded him.

"I'm aware of that, but you've seen her. Who would deny such beauty something as common-place as a bed?"

"Slavery is an ugly business, as we all know," said Esteban.

"True, and I suppose I shouldn't be so outdone, but she speaks three languages besides English."

"And curses in them very well, I noticed." Gaspar chuckled.

Dominic smiled. "She presents a dilemma."

Esteban shrugged. "Offer her freedom, and maybe she will find you more to her taste."

"I did. She turned it down."

"She's a content slave then?"

"No, quite the contrary, but she wishes to return to her mistress."

"And her reasoning?" James asked.

"She said better the devil she knows than one she does not."

"So, let her go if she is so unwilling," Esteban tossed back.

"No."

In the silence that followed, they all studied what they could see of his shadow-shrouded face.

"And your reasoning?" Gaspar wanted to know.

"In truth, I have none, other than wanting to know her story."

"Preferably while she's in your bed."

That drew laughs and a shrug from Dominic. "That I cannot deny; however, I will not force my attentions on her. Who knows what degradations she's already had to endure."

Gaspar offered sagely, "Slavery for one."

"Exactly. So I will bide my time, and if she continues to refuse me, *c'est la vie.*"

"I don't believe that for a moment," James replied, "but I do know you to be an honorable man, Dominic."

"For a pirate," Esteban added.

More laughter.

Dominic took no offense at their good-natured teasing because they were a brotherhood. Having sailed together for the past three years, they knew each other fore and aft, and would sacrifice their lives for the common good, if need be. "Did we incur any damage during the fight?"

"Nothing significant," Gaspar responded. "The long cannons we took from that Dutch ship last month are worth their weight in gold. They kept us well out of range of the British guns today. Be nice if we could get more."

Dominic agreed. "Maybe someone knows of another ship similarly equipped that's willing to *share.* When we reach port, we'll keep our eyes and ears open. Any significant injuries to any of the crew during the fight, James?"

"Other than Watkins running into the mast, no."

Grins showed in reaction to that news.

Dominic said, "He doesn't usually participate in the fighting."

"And he wasn't today. He was trying to escape to the frigate. Found him lying on the deck out cold."

Esteban asked, grinning, "You are going to release him when we reach home, aren't you, Dominic?"

"Only if we can find a replacement, and I pray we will. His constant whining rankles the crew."

"Well, he is here against his will, *mon frere*," Gaspar pointed out.

"And he'll be paid generously for the inconvenience," Dominic replied. Because ships were made of wood, one of the most valuable members of any crew was its carpenter, but with so many vessels on the water, there were not enough of the skilled men to go around. As a result when one was found, whether it be on an opposing ship or in an alehouse, he was asked to join. If he refused, then the tradition set forth by the British Navy was employed and the man was impressed. Thus was the case with Hugo Watkins. They'd taken him from a Portuguese slaver off the African Gold Coast four months ago, and he'd done nothing but complain since. He was an excellent carpenter, but Dominic and his men couldn't wait to be rid of him. "I will leave you to the accounts. Give me a report in the morning on the totals. We'll add the profits from the rebel guns to everyone's share after they are sold."

Gaspar nodded. "Shall I again wish you luck with fair Clare?"

"No."

Laughter accompanied Dominic's exit but he smiled and ignored it.

Back up on deck, the crew prepared themselves for the onset of the evening. Dominic went to the stern's rail and looked out at the sun setting over the open water. He loved the sea. Be it dusk, dawn, or midday, the rolling waves and the sights and smells of the ocean fueled him like nothing else. His father had been a captain in the French Navy and Dominic had served as his aide. He'd been only thirteen on his initial voyage, but from the first day he drew the salty air into his lungs, he knew that sailing was what he'd been born to do. Since then, he'd swabbed decks, loaded cannons, climbed riggings, and been voted captain. No matter the job, as long as he had a ship rolling beneath his feet, he was content.

Out on the horizon, seabirds flew against the dying sun. He grinned at the sight of a pod of dolphins racing beside the ship. Long day, he mused. Profitable, but long. The muskets they'd confiscated from the British frigate would go to a merchant who'd arrange for them to be turned over to the Continental Army, for a profit of course. The gold would be divvied up according to the percentages specified in the *Marie*'s articles, and once they reached home, the crew would all go their separate ways until the sea's siren call lured them back to her watery embrace.

Dominic had been answering that call for fifteen years in capacities both legal and non; mostly non. He was a wealthy man now in both fortune and property. His dear brother, Eduard, would undoubtedly foam at the mouth were he aware of how much his bastard half brother was truly worth, but Dominic had no plans to enlighten him, nor reveal the whereabouts of the families he'd planned to enslave. Eduard could rot in hell.

The *Marie*'s bell rang the hour, refocusing his

mind on the present. He wondered if his guest was sleeping. Thinking of her, he was again struck by her novelty, and he asked himself, why would a slave woman not want freedom? In truth, the answer she'd given had been logical, but he sensed something more at play. Did she have a lover she longed to return to? Was that the reason, or were her protestations about hating her privileged captivity nothing more than a lie? Because he didn't have an answer, he spent a few moments trying to unravel the conundrum. His own mother, Marie, had been enslaved on the island of Martinique before being plucked out of the cane fields by his father to be his mistress. Antoine had loved her so deeply, he'd freed her, and nine months later, she gave birth to a son. She died when Dominic was twelve, but she'd loved him as he loved the sea; unconditionally and with every breath. Could anything have made her turn her back on the offer of freedom that day in the cane field?

Thinking about her sent his mind back to Clare's response when he asked about her children. Three words: *They were sold*. A grimness settled over his soul. *Her children!* That was it. Her children were somehow involved in her stance. He was as sure of it as he was of his mother's love.

And now his impetuous decision to take her from the frigate weighed even more heavily. He had no explanation as to why he'd done what he had. Yes, he was a pirate, but where other men of his profession made a practice of defiling women, he eschewed such behavior. With the bevy of women willingly raising their skirts for him all over the world there was no need for him to be so crude, yet he'd taken Clare. The sight of her on the deck of the British ship had been surprising enough, but the beauty of her face partially framed by the hood of her cloak took his breath away. By European standards her small nose was too wide, her lips too beguilingly lush, but by his standards just the sight of her stirred his manhood, and therein lay his humbling. She didn't seem to care that he found her as attractive as the sun setting over the ocean. All she wanted was to go home, and now that he was fairly certain he knew the reason why, and because this was all his fault, it was his responsibility to get her there.

Sighing, he looked up at the night sky. No moon. Good. If the British Navy was out trawling for privateer prey, the *Marie* wouldn't be easily seen. Shivering slightly at the drop in the temperature, he left the rail. After paying his respects to the men on the night shift, he went to his quarters.

Aided by the flame of the torch burning in the sconce outside his door, he quietly turned the key and opened the door. As he removed the torch to aid his sight in the darkness, his equally quiet entrance showed her asleep on the pallet. Her soft snoring barely ruffled the silence so he carefully closed the door behind him so as not to awaken her. Soundlessly crossing the room, he lit a few candles on the desk off the torch, then used its flame to fire the logs in the small stone hearth. Although the calendar showed it to be late April, the ocean was still cold at night, and the chill in the room reflected that.

He doused the torch and set it on the hearth's apron, then moved to the chair at his desk to sit and remove his boots. Glancing her way, he stilled. She was awake, sitting up watching him. Her hands were tightly clutching the cloak, and even in the shadows he could see the wariness and distrust in her face.

"Good evening," he said in hushed tones. "My apologies for waking you. I'd hoped I was being quiet."

She didn't respond. As the seconds passed, the light from the fire in the grate had grown strong enough to quell some of the darkness enabling him to see her face and expression more clearly. She looked ready to flee so he sought to reassure her. "The room is cold. Why don't you sleep in the bed. You'll freeze with just the cape for covering."

"I'm fine."

He knew she was lying, even he was shivering in the chill. It bothered him that she was being so stubborn when his sumptuous bed could offer her both comfort and warmth.

"I'll not share your bed."

"That isn't what I'm asking, pigheaded woman."

"Indulging in name calling is rather childish, don't you think?"

He sighed and then chuckled softly. Silently praying for strength, he offered her a gallant inclination of his head. "My apologies. My concern is for your comfort and warmth only."

"But the question remains. If I take the bed, where will you sleep?"

"On the pallet. In a chair. It won't be in the bed, so don't worry."

"Is this a ploy to stoke my guilt?"

Amazed and amused by her tenacity, he shook his head and responded, "No."

Waiting for her to react further, Dominic knew there and then that taking her home without learning just how truly fascinating she was would haunt him for the rest of his life.

Clare wasn't sure if he was telling her the truth but it didn't much matter. She wouldn't be changing her mind. Waking up in the dark and in unfamiliar surroundings had startled her, but as the memories of the day came rushing back, they were accompanied by the realization of how vulnerable she was by being alone with him in his quarters, so she remained on her guard.

"So will you humor me and sleep in the bed?"

Clare noted that he was handsome even in the dark. The firelight played off the strong lines of his dark features, the smoothed, tied-back hair, and the gold hoop hanging from his earlobe. Shaking her mind free of the distracting thoughts, she instead contemplated her reply. He was correct in his assessment of the room's temperature. In spite of her heavy cloak the air in the room was cold, and although she was accustomed to discomfort she didn't want to risk contracting a sickness. "Yes. I'll sleep in the bed."

"*Bon*. And I'll take the pallet."

Clare rose to her feet. The light from candles that

must have been lit while she slept mingled with the crackling flares of the fire and gave the otherwise silent room a hushed glow. As he left his chair and slowly walked over to where she stood, wariness and something she couldn't name increased her breathing. He came to rest before her and captured her with his shadowy gaze. Although she knew it was only her imagination, the heat of his body seemed to blend with hers. She forced herself to take in a deep breath to calm her now pounding heart.

When he reached up to touch her cheek she leaned away. "Please, don't," she whispered.

Hearing the anguish in her voice, Dominic dropped his hand. "I don't mean to frighten you, Clare. It's just—" How could he explain to her that he'd been moved by the play of the light flickering over the smoothness of her silken skin? He stepped back. "My apologies again. That seems to be all I'm doing this evening."

The unease in her face and in the way she was gripping her cloak caused him to say, and with passion, "I would never hurt you, *petite*. Never. Please don't be frightened of me."

When she didn't respond he told her, "I'm going to take you home."

Her surprise was plain.

"I am. I've a responsibility to my crew first, but after—"

"What changed your mind?"

He shrugged. "You, and because it is my fault that you are here."

"Nothing more?"

"*Non.*" He didn't want to tell her about the conclusions he'd come to.

Clare wasn't sure she believed him. Did she dare hope he was telling her the truth, or was this just a ploy? "And your conditions?"

"None."

Clare studied him. Because she didn't know him well, it was impossible for her to tell by his eyes or manner if he was speaking truth, but she decided to give him the benefit of the doubt. "I thank you then. I truly and honestly do."

"You're welcome."

"How long will your other duties with the crew take?"

"A month at the most. After that, Gaspar and I will escort you home. Which is where?"

"Savannah." She thought about her children. The happiness filling her heart made her eyes shine with tears of relief. "Thank you," she said again, this time with emotion. "Thank you."

"My pleasure. So now to bed. We get up early on the *Marie.*"

"Is that the name of the ship?"

"Yes."

Dominic was pleased with her reaction to his news. He hoped it would help alleviate the fear and mistrust brought on by his impetuous actions. "If you'll pardon me for a moment, I'll take these sheets and replace them with the ones on your pallet."

Clare watched and waited while he went about the task of stripping the bed. Moments later, the sheets from the pallet were in place. He tossed the pillow she'd slept on onto the bed and bowed. "M'lady, your bed awaits."

"You'd do well as a lady's maid, Captain."

"Only if the lady I serve is you."

His manner was light, but there was an underlying tone in his voice that touched her and caused her to wonder what it might be like to have such a man in her life. Had she been born in another time and place . . . Her thoughts trailed off. A woman like herself knew better than to envision any reality that softened or did away with the true circumstances of her life. To dream of another existence accomplished nothing.

Dominic saw her mask slip, and for just a moment her myriad emotions became visible. Before he could get a true handle on what she might be thinking, the barrier hiding her inner thoughts was firmly back in place and she was looking up into his eyes. *Who are you, Clare Sullivan?* he wanted to ask. *What would you have your life be were you not a captive?* "Your trunks are there if you wish to change out of your dress."

She went to her trunk and found it empty. All her clothing, which consisted of nothing more than two day dresses and her unmentionables, had been in the armoire when the frigate came under attack, and was apparently still there. Violet or whoever had directed Gaspar to her trunk hadn't looked inside.

She turned back to the captain. "All of my things are still on the frigate, so this dress is all I have to wear. It belongs to Violet and I'm certain she'll want it returned in good condition, but it won't be if I have to sleep in it."

"I have a nightshirt you may borrow, if you'd like."

"That might be best."

Dominic opened another trunk and withdrew a clean nightshirt. Since he preferred to sleep naked as Poseidon, the garment was clean. "It'll probably cover you to your toes."

She took it from his hand. "Thank you."

"You can use the screen over there. I'll step outside. Call me when you're decent."

She nodded and he made his exit.

Behind the screen, Clare hastily removed her gown. Leaving on her shift and stays, she pulled on the large cotton nightshirt. The captain's assessment had been correct, it did indeed cover her to her toes, and its long sleeves hung past her fingertips and warmed her wonderfully. It had a slight smell of mildew as was to be expected on a seafaring vessel, she supposed, but the well-worn fabric felt good against her skin. The knowledge that she'd be going back to Savannah felt good as well, and the faces of her children filled her mind. She couldn't wait to see them. Buoyed by her happiness, she covered herself with the cloak again and left the screen. After laying her gown over one of the chairs, she crossed the floor and climbed into the big four-poster bed. The quilts were fat and heavy, the mattress beneath her firm yet soft. Removing her cloak, she hung it on the bedpost. Pulling the quilts up to her chin, she called out for the captain to return.

When Dominic entered, the sight of her sitting up in his bed set off a physical reaction common to all men attracted to a beautiful woman. His form-fitting breeches left little to the imagination, so he stuck to the shadows and took a seat at his desk so as not to embarrass her with the proof of his arousal. "Warm enough now?"

"Yes."

"Go ahead and lie down. I'll douse the candles. Good night, Clare."

"Good night, Captain."

The dousing of the candles left the glow from the hearth the only light in the room. After the tumultuous day, the now warm Clare was quickly asleep once again.

Dominic placed his head down on the table, intending to let some of the long day drain away before moving to the pallet, but moments later he was asleep.

Chapter 3

Powder monkey Richmond Spelling also served as the captain's aide, so when he entered the captain's quarters at dawn to bring breakfast, he expected to find the captain in bed with the lady. The lady was in the bed, but to his surprise Captain LeVeq was fully dressed and asleep with his head on the table. Bets had been flying all over the ship that she'd be bedded before sunrise but those who'd put their money on the captain appeared to be losers. "Ahem," he called loudly, clearing his throat just as Gaspar entered the cabin, too. The quartermaster took in his captain and then the woman asleep in the bed and grinned. "Who'd you place your money on, Spelling?"

"Her, sir."

"As did I," Gaspar replied with great satisfaction.

Clare stirred awake and upon seeing the men, hastily dragged the quilts to her chin.

"Good morning, miss," Richmond said politely, averting his eyes. "Sorry to wake you, but I brought you and the captain breakfast."

Dominic raised his head and stared around blearily. Upon seeing Gaspar's amused eyes, he groused, "One word, and I'll maroon you on the nearest isle." Forcing himself to sit upright, he swiped his hands across his weary face and turned his attention to Clare. "You've already met Gaspar. This is Richmond Spelling."

"Good morning," she replied.

Richmond nodded. "Cook sent turtle soup and biscuits. There's tea here, too."

"Thank you."

"Just set the tray down and leave us," Dominic grumbled. "Both of you," he added pointedly for Gaspar's benefit.

In his own defense, Gaspar replied, "I came to give you the report on the gold you asked for last evening."

"Later."

The two intruders shared knowing looks, then departed, leaving Dominic and Clare alone.

"Did you sleep well?" Dominic asked her, trying not to wince from the knots in his neck.

"Yes. And you?"

"No. Tabletops only make good pillows when you're too drunk to care."

She responded softly, "My apologies for taking your bed."

"None needed. It's the price one pays for being a gentleman." He stood. "Take care of your needs. I'll return shortly."

Clare was sorry he'd had an uncomfortable night, but not enough to have invited him into the bed.

Dominic made use of the ship's facilities, then walked through the gray dawn to let the ocean breeze lighten his mood. He never felt fully awake until he took in his first deep breaths of fresh air, and this morning the assistance was dearly needed. There was a strong wind blowing out of the east, and the sails fluttering high above on the masts were taut and fat. He mumbled good morning to the men he passed while on his rounds. Considering how he felt, engaging in a detailed conversation was out of the question, but none of the crew seemed to mind, and continued with their chores, ranging from mending fishing nets and cleaning weapons, to handling the sails. He stopped for a moment to greet Esteban, who was at his post expertly piloting the *Marie* through the water.

"So, how was your night, Captain?"

"Don't ask. How far are we from port?"

"About four, maybe five days."

"Good."

"How's the lady?"

"She's well. I've decided to take her home."

Surprised, Esteban asked, "When did this come about?"

"It doesn't matter. I'm taking her home." Dominic could see some of the nearby crew discreetly listening in, but that didn't matter, either. On a ship there were very few secrets.

"Where's her home?"

"Savannah. I'll need a small crew."

"Give me a few days at Levine's and I'll join you."

Surprise and disbelief cut through Dominic's

foul mood. "A few days?" He laughed. "Once you're inside we won't see you for a week, at least." Levine's was a tavern whose ale was almost as well known as its whores.

The Spaniard shrugged. "The women like me. I can't help it if it takes the lot of them a while to welcome me home."

Dominic chuckled, "When it's time to set sail, if you're still of a mind—and can walk—you're welcome to come along."

"I will be. I'm enjoying watching you humbled by the *pequeno senora*."

Dominic rolled his eyes. "I'll be back up after breakfast."

As he walked away, Esteban called out in a voice tinged with humor, "Give her my regards."

Dominic ignored him.

When he entered his quarters, he found her dressed in the blue gown and seated at the table; she was a lovely sight, but the breakfast tray was no longer where he'd seen it last. "Our meal?"

"In the grate keeping warm. I was unsure how long you'd be away."

The soup tureen was perched atop the dying embers of last night's fire. The teapot was at its side. "Thank you, but you didn't have to wait for me."

"I didn't want to appear rude."

"I would never think that." He retrieved the items and set them on the table.

As they began the meal, he told her, "Been some time since I shared breakfast with a beautiful woman."

"And this is the first time I've not had duties to complete before I could eat."

"How does it feel?"

"Odd," she offered truthfully. "I feel as if I should be up pressing Violet's gowns, and emptying chamber pots and bringing breakfast instead of having it brought to me."

"I promise, there'll be no pressing, emptying, or bringing while you're here."

"I thank you for that, but I mustn't let myself become accustomed to such luxury."

The sadness of that touched his heart. "Then don't go back. We'll figure out a way to free your children."

She froze. "My children?"

"That is the reason you wish to return, is it not?"

She stared at him with wide eyes. "How could you know?"

"A guess, really. My mother was a captive."

Clare was speechless.

"What are their names and ages?" he asked gently.

"Sarah is ten and Benjamin twelve." She was dumbfounded by his insight. How could he know the secrets of her heart?

"I guessed it was either children or a lover."

Embarrassed by his latter choice, she lowered her eyes for a moment. "No, it's my children, and if I don't return, they could be sold again."

Dominic knew that was a very real concern, but wished he could present her with an alternative that would guarantee liberty for all three of them. "Do you get to see them?"

"Sundays." Which made Clare luckier than some of the other captive mothers with children. Many children auctioned on the block were lost to their families forever. Her mind went back to the brief reference he'd made to his own mother. "How long was your mother a captive?"

"Until her sixteenth year."

"Is she still living?"

"No, she died when I was young. In many ways her death seems a long time ago, but in others, it's as if it happened only yesterday."

She heard his wistful tone. "You sound as if you loved her very much."

"I did."

Clare realized there was more to the captain than the pillaging and thievery she'd accused him of yesterday. "I love my children very much, as well."

"That's apparent."

"Would you do less?"

He shook his head. "No, and you are to be commended."

For a few moments they ate in silence.

"I'd like to help," he said.

"Help with what?"

"Your children's freedom."

For a long moment she said nothing, observing him instead, before asking, "And how might you accomplish that?"

He shrugged. "No idea now, but I'd like to put my mind to it, if it is agreeable."

"Thank you, but no."

"You're refusing my help?"

"I'm refusing to pin my hopes on something that is beyond our reach."

"You don't want them to be free?"

"Of course I do. I'll go to my grave content if I could see them free."

"Then let me help you, and them."

"I appreciate your concern but your efforts, whatever they might be, could put them in great jeopardy."

"I understand, but—"

"So great a jeopardy that they could be sold to the Indies." Being sold to the French- and English-controlled islands of the Caribbean was to live a nightmare. The French led the world in human trafficking because of the constant need to replace their slaves that they worked literally to death.

The last thing Dominic wanted was to begin their day with an argument, but her misgivings were legitimate ones. Exposing her children to the block would not be helpful in any way, so he dropped the subject for the moment with the idea of presenting her with a well-thought-out solution sometime in the future.

They finished breakfast soon after, and he asked, "Would you like some air?"

Clare nodded. Being confined to the cabin all day wasn't something she was looking forward to since it would only add to her sense of being closed in. Having the sun and the wind on her face might be a refreshing alternative. "Let me get my cloak."

Once she was ready, he escorted her out.

Up on deck the first things she noticed were the

scents and sight of the open ocean. Its undulating blue-gray tone stretched to the horizon beneath a cloudless sky and a breeze strong enough to tease the hem of her cloak. The second thing she noticed was the men. There were scores of them and they'd all dropped what they were doing to stare her way.

"This is Miss Clare Sullivan," the captain announced in a voice loud enough to be heard over the elements. "She will be our guest until we drop anchor."

The introduction was met by a series of "Welcome, mum," "Good morning, miss," and "Pleased to meet you."

Clare nodded in response. They were all heights, sizes, and races. Many sported beards framing dirty faces. Some wore breeches; others tattered trousers. None looked like he'd visited a laundress in months. All were smiling, however, and that was surprising. Not the leering treacherous smiles one might expect from a band of hardened men who made their living on the high seas, but genuine welcoming smiles made her feel at ease.

The captain helped her put names to the faces by introducing some of them: like Lloyd Beekum, an Irishman, she guessed by his thick brogue, and Washington Julian, a member of the Cherokee nation and an escaped slave. She was also introduced to Pierre Tait, a short Frenchman whose face showed only a puckered piece of skin where his left eye should be.

"Sail!" a loud voice shouted.

Everyone glanced up. The call had come from the lookout riding high up on the mast.

"Flag?" Dominic shouted back.

They all waited while the man peered through a long-barreled spyglass. "Dutch!"

Clare noticed that the *Marie* was flying the French flag now.

"Can you make her out?"

The seaman took another look. "Aye! It's the *Amsterdam*!"

Dominic froze. "Are you sure!"

"Sure as my name!"

Dominic looked into the faces of his crew. "You all know how I feel about the *Amsterdam*'s captain and crew, but I'll take a vote. Do we keep heading south for home or do we go after her?"

A man Clare hadn't seen before rushed up and said, "LeVeq, if you go after another prize and delay my passage home, I will see you hang!"

Dominic eyed the short, squat, balding complainer and asked sarcastically, "Are you voting no, Mr. Watkins?"

"Damn right I am!"

Dominic turned to the crew. "Our carpenter votes no. What say the rest of you?"

"I vote with the captain!" shouted Gaspar.

"As do I!" echoed Dr. James Early in a louder voice.

Man after man raised his voice in increasingly exuberant support of the captain's plan. Soon the entire crew was roaring.

Dominic called over the din. "You're outvoted,

Mr. Watkins. For the rest of you, we're going to run her down! Prepare yourselves!"

The men scattered, running to their stations to ready themselves and the *Marie* for the upcoming fight.

As cannons were dragged into position, sails were adjusted to heighten their speed, and Esteban altered course, Clare stood in the chaos swirling over the deck. Surely she wasn't going to be party to another sea battle!

Dominic stopped in the middle of shouting orders to call out, "James, please escort Miss Sullivan back to my quarters."

"Come, miss."

But she wanted to speak to Dominic about his decision to engage the other ship. "Captain, I—"

"Clare, go with James."

"Why can't we ignore the other ship and go on our way?" she asked.

"Because the *Amsterdam* is a slaver, and her captain specializes in African children."

Her knees turned to water. Without another word, she followed the doctor below deck.

Alone in the captain's cabin, Clare was sure her pacing had carved a trench in the floor. She agreed that the slaver needed to be stopped, but questions about the captain's decision and how it would affect her journey home did battle with others centering around her fate should the *Marie* be forced to surrender. More than likely she'd be sold again, if she lived to be sold. Imagining the worst only increased her anxiety but she couldn't focus her mind anywhere else.

Suddenly the door opened and the captain walked in.

The unexpected entrance startled her but seeing that it was he made her relax.

"Came down to see how you were faring," he explained, closing the door behind him.

"As well as can be expected, I suppose." She didn't want him to know the extent of her worry. "Have you closed in on the other ship?"

"Almost. She's trying to outrun us, but it's only a matter of time. The ship's riding low in the water, which means she's carrying a large cargo in her hold. That great weight is slowing her down."

"Captives?"

"I pray not, but we won't know until we board her."

Clare prayed, too. "So you've had encounters with the captain before?"

"Most recently, eight months ago off the coast of Florida. His name is Paul Vanweldt. Spawn of the Devil himself. British Navy's been after him for many years."

"And he was carrying children the last time you encountered him?"

His eyes went cold. "Yes, and he dumped his cargo when we got within range."

"What do you mean?"

"He threw the captives overboard. It's a common practice amongst slavers. When we stopped to help those we could, he of course was able to sail away—laughing at us, no doubt."

Clare shook her head at such heartless cruelty. "Were you able to rescue them all?"

"Only a few. Some of the smaller children were being transported inside cooper's barrels that went straight to the bottom. Them we couldn't save."

She now understood why the captain wanted to hunt down this particular slaver. "What will you do if you catch him?"

"We'll see when the time comes."

The stony set of his features said he already knew the answer, and she shuddered in response.

He told her, "I recommend you stay here while the fighting is going on."

"Of course," she responded. "I've no wish to be in the way."

"*Bon.*" Being alone in the cabin with her made Dominic want to forget about the outside world and spend the rest of the voyage cajoling her into letting him explore the taste and sweetness of her lips, but the desires would have to wait. Vanweldt took precedence for now.

Clare could tell by the way his eyes were blazing down into hers that Vanweldt wasn't the only thing on his mind. Mixed feelings coursed through her. On the one hand, he represented danger and a way of life she found reprehensible, but on the other hand, she was attracted to him in ways she had yet to understand. Even though she didn't wish to be, the burgeoning awareness was impossible to ignore.

"You will keep yourself out of harm's way?"

His lips curved upward. "Anything for you."

His teasing tone made her shake her head with muted amusement. "I merely want to be certain I get home to Savannah. Nothing more."

"You don't lie very well, *petite*, but your concern will be my armor."

He reached out to stroke her cheek, and unlike last night, Clare did not back away. Although she steeled herself not to react, the slide of his warm finger against her trembling skin made her eyes close and her heart pound.

"I will send someone to sit with you, once we overtake Vanweldt." The heat in his gaze was almost palpable.

"That isn't necessary."

"It is to me. I don't want to worry if you're safe."

His nearness was making it difficult to keep her breathing even. "Thank you."

"I'll return later."

Giving her one last affectionate look, he departed, leaving her alone with her jumbled emotions.

An hour later, the *Marie* closed in on the *Amsterdam*. The Dutch ship took issue with the encroachment and fired seventeen of its twenty-five guns. Although the balls fell short, it was the moment Dominic had been waiting for. "Fire!"

Fifteen long-range cannons fired as one, striking the *Amsterdam* on its port and stern, and exploding with brilliant colors of gold and red.

"Fire!"

A second volley barked, this time hitting the deck

and toppling the masts down onto already screaming, dying men. Even as the *Amsterdam*'s answering cannons continued to boom, fires flared from its bow to its stern and the ship was beginning to take on water, but Dominic was offering no quarter. "Ready the chains! Fire at will!"

The *Marie*'s cannons thundered again, this time sending bar and chain shot hurtling towards the target. The halved cannonballs, held together by an iron bar or lengths of reinforced chain, reached their destination as whirling dervishes of destruction that splintered the *Amsterdam*'s remaining mast and ripped the sails and riggings to shreds. Shards of wood, some as long as a man's arm, pierced limbs, faces, and eyes, plunging the defenders into screaming chaos.

In the aftermath of such carnage, most ships were ready to surrender, but the *Amsterdam* seemed to be an exception. No white flag could be seen waving from the burning deck, even though some of her crew were jumping overboard into the chilly ocean water. "Lower the longboats!" Dominic ordered.

The boats would rescue all who wished it, and Dominic doubted any of them would refuse. With all the blood and turmoil in the water, sharks would be arriving soon.

The longboats hit the surface, and while the crewmen from the *Marie* rowed out to rendezvous with the deserters, Dominic called up to his pilot, "Put us closer, Esteban!"

"Aye!" the pilot replied.

As the *Marie* came alongside the crippled vessel,

bodies could be seen lying on the burning deck and draped over the splintered, severed masts. Cannonballs were capable of decapitating ten to fifteen men at a time during a battle, and some of the dismembered dead bore evidence of that grim truth.

"Prepare to board!"

Token pistol fire was returned by the other side, but grappling hooks sailed from the *Marie* like nests of metal-headed snakes and held the *Amsterdam* fast.

"We have less than an hour before she sinks!" Dominic informed his crew. "Find out what she's carrying. I'll find Vanweldt!"

His men swarmed the burning boat. Armed with short swords, cutlasses, and clubs they took on what remained of the opposing crew. With his linked pistols hanging around his neck and a short sword in his hand. Dominic fought his way through the smoke, stepping over the dead and wounded as he searched for the enemy captain.

"Where's Vanweldt!" he barked at an injured man covered with blood and powder lying on the deck.

The sneering man coughed and spat, "To hell with you, LeVeq."

Dominic grabbed him up and stuck a pistol in his mouth. "Shall I send you ahead to reserve a seat for me?"

The man's eyes widened with fear.

Dominic drew the weapon free. "Where's your captain!"

"His quarters," he snarled. "Below deck."

Tossing the man aside, Dominic angrily strode away.

He met no resistance below decks, and when he reached the door, he didn't bother to knock. He kicked it in, shattering the wood and the lock that was supposed to keep intruders like him out.

Upon his entrance, the fear and surprise in the eyes of the two men inside put a sharklike smile on Dominic's face. Pistols turned ominously their way, he asked, "Going somewhere, Vanweldt?" Trunks and valises were set out on the bed. Dominic had interrupted the slavers' attempts to fill them all with gold and other booty. The man beside him was the mute giant Yves, the captain's bodyguard. At six feet, eight inches tall and over three hundred pounds, Yves was no smarter than the average flounder, but could tear a man apart as easily as most people tore apart a chicken wing.

"Bastard!" the Dutchman swore. "I should have killed you the last time we met."

"But you were too busy throwing children to the sharks, then slinking away like the cur you are rather than fight with any honor."

Yves made a move to advance, but was stayed by a warning touch of his captain's hand. In the eyes of many women, Paul Vanweldt was a handsome man. He was of Dutch and African descent, but in the eyes of those he stole from the Mother Continent, the slaver was an abomination. "What's in your hold?"

"You tell me."

The ball fired from Dominic's pistol exploded

in Vanweldt's shoulder, and he let out a scream, clutching his injured flesh. His eyes widened in disbelief.

"That appears to be the wrong answer, *non*?"

Yves took another menacing step forward, only to have Dominic promise, "One more step and I'll shoot you and then him in the balls."

Yves stopped, his ugly dark face blazing with hatred.

Dominic saw Gaspar enter the room. The quartermaster was holding two large-bore pistols.

"Thought I'd come join the party," he said to Dominic, but his attention and his guns were focused on the men across the room.

"The more the merrier. How goes it above?"

"We're mopping up. I sent some men to the hold. No captives."

Dominic's eyes had never left Vanweldt. "Then we may let him live."

"I vote no."

"I'll take that into consideration. Let's go above, gentlemen. After you."

Up on deck, the air was thick with the mingled scent of smoke and gunpowder. The fires had been doused, leaving behind a blackened and shattered deck stained with blood and littered with the dead, broken masts, and pieces of tattered sails.

Vanweldt surveyed the damage with wide eyes, then turned to glare at Dominic, who responded by saying, "Maybe you should have been up here commanding your crew instead of trying to save your loot."

Vanweldt promised coolly, "The next time we meet, LeVeq, plan to die."

"Who says there will be a next time?" He turned to Gaspar. "Get our men back on the *Marie*."

"What about the cargo in the hold?"

"Let it go down with the ship."

Vanweldt stared in stunned disbelief. "There's a fortune down there!"

"I don't care. My only intention is to sink this ship. I'd kiss the Devil himself before making a profit from anything carried in a slaver damned by the blood and souls of dead children."

Dominic called to the surviving members of the Dutchman's crew, "Anyone who wants to join the *Marie* is welcome to sign the articles. Otherwise, I'd unlash the longboats and take to the oars. By the next bell, our cannons are going to send this whore straight to the bottom."

Filled with the memory of those screaming, drowning children, the stone-faced Dominic walked back to board the *Marie*. In the wake of his exit, Vanweldt, Yves, and the remaining crew scrambled to get to the longboats before it was too late.

"Come on, miss, before he sees us."

Clare left the spot where she and the Cherokee Washington Julian had secretly watched the battle, and slipped back down the stairs to the captain's cabin. Once they were safely back inside he told her, "He ever find out I let you watch, he'll maroon me for sure."

"And that means what, exactly?"

"Back in the old pirate days, a man who disobeyed orders could be voted off the ship and taken to a deserted island and left there. They'd be given a pistol and enough food and water to last a few days."

"And then?"

"You were either rescued by a passing ship or you died there—thus the pistol. In case you wanted to put yourself out of your misery."

Clare shuddered faintly. "I will keep our secret."

"Good."

Clare liked Mr. Julian. In the time they'd spent together during the hours-long battle, she'd learned that before the European slave trade settled on Africans, peoples like America's Indians and other natives in places like South America had been enslaved first, only to die by the thousands under the harsh conditions. His Cherokee clan had been arrested and sold into slavery a generation ago for refusing to turn over their land to newly arrived English colonists in upper Georgia. After a series of escapes and recaptures, he escaped for good ten years ago.

As they took their seats at the table to renew their game of backgammon, he said to her, "Every man on the *Marie* is an escapee from something—slavery, the British Navy, debt, family, unjust accusations."

"And the captain?"

"His brother, Eduard."

Clare knew the captain and his brother were at odds over their father's estate but wondered if there was more to the story. Having no answers she looked down at the game board in front of her and let go of the tension and excitement brought on by the battle she'd just witnessed. She knew the captain wanted revenge on the *Amsterdam*, but to let the valuable cargo sink with the ship was something she wouldn't have believed a man like him capable of had she not heard and seen the drama unfold for herself. It came to her that once again, her preconceived notions of what LeVeq was because of how he made his living were deeply flawed, or at least seemed to be.

The captain entered a while later. "Thank you, Mr. Julian. You may leave us now."

"Aye, sir. I enjoyed our visit, Miss Clare."

"As did I. Thank you."

After his exit, Dominic walked over to where she sat and asked, "All is well?"

She nodded. "And you?" There were blood and smudges of black powder on his red coat. Similar stains could be seen on the blousy white shirt he wore beneath. She noticed a cut on his throat. "You've been cut. Your neck is bleeding," she said, rising to her feet to get a better view.

His fingers went to the wound as he walked over to the mirror atop the armoire. "A gift from one of Vanweldt's men. I'll live." He felt the weariness of the day begin to take hold.

"It should be cleaned and dressed."

"Right now, I just wish to sit." He was exhausted and wondered if he might be getting too old for the spirited life of a privateer. He felt good about sending the *Amsterdam* to the bottom, though. Depriving Vanweldt of his profits was an added boon.

"Then come and sit and let me clean it. You don't want a poison to settle in."

"Clare—"

"Sit, Captain."

Her firm tone garnered a weary smile, "Yes, ma'am." He took a seat in the chair Julian had vacated.

"Where are your medicinals?"

"James has whatever is available, and I am not going to bother him for such a small prick."

"You'd rather wait until your neck swells up like a gourd, I suppose."

He studied her for a long moment. "I didn't know you had a stubborn streak."

"You don't know a number of things about me."

"Sassy, too."

"Only with you it seems."

That made him smile. "All right, if I go and get a plaster from James, will you stop bedeviling me?"

"Yes."

He sighed heavily. "Fine." Hoisting himself out of the chair he'd just gotten comfortable in, he added, "I'll expect a boon for this."

"Your boon will be a treated wound."

He shook his head as he looked down at her. "I'll want a kiss."

Her heart stopped, taking with it her ability to breathe. Captured by the mischief in his eyes, she finally found her voice. "Well, you shan't have one."

His gaze lowered and then lingered on her lips. "I call it payment for putting up with your nagging."

"Then forget the plaster. Maybe you'll end up

with so much poison James will have to cut off your head."

"You're a bloodthirsty little wench," he responded, chuckling.

"Who will not be handing out kisses like Christmas treats." Even though she was so aware of him, she seemed to be warmed by an inner heat that flowed directly from him.

As she stood before him with her arms folded firmly, Dominic felt a strong urge to take her in his arms and give her bewitching and sassy mouth something else to contemplate. "A kiss, *petite*," he warned, and left the room.

Alone, Clare wondered if it was normal to be so affected by a man. Did he really expect her to fulfill his request? After his heartfelt words last night, she no longer feared he'd do her harm, so she was certain he wouldn't force a kiss on her. He was just trying to needle her, she supposed, and he did like to tease. In the middle of those logical thoughts the remembrance of last night and his warm touch against her cheek came back unbidden, and she relived the moment all over again; the way her eyes lidded closed, the way she'd trembled. What might it be like to give herself to him fully and without inhibition? she wondered. The thought was scandalous, true, but once she returned to Savannah her captivity would resume. Should she give in to him and see where this small respite might lead? But she had no answer.

Chapter 4

He was gone for such a long time, Clare thought
maybe he'd decided to seek his rest elsewhere,
but moments later the door opened and he strode
in. He'd washed up while away. The damp, jet
black hair hung loose behind his ear, brushing his
collar. He'd changed his shirt, breeches, and stockings as well. None of the replacements appeared
newly laundered, but they were far cleaner than
the ones he'd worn previously. He'd shaved, too.
The fresh-clipped beard rode his jaw with a shadowy rakishness that only added to his dangerous
countenance.

"James sent some plaster, and I'm still wanting
that kiss," he pronounced, eyes holding hers.

Ignoring his declaration, she took the battered tin
cup from his hand and stirred the dab of sticky plaster with the small tarnished spoon resting inside.
"You'll have to sit, please."

He took a seat in the chair at his desk and his
manner was easy as he watched her intently.

Only then did she realize that she'd set herself
up. In order to get close enough to apply the plaster

she'd have to do just that, get close; close enough to touch his skin, close enough for the heat of his body to brush her own.

"Something wrong?" he asked.

She shook her head quickly. "No." Taking in a deep breath to buttress her resolve, she moved to the side of the chair so she could begin.

"Might be easier if you stand in front of me, *petite*."

She paused. The gaze she met fairly sparkled with amusement.

He tipped his head back so that the cut was exposed. "I'm ready when you are."

He had her over a barrel and they both knew it, but she refused to tuck tail and run. Determined not to look into his face, she leaned in and spread a thin line of the plaster down both sides of the open wound. Although she tried to remain unmoved by his nearness, warmth, and clean fresh smell, it was impossible. A quick look up showed him watching her, so she just as quickly refocused on her task. "Did the doctor send something to bind this with?"

"Yes." He handed her a thin short strip of black silk.

She gently placed one edge of the silk against the outer edge of the wound, then just as gently pinched the skin closed, and pressed the unattached edge of the silk over it. The plaster and silk would hold the wound together and keep out any dirt while it healed. "There," she said approvingly. "Now you won't have to worry about poison or decapitation."

"And my kiss?"

She viewed him silently at first, taking in the chiseled features, the shape of his mouth, and the gold hoop gleaming in his ear. To her surprise and to his, she tossed back the same question he'd posed to her earlier. "If I say yes, will you stop bedeviling me?"

He grinned and confessed, "Probably not."

She looked away hoping to hide her smile, but he gently turned her chin back and gazed at her long enough for time to stand still, and for all her defenses to crumble and melt away. Warm lips brushed hers as he whispered, "Probably not, because one kiss will lead to another, and another, and another . . ."

It was the most arousing moment of Clare's life. His mouth was firm yet fleeting, bewitching her with a series of short, slow kisses that sparked, seduced, and promised more. She'd never experienced anything so deliciously overwhelming, and for a moment could do nothing but let him have his lazy, heated, feasting way. In response she was breathless, drowning. When he gently tugged her down onto his lap, she complied without protest. Easing her closer, he deepened the kiss.

"You are sweet, *petite*," he husked out, pressing slow hot touches of his lips against her mouth until it parted passionately. When he teased the tip of his tongue against the trembling corners and then nibbled possessively on the ripe, lush flesh of her bottom lip, she moaned.

Dominic knew from the moment he kissed her that the longer she sat on his lap, the more likely she'd wind up with his hands touching her everywhere. He'd sensed she'd be passionate, but not this beguiling. Her lips were like manna, and all he wanted to do was slide his hands over her silk-dressed curves and then beneath to sample the damp fullness he knew awaited him there in the warm darkness. Wanting to pull away from her tempting mouth before things got out of hand, but unable to do so, he murmured over his racing blood, "Clare, unless you want to surrender to me fully, we should stop."

Her lips stinging, her breathing heightened, Clare pulled back just enough to break the contact. She closed her eyes for a moment in a vain attempt to find herself.

He placed his lips against her ear, murmuring, "I could kiss you until the sun becomes the moon."

There seemed to be a haze over her vision and her whole body felt awake in a strange and wonderful way. Her nipples had tightened to hard points and her blood seemed to be singing a slow undulating tune. "Is this the way it should be?" she asked.

"Is this the way what should be?"

"The beginning of coitus between a man and a woman."

"Yes," Dominic responded, noting her now serious manner. "Was it not this way when you conceived your children?"

She shook her head and whispered, "No."

He wrapped his arms around her and held her close. "Was there violence?"

Clare knew what he meant. "No."

"Good, then I won't have to find the man and kill him."

She pulled back so she could see his face. The hard glitter in his dark eyes revealed him to be quite serious. She fit herself back against his broad chest and let his strong yet gentle arms enfold her again. "He was a stranger chosen by Violet from amongst her brother's field slaves. I didn't know what to do, but he did, so I—I just lay there. I knew it would hurt, and it did. When he was done, I wasn't sure how I felt. Shamed. Soiled."

He nodded his understanding.

"A year after Benjamin was born, she chose another man, another stranger, and I sent my mind elsewhere until he was finished."

Dominic wanted to send Violet Sullivan to the bottom of the sea for her callousness, but putting his anger away, he said genuinely, "Coupling doesn't have to be so joyless, *petite*. When our time comes, I shall be especially attentive."

Their gazes met.

"I promise," he declared, using a finger to tenderly stroke her cheek before placing a solemn kiss on her brow. "With all my heart."

"Do the women you have coitus with just lie still?"

"I should hope not. That would make me a very poor lover." Dominic had never had a conversation quite like this one, but he would cut off his own arm before mocking her for her inexperience.

"And you are not considered a poor lover, are you?"

"*Non.*"

She sat up and he watched her appear to mull something over. After a few silent moments, she looked to him, asking, "Do you think I will be damned for all eternity if I choose to give myself to you?"

The earnestly stated question made his heart swell, even as he shook his head negatively. "The people enslaving you are the ones facing damnation." He traced a slow finger over the curve of her lips. "And I would be honored to accept such a precious gift. In return, I will teach you a love that will make you forget all about what happened before."

Moved by his husky declaration and filled with an uncharacteristic boldness, she kissed him to show her thanks, and whispered against his lips, "I don't have the experience your others likely had."

He kissed her back and ran his hand slowly up her spine. "That matters not."

"You'll show me what to do?"

For a long moment, while they lost themselves in the tastes and warmth of each other, all words and responses were set aside.

"Will you?" she asked humidly as the languid kissing continued. Only the sounds of their breathing could be heard against the silence.

"Gladly," he whispered. "But the first time I make love to you, I want it to be in my home, and in my bed."

His voice was so potent her eyes slid closed and her body shimmered.

He moved his lips to her ear and asked, "Do you know why?"

"No," she breathed as he rubbed the tip of his finger slowly over one tight nipple and then the other.

"So that there will be no one to disturb us."

Too shocked and overwhelmed by his decidedly bold fondling, Clare felt as though she were in the middle of a powerful storm that was threatening to sweep her away. Her breasts crooned in response to his glorious stroking, and there was a warm restlessness between her thighs she'd never felt before.

Dominic met her eyes and smiled. "Are you enjoying yourself?"

"Very much."

"*Bon.* You are a passionate woman, Clare. We will have fun together, you and I."

"I've not had much fun. Ever."

"I know, but we'll make up for that while we are together. Agreed?"

"Agreed." Clare realized that in less than a day, he'd turned from a man who terrified her, into one with the ability to see into her heart, while at the same time offering her something she'd never tasted before—passion. And even though their time together would be finite, she planned to take full advantage of each and every moment, so that when she returned to Savannah she would at least have the memories.

"Would you like more?" she heard him ask through the haze floating around her. A drum seemed to be beating softly between her thighs.

He filled his hands with her breasts and she moaned again when expert fingers gently tugged and plucked. "Or do you wish for me to stop . . ."

There was so much sensation flowing through Clare, she couldn't even recall her name, but she did know that she didn't want him to stop. "No, I don't want you to stop."

"Then say . . . Don't stop, Dominic. . . ."

He teasingly bit each of her breasts and she came apart, crying out softly. Her hips rose, her body stiffened, and an unnamed force took hold and spun her out over the ocean.

Dominic closed his eyes and employed every calming thought he could muster in order to fight down the smoldering urge to take her over to his bed and have her. Now. He was so close to the edge, he knew that if he even looked at her he was going to spill his seed like a youth visiting his first bordello, so he kept his eyes closed.

She asked in a dazed voice, "What was that?"

Against his better judgment he looked down and swept his vision over her lidded eyes and passionfull lips. She was in the final throes of her orgasm, and the sight threatened to shatter the tenuous hold he had on himself. Closing his eyes again and forcing himself to think of the snows of Greenland, he said quietly, "Orgasm."

"Is it a normal occurrence?"

"It is when you're with a proper lover."

"Are you in pain, Dominic?"

Her usage of his first name garnered a smile. "No, *petite*."

"Then what—"

"Up with you now," he said, giving her one last stirring kiss before placing his hands on her waist and guiding her to her feet. "I have a ship to captain and some charts to look over. Having you so close will distract me."

Her reply, a saucy pout, drew his laughter. "Go sit on the bed. I'll only be a few minutes.

She nodded and complied.

Watching her retreat, Dominic forced himself to look at the chart in front of him. In reality, the chart was a ruse. He'd needed to distance himself to allow his erection to subside. Her tempting kisses had him in turmoil. Being at the desk gave him the opportunity to sit in tortured silence until he could stand and not embarrass her with a show of how much he physically desired her.

A short while later with everything back to something akin to normal, Dominic stood. "I'm going up on deck. I have to meet with my officers. Would you like to get some air?"

Clare doubted she'd ever be the same after such a novel experience. Even now her breasts were whispering his name. "Yes, I would." She hurried to get her cloak.

When she joined him at the door, he touched her cheek and said, "I'll be very discreet in my dealings with you in front of the crew. I don't wish for them to think you are anything but the lady that you are."

"That's very generous."

"You should expect no less." He gave her another

long, lingering kiss, then let her precede him from the room.

Up on deck, he walked her to the stern rail. "I'll return as soon as I can. If you need anything just ask one of the crew."

She nodded.

He bowed and departed.

Alone, Clare stood and watched the late afternoon sunlight sparkle like jewels strewn across the water. Her body was still echoing from her passionate encounter. Her lips stung from the many kisses they'd shared, and the restlessness between her thighs had lessened somewhat after the orgasm, but her awakened senses craved more. Her enslavement, with its puritan influences, had left her unprepared for such a stimulating interlude, and she again wondered if she would be damned for seeking the pleasures of the flesh with such a man. In the end, she decided she didn't care. Returning to Savannah and the fetters of captivity would occur soon enough.

Whether due to the captain's orders, or of their own accord, the deck crew didn't disturb her. Those who came near nodded greetings but continued on their way; however, the sudden sound of someone calling out, "Miss Clare," caused her to turn with curiosity.

Dr. James Early was approaching. The tall blond Scotsman was in his own way as handsome as the captain. "You did a fine job patching up the captain," he told her in words laced with the brogue of his homeland.

"Thank you, and thank you for the plaster."

"You're welcome. The captain's still meeting and asked that I come and make sure you are well."

"I am."

He came closer and stood beside her at the rail. "Quite the day."

She knew he was referencing the battle and she agreed. "Is it always this frenzied?"

"At times yes, and at others no. Sinking the *Amsterdam* was a boon though."

"What will happen to its captain and the men who chose to leave with him?"

He shrugged. "Hopefully, they'll be picked up by the British Navy and hung for their crimes. Even better would be to have their longboat sink so they could turn into a shark's supper. I've no sympathy for slavers."

Neither did Clare.

"More than likely, though, they'll find refuge on a passing ship and live to sell more human cargo." He didn't bother masking his disgust.

"How long have you sailed on the *Marie*?"

"Two and a half years. Met the captain and Gaspar at a tavern in Kingston. When I learned they needed a doctor, I joined the crew."

"Do you have family where you are from?"

He shook his head. "I left nothing behind in Scotland but a date with the hangman."

Surprise filled her eyes.

He shrugged and explained, "I treated a lord back home who died a few days later. His family accused me of hastening his demise. I was arrested, tried, and sentenced to hang, but having no desire to dance on the end of a noose, I bribed a jailer and escaped. Made my way to the coast and signed on with a merchant captain heading south. When I told him I was a doctor he didn't care about my past."

"And you went from his ship to the *Marie*?"

"Not at first. The merchant ship that I was on initially sank in a storm and the survivors like myself were picked up by another ship. A slaver."

Clare went still.

He looked out over the ocean and said nothing for a moment as if recalling the times, then in a voice filled with emotion, continued. "For three months, I sailed on a filthy, godforsaken vessel with two hundred Africans stuffed in its hold like stacked grain. The captain refused to let me aid the ones who were sick or near death, and those who mercifully did pass on were tossed overboard as if they had no right to expect better. It was the most horrific experience of my life. When I continued to protest the treatment, he threatened to throw me overboard, or maroon me, so I kept my mouth shut for the rest of the voyage."

Tight-lipped, she watched the ocean undulating silently.

"I'd lie in my bunk at night and hear them singing below decks in soft, mournful melodies that I learned later were their death hymns."

Tears filled Clare's eyes.

"Changed me forever. When we reached the Indies where they were going to be sold, I walked away from the ship and never looked back. Men like Vanweldt have a special room in hell. There's not a crewman aboard the *Marie* who didn't applaud the captain's decision today. As I see it, every slaver should be sent to the bottom, and the faster the better."

Only then did he turn her way and notice her reaction to his tale. "Oh, miss. Forgive me. I didn't mean to make you cry. The story seemed to come out on its own. Captain finds out I made you cry, he'll hang me from a yardarm for sure."

Clare wiped at her eyes with her fingers and sought to reassure him. "No, it's just that I came over in a slaver, too. Your words brought back memories. I thank you for letting me know I am amongst honorable souls who find the trafficking as much an abomination as I."

She saw that he still looked doubtful. "Please don't fault yourself. Your story shows you are a good man, Dr. Early."

"Are you certain?"

"Very much so."

He bowed gallantly. "You're very kind, miss. Again, my apologies."

"None are needed."

"I'll let the captain know you are faring well."

"Thank you."

He made his departure, and Clare directed her eyes back out to sea. She thought back on her first few months as a captive and how frightened and confused she'd been. Before being torn from her home, she'd never seen a White person and therefore knew nothing of their language, food, or customs.

In many ways, dying during the Middle Passage might have been preferable, but then she would never have given birth to her precious children. No matter the circumstances of their conceptions, they were the fruit of her loins, and she loved them with every breath. She also worried about them, Benjamin mostly. Sarah worked in the kitchen, but he toiled in the fields, and at twelve years of age was amassing the size and height of his sire. Healthy male captives were fetching higher and higher prices on the slave block. Although the Hamptons had given her no indication that her son might be sold, they didn't have to. He was their property, and could be auctioned in an instant to settle a debt, pay for feed, or for any other reason they might decide. She tried not to think about the terrifying prospect, but the fear was something she carried in her heart, also. If Dominic kept true to his word, she would see both Ben and Sarah in the months to come. As their mother she felt it could not happen soon enough.

"Clare?"

This time it was Dominic walking towards her and her senses leapt. "Are you finished with your business?" she asked when he neared.

"I am. My officers and I would like for you to join us for supper if you care to."

"I'd enjoy that."

He extended his arm. She placed her hand across it, and let him lead the way.

The meal was served at the table in his quarters, and she found herself seated with Gaspar, the doctor, and the pilot Esteban. Richmond Spelling acted as their server.

"It's turtle soup again, sirs," he told them, setting down two tureens. "Miss, Cook says he'll prepare you a feast once we reach home and begs your pardon for the plain fare."

"Tell him I find his soup to be very good so there's no need for him to apologize."

"He'll appreciate you saying that, even if it's not the truth."

He left them a plate of hardtack, then departed.

Clare declined the hardtack when the plate was passed her way. The hard, breadlike staple was known to harbor weevils and worms.

Gaspar put a spoon into his soup and said, "We've eaten so much of this, it's a wonder we haven't grown shells over our backs."

"Beats months of dried fish," Esteban told him.

"Aye," Gaspar responded.

The men were all so large in stature, Clare felt as if she were dining with the sons of Hercules. She also thought the soup much better than the boiled bland fare she'd eaten on the frigate. She wondered about the fate of Violet and the others, but she supposed she'd find out when she returned to Savannah.

A bottle of fine French wine taken from the captain's store was added to the meal. Clare declined it as well. She was content to eat her soup and watch and listen while the conversation flowed around her. It became readily apparent that the men were not just crew members, but friends as well, and seemed to enjoy poking fun at each other.

James asked, "Think we can convince Esteban to hunt us down a boar for the homecoming feast?"

Uproarious laughter erupted, and Esteban chided Clare, "Do not believe a word they say, Lady Clare. They lie every day of their lives."

Howls greeted that, and Clare looked around in confusion.

Dominic asked, "Were you or were you not screaming for help up in that tree?"

"Spaniards do not scream. We may shout, but scream? Never."

James was laughing so hard he was gasping for air.

Gaspar said sagely, "Sounded like a scream to me. No, I take that back. It sounded like *many* screams."

Clare had difficulty masking her smile. "May I ask what happened?"

James gestured with his shoulder. "Don Juan da Silva over there got himself treed by a two-hundred-pound boar."

Clare turned to Esteban, who was pouring himself more wine, and he explained further, "Let's just say the boar caught me and a young lady at an inopportune moment. I fended the thing off with a pistol long enough for her to run to safety, but the ball I put into it only made it angry, thus the tree."

Dominic picked up the story. "The boar was so angry that not only was it charging the tree in attempt to shake Esteban down, it ate his breeches!"

Screams of laughter filled the small cabin.

Clare stared. "If you were in the tree, how on earth did it get to your . . ." She then remembered him referencing an inopportune moment. "You were undressed?" Genteel women never uttered the word *naked*.

"As a newborn babe," Gaspar answered for him.

The smiling Esteban sipped his wine and didn't respond.

She was astounded by the implication. Surely he and the lady weren't . . . ? Out of doors? The look of sheer wonder on her face brought forth even louder peals of glee.

Dominic said, chuckling, "Our apologies, *petite*."

"It's quite all right. I know my naiveté is showing."

"But it is very sweet," he told her. He lifted his goblet high. "To Clare. May she never be treed by a boar!"

The others raised theirs. "Hear! Hear!"

She laughed at the outrageous toast and at them.

Later, as she climbed into the bed with the sweet sounds of Tait's fiddling floating in through the open porthole, she thought back on their antics and smiled. What a merry band of men. After the meal, they'd returned to their duties, the captain included. Now, with night falling, she'd lit the fire and a few candles, and changed out of her dress and into his overly large nightshirt.

Making herself comfortable in the firelit room, she leaned back against the pillows, listening to the haunting music and wondering what might happen when Dominic returned. She doubted she'd be so bold as to let him share the bed, but she did wish to share more passion. It was shameless, she knew, but she couldn't turn her mind anywhere else.

A short while later, a knock sounded, and his voice carried through the door, "May I come in?"

"Yes," she called in reply.

The moment he entered and her eyes swept over his tall perfect frame, the heat lingering from this afternoon's encounter rekindled like fresh wood on embers.

"Are you well?" he asked, standing across the room and observing her with eyes that seemed to catch the firelight.

"I am, and you?"

"Yes."

He walked over to the foot of the bed. "My men enjoyed your company at supper."

His steady gaze made her heart pound. "I enjoyed them as well. Especially the toast."

"We didn't mean to offend with our laughter."

"I wasn't by any means."

"Good, because they like you."

"I like them, as well."

The idle chatter was a masquerade. What they wanted was to pick up where they'd left off this afternoon.

"May I ask you something?" she said.

He nodded. "What is it?"

"The story about Esteban and the boar."

"It is a true story," he replied.

"Not that, but the part about him and the lady.

Were they engaging in coitus when the boar surprised them?"

"Yes. Why?"

"I just—" Articulating what she wanted to ask was difficult because females weren't supposed to discuss such things.

He cocked his head at her and waited for her to continue.

She looked back up into his face. "I always thought the act was supposed to be done inside at night."

"Inside, outside. At night. Midday. There are no rules. Those who believe there are probably aren't enjoying themselves much." He sat down next to her on the edge of the mattress. "Take the enjoyment I gave you this afternoon, multiply it by as high as you can count, and that's how good it can be."

She found that amazing.

"There's a grand difference between the coitus that led to your children and true lovemaking, *petite*."

The unspoken desire in his eyes stroked her like a touch from his hand. When he leaned over and kissed her softly, she rippled like a wave on the ocean. There was power in the contact, but also a gentleness that cajoled and invited her to join in. She met him gladly. Having a bit more experience than she'd had earlier, she slid her palms over his lean, muscular arms and thrilled at the feel of his mouth moving over hers. When his arms gathered her in, she answered with all the ardor she could muster. He groaned and pulled her onto his lap, quilts and all, and eased her close until she was flush against his chest.

Lips against her ear, he breathed, "Inside. Outside. Midday. I'm going to make love to you everywhere."

Clare couldn't breathe. His hand was roaming up and down her spine and over her breasts. Heat burned through the layers of clothing to her skin, making her nipples bud and plead. Hot lips flamed against her jaw as he promised, heatedly, "I'm going to take you in the moonlight, and the next day, under the morning sun."

The scandalous words set off a series of smoldering sensations that made her body flow and sing.

"Inside. Outside. Midday," he echoed.

Being with him made her forget all about the Old Testament morals she'd been raised with and want to experience all the pleasures of the flesh his could offer hers. Mimicking him, she slid the tip of her tongue against the parted corners of his mouth. Savoring the low groan he gave in response, she boldly repeated the move.

They soon lost touch with time and place. The possessive slide of his large hands over places no man had ever explored until he entered her life, left her yearning and breathless. The torrid pressure of his lips worshipping over the silken skin above the nightshirt's collar dropped her head back and made her world spin. He brushed kisses over the silent offering and her soft sigh drifted up like a note from Tait's fiddle. He worshipped his way down the front of the shirt to her already budded breasts. Once there, he filled his hands with their delicate weight, toyed with the nipples, then recaptured her lips with a fierce yet gentle thoroughness.

"Let me touch you," he whispered passionately.

While his mouth continued to ply hers, his fingers pleasured the hardened crests with magical expertise. The storm inside rose and expanded. Desire had her in such a mindless state, she didn't protest as he undid the nightshirt's buttons. The thin shift she had on underneath seemed nonexistent when he bent to pay her tribute. The licks and tugs of his wordless devotion rocked her like small strikes of lightning. She sensed the nightshirt moving up her thighs but she was too caught up in the storm to pay it much mind. When he finally raised his head and looked into her eyes, her nipples were hard as diamonds and her shift damp.

Dominic was in turmoil. The pirate in him wanted to lay her down and have at it, but the gentleman who also lived inside held back. The two entities warred with each other for a long moment. In the end, he gently but firmly moved her off his lap. He turned away from the tempting sight of her and ran his hands wearily over his face.

"What's the matter?"

"You're too damn tempting, woman."

There was silence for a moment as Dominic continued to fight against himself. "I'm not accustomed to having a good woman in my bed."

"Is that so wrong?"

"It is when I want you nude."

"Nude? You're jesting?"

"No, I'm not."

"Why would you want me nude?"

He chuckled softly. "You truly are an innocent, aren't you?"

He came to a decision. "I have to leave you. If I stay here one more moment, not only will you learn why I want you nude, every man on this ship is going to know I'm making love to you, and that wouldn't be fair to you or to them."

"Dominic—"

He stood. The tumult raging below his waist was going to make it difficult to leave the room gracefully, but it couldn't be helped. "I'm going to be busy with the ship until we drop anchor, so if I don't see you until then, I'm offering my apologies in advance."

"What?"

He bowed. "Good night, Clare."

Her astonished face was the last thing he saw before turning and exiting the room.

Alone, in the firelit darkness, Clare fell back on the bed. The logical parts of herself understood his reasoning, and in a way applauded him, but the parts of herself that he'd left pulsating and open were bereft and disappointed at his abrupt departure.

Dominic entered the quarters shared by Gaspar and James. Both men took a look at his tightly set features, but before they could say anything, he warned, "Not one word."

They continued to watch as he availed himself

of a spot on the floor and covered himself with the blankets he'd taken from the ship's stores. Turning away from them he growled, "Don't ever let me steal a good woman again. Ever!"

When it became apparent that that was all he had to say, they shared a knowing smile and resumed their backgammon game.

Chapter 5

Accustomed to rising early, Clare was up and dressed when a knock sounded and a voice called out, "Miss Clare, it is Gaspar. May I enter?"

She went to the door and opened it to find the quartermaster standing on the other side, breakfast tray in hand.

"The captain is busy, and asked if I'd share your meal with you this morning. If that meets with your approval?"

Even though Dominic had prepared her for his absence, disappointment stung. Hiding it, she nodded. "It does, please come in."

He set the tray on the table and then helped her with her chair before seating himself. "It's more turtle soup and hardtack, I'm afraid."

"That's quite all right. I'll decline the hardtack though."

"I don't fault you. It's difficult to get excited about weevils and worms so early in the morning."

The jest made her smile. "May I pour?" she asked, indicating the pot of tea also on the tray.

"Please."

She poured them each a bit and then started in on her soup. "How long have you known the captain?"

"Since we were boys. His father was kind enough to purchase me from the block."

That surprised her. "You were a captive?"

"Yes, and Vanweldt's father was the slaver responsible."

Her lips tightened. "So, it is a family tradition for the Vanweldts to traffic in children."

"Yes, and yesterday's sinking of the *Amsterdam* partially satisfied my lifelong dream of revenge against them."

She confessed, "I, too, was captured as a child, and wonder if the Vanweldts were the ones responsible."

"Without access to the slave ship's manifest, it would be difficult to determine, because unfortunately there are others who capture and sell children as well."

Clare shook her head in disgust. "May they all be damned."

He raised his mug of tea in agreement.

"Have you attempted to find your true family?" she asked him.

"No. Dominic and I talked about it when we came of age, but it is too dangerous. A man like me, with my size and brawn, would risk recapture in Africa were I in the wrong place at the wrong time. I'm certain I was taken from the western interior, but that is all."

Clare wondered how and if the hundreds of thousands of souls stolen from the continent would ever reestablish ties to their real families. How many mothers cried themselves to sleep each night grieving for their children? How many fathers had lost their sons and brothers, and children their parents? The slave trade was an insidious, rampant evil that appeared to have no end. Even though some voices in England and in the colonies were beginning to be raised against it, she saw little change on the immediate horizon. "Were you treated well by the captain's father?"

"Oh yes. Antoine LeVeq's workers had been freed for years prior to my coming to the block, so when he purchased me, he freed me as well. Dominic and I grew up as brothers. We were schooled together, sailed the world together, and grieved together at his mother's graveside after her untimely death."

"She was ill?"

"No. Poisoned."

Her mouth dropped in astonishment. "Do you know by whom?"

"Antoine's wife, Nancine."

Clare continued to stare.

"Antoine and Nancine's marriage was an arranged one, but his love for Dom's mother, Marie, was born of his heart. Nancine hated her."

"Was she ever punished?"

"No, she's a duchess of the realm, and her family had the ear of the king. The doctors didn't dare go to the authorities."

"And the captain's father had no recourse?"

"Other than to never see nor communicate with

Nancine or Eduard for the remainder of his life, no. After Marie's death, he went to sea and took me and Dominic with him. He never set foot in France again."

"That is a sad tale."

"Indeed.

And a telling one in that it added more flesh to Dominic LeVeq the man. She knew from speaking with him how much he loved his mother. Her death and the horrible circumstances surrounding it must have caused him tremendous sorrow.

"I'm to be your escort for today, if you'd like to take some air after we are done here."

"Are the captain's duties so pressing?" she asked, going along with the ruse.

He nodded. "If you would prefer James—"

"No, your company is fine. I just don't wish to take you from your duties."

"Escorting a beautiful woman is far more of a joy than any duty."

"Then I'd be honored to have you as an escort."

Up on deck, the winds were warm. The crew members she passed gave her nods of greeting, while others called out theirs. She acknowledged both warmly. Regardless of how the men on the ship were viewed elsewhere, in her presence they'd been gentlemen, and she appreciated their kindness. She spotted the captain up by the helm, but if he saw her he didn't let on. Disappointment filled her again, but she refused to let it cloud such a beautiful day or her response to Gaspar's wonderful company.

Standing by the rail, she saw land off in the distance, and when she asked Gaspar what it was he answered, "Santo Domingo, or Haiti as it is sometimes called. By either name it is a French-owned hell for the hundreds of thousands of captives there. Many believe the island will be awash in blood soon if conditions do not improve."

"They think there will be a revolt?"

"Unlike anything the European masters have ever seen."

"There have been uprisings in the colonies. None have been very successful, but it is the single most fear of the masters that their captive will someday revolt and kill them in their beds."

"As well it should be. Slaves may have the legal status of oxen but they are human beings and have a God-given right to be free."

They watched silently until the island slowly passed from view.

Clare noted that the weather was considerably warmer than it had been a few days ago and she supposed it was because they were traveling south. "Where are we destined?"

"Eastern region of Cuba."

"There is still slavery there, am I correct?"

"Yes. Thousands of Africans are sold in Havana each year, but we pay the governors enough to leave our people alone."

She knew from her geography that the Spanish-owned island was not very far from the colonial mainland, which meant it would be the closest she'd be to Savannah since leaving for England with the

Sullivans. Thinking of home naturally made her muse on her children and she prayed again that they were faring well.

"Our home is paradise on earth," he interrupted her thoughts to say. "I'm certain you will enjoy your time there."

She was certain she would also. For the past few days being able to rise every morning with nothing to do but see to her own needs was still taking some getting accustomed to, so she couldn't imagine how it might feel to walk in a world where she'd be completely free.

"You may enjoy it enough to consider staying permanently."

"I can't. I've two children in Savannah I cannot leave behind."

He studied her for a long moment. "The captain knows?"

"Yes."

"Then the men of the *Marie* will do everything in our power to remedy that."

Clare had already stated her misgivings to the captain on the matter, so rather than resurrect the debate, she replied simply, but sincerely, "Thank you."

Although Clare was enjoying having no duties while on board, deep down inside she was growing bored living such a pampered life, not to mention Dominic's decision to avoid her, so she asked Gaspar, "Is there anything that I may help with?"

He looked confused. "Help with?"

"On the ship. May I help with the wash, prepare

meals, darn socks? I'd like to contribute while I'm on board."

"Have you spoken to the captain about this?"

"No. He's busy," she said pointedly.

He smiled. "In truth, we have nothing suitable for a lady's hands."

"How about hands that have worked since the age of seven? I'm aware that I can't climb the riggings or clean the cannons, but there has to be something I can help with that needs doing."

"You're serious."

"Yes, Gaspar, I am."

"Let me talk to the captain."

"He will only tell you no."

"Let me speak with him anyway. Will you wait here until I return?"

She nodded. As he walked away, she was certain Dominic would deny her request, so because she knew the ship's layout, she decided to see what task she could find to do on her own.

Her mission took her across the main deck to where Pierre Tait and two men were seated repairing sails. "Mr. Tait?"

He looked up out of his one eye and immediately jumped to his feet and bowed. "Mademoiselle Clare." For a moment, he glanced around as if confused. "Is the captain not with you?"

"No, he's attending to duties."

The men working with Tait eyed her with varying amounts of wariness.

"Is there something you need?" the fiddler asked.

"Yes, Mr. Tait. A job. May I help you with the sails? I am a very good needlewoman. If you would just show me the stitches you employ, I'd be glad to assist."

They all stared.

Tait seemed speechless for a moment before finally replying, "This is no work for a lady, miss. The sails are dirty, full of salt . . ."

Clare interrupted his explanation by taking a seat on the deck. "Please hand me a needle and show me what to do."

One of the men warned, "Captain's not going to like this, mum."

"We'll tell him I threatened you with marooning."

Peals of laughter greeted that. It seemed to break the tension. Tait studied her for a few seconds longer. With an amused shake of his head, he surrendered. He handed her one of the whalebone needles, showed her how and what to do, and she and the men set about the task.

Dominic was in the hold cataloging the goods they'd be unloading once they reached home. At Gaspar's entrance he looked up and asked, "How's Clare?"

"Looking for work."

"What?"

"She wants a job."

Dominic stared, confused. "Why?"

"Wants to contribute."

"She doesn't need to contribute."

"Go up and tell her that. She's waiting for me to return with a reply. She's also not happy with you avoiding her."

"I'm not avoiding her," he lied.

"You can tell her that, also."

In reality, Dominic was avoiding her and they both knew it. He'd never been around a woman who affected him so intensely. After being with her last night, he figured the best way to deal with the tempting dilemma she presented was to avoid her until they dropped anchor. It wasn't working because since waking up this morning, his every thought had been tied to her smile, the taste of her mouth, and her soft sighs of pleasure. "Where is she?"

"Stern rail."

"All right, I'll go speak with her."

He never made it to the stern, though, because he found her seated on the deck beside Tait repairing sails. Surprised, he studied her and the men with her. "Clare?"

She gave him a smile that warmed him through the soles of his boots. "Captain. How are you?"

"I'm well. May I ask what you're doing?"

"Repairing the *Marie*'s sails."

Tait and the others didn't look up.

"I see. I'm certain Mr. Tait told you this was not a task for a lady."

Clare studied the last few stitches she'd put in, and upon finding them to be sufficient, said, "He did, but I threatened to maroon him if he refused my help."

"Really?" Dominic eyed Tait. Although the fiddler had his attention focused on the sail it was obvious that he was also trying to conceal his amusement.

"So, he had no choice but to agree. Right, Mr. Tait?"

"Aye, miss."

"Well, would you at least sit on a tarp so that you don't ruin your gown?"

"Certainly."

A tarp was fetched and Clare positioned herself atop it. Once she was settled she looked up into Dominic's eyes. "Is there anything else, Captain?"

He wondered when he had lost control of this situation, but since he had no answer, he said, "No. Carry on."

She nodded and resumed her task.

Clare spent the rest of the morning working beside Tait. She enjoyed the company. She took pleasure in the work as well, mainly because it was a chore she'd chosen to do as opposed to being ordered to and having no say. She saw it as yet another boon of the freedom offered onboard the *Marie*.

Later, the ship's bell sounded the midday hour.

Tait looked her way. "Time to eat. Would you care to join us?"

"I'd be honored."

Tait turned to his mate, a man named Barney. "Would you fetch us our share?"

Barney was a rail-thin Englishman with three teeth. "Sure." Flashing Clare a shy grin he hurried off.

A pair of muscular legs encased in boots, hose, and breeches appeared beside Clare. There was no need for her to look up. She knew who it was. "Captain."

"Would you care to share the meal in my cabin?"

"I just accepted an invitation from Mr. Tait."

If he was disappointed he didn't show it. Instead he bowed. "I'll let you enjoy yourself then."

He strode away.

Tait eyed her speculatively.

She met his gaze silently, then turned her attention out to the blue-gray water of the ocean.

Dominic went down into the hold and found Gaspar and James still working on the inventory. The *Marie* had preyed upon sixteen enemy ships since setting out for sea last fall. The final accounting of everything from bottles of wine to grain would take some time.

"Thought you were eating with Clare?" Gaspar asked.

"Tait asked her first."

James hid his smile.

Dominic took a seat. "Why couldn't she just be a doxy I met in a tavern?"

"Because she isn't."

"You're so astute, Gaspar."

"Just stating the obvious."

Esteban walked in. Taking in the frustration on Dominic's face, he asked, "Is the lovely Clare still putting him through his paces?"

James and Gaspar nodded.

The Spaniard shook his head. "And that is why it is best to stay away from good women. They leave you hard and frustrated."

"I'm hard and frustrated because I don't want the crew to know I'm making love to her."

"You always were noisy. Remember that time in Venice when you—"

Dominic's sharp gaze cut him off.

Esteban replied, "Never mind."

Gaspar and James laughed.

Their captain skewered them with a look. "Aren't you two supposed to be working?"

"Aren't you?" Gaspar tossed back.

Dominic picked up a nearby crowbar and took out his foul mood on the crates.

By the second bell of the afternoon, all the sail repairs were done.

Tait put the needles in a metal snuff tin and said to Clare, "You should probably go back to the captain's cabin now, miss. Thank you for your help. We accomplished a lot today."

Clare agreed and stood. "Thank you for your kindness, gentlemen."

They each nodded in reply and she went on her way.

In the captain's quarters, she spied a book on the table. On top of the book lay a note upon which her name was penned. The book was John Milton's *Paradise Lost* and the note was from Dr. Early. He thought she might like to borrow it to pass the time. Silently blessing him, she settled into one of the chairs and began to read.

She was midway through the opening verses when a knock sounded on the door.

"Clare? May I enter?"

She set the tome aside. "Yes."

His entrance set off a familiar rush in her blood, but she did her best not to reveal it. "Good afternoon, Captain."

He bowed. "I came to make sure my crew has been treating you well and to see if there is anything you need."

"They have, and all needs have been met. How has your day fared so far?"

"Well. Things would be better if we were dropping anchor but that will come soon enough."

"How many more days?"

"Two at the most."

"Good. I've never been partial to ships, so it will feel good to be on solid ground once again."

"You don't care for sea travel?"

She shook her head. "In the past every ship reminded me of the slaver, until this one."

"That's good to hear."

"I've had good company and the *Marie* is not overly uncomfortable. The entire time the Sullivans and I were in England, I was not allowed to leave the ship or go above deck. Violet was afraid if I were seen the British would declare me free."

"Because of the Somerset case?"

"Yes." Clare had read in one of Teddy Sullivan's

English newspapers about a slave named James Somerset who'd won his freedom back in 1772. The British judge presiding over the case declared slavery to be so odious that not even law could support it. Although the controversial ruling didn't force slave owners in the colonies or in the British West Indies to free their captives, it did call into question the legality of bringing captives into England.

"We'll drop anchor in a few more days," he told her.

"I'm looking forward to it."

In the silence they fed on each other with their eyes. The undisguised desire she saw reflected in his ignited a yearning inside her that was embarrassing because of its strength.

"I must get back," he said quietly. "I'll see you at the evening meal."

She nodded and he exited.

Dominic didn't want to leave her, but was in a way glad that his captain's duties made it necessary. When he was with her, she was all he could think about. When he wasn't with her, she was all he could think about. He didn't want to study charts, settle disputes, or help catalog all the gold and booty in the hold. All he wanted to do was avail himself of her kisses while holding her in his arms. Soon, he'd be able to spend as much time with her as he craved, but for the present it would be better for the *Marie* and her crew if he continued to distance himself from the tempting Clare Sullivan.

As he made his way back down to the hold, he admitted that this constant wanting of her was not something he was accustomed to. In the past, no woman had ever occupied his mind to the point of distraction; women were women. They had their uses, and when he was done he moved on to the next. However, Clare was affecting him like an uncharted sea, and he had no stars to steer by. So far, they'd shared nothing but kisses, which made him wonder how he might be after they shared a bed. It was his hope that once they made love he could shake himself loose of her spell and regain full charge of his faculties, but she was so unlike the women that usually sailed in and out of his life that there was no guarantee.

At dinner that evening with the captain and his officers, Clare made a point of not focusing on him. By concentrating on the others she hoped to remain unmoved by his presence, but each time she stole a glance his way, his eyes were waiting. In response, her look would go chasing off, but the heat he evoked would remain, a vivid reminder of his power over her newly awakened senses.

Esteban was recounting the tale of an ancestor who'd been captain of one of the many Spanish ships sacked and plundered by the English privateer Sir Francis Drake on behalf of Queen Elizabeth. "Drake hated Spain and its people," he said, "but we hated him and the English more."

James grinned over his wine, "My ancestors hated them more. Remember Queen Mary of Scots, the sister of Elizabeth? She had her head chopped off."

"Which in no way compares with what he stole from the Spanish when he sacked Panama. For example, the one hundred and ninety mules he and his men ambushed carried three hundred pounds of silver each. Add to that fifteen tons of silver ingots, and an additional amount of gold coins said to have equaled one hundred thousand English pounds."

Gaspar whistled.

James said, "Doesn't equal a queen's head, my friend."

"You're right. It equals *more* than a queen's head. We've hated the English for two hundred years."

"Everyone hates the English," Dominic said. "So let's all agree. You're boring the lady."

"No they're not. I'm impressed that he can trace his ancestry back two hundred years." Clare countered, "Were all the men in your family sailors, Mr. da Silva?"

James cracked, "Only the ones who weren't pirates."

They all laughed including Esteban, who raised his glass to James. "He's right. I'm hoping to be the first male in my line to die of old age and not by noose."

Gaspar raised his glass, "To old age!"

The rest shouted, "Hear! Hear!"

After the humorous and vocal toast, Clare had a question, "Are you really allied with the American rebels?"

The officers turned to Dominic with knowing smiles.

He shrugged. "When it's in our best interest. We do have a letter of marque, and we do harass the British, but only if it suits us. We first take care of ourselves and those who depend upon us."

"So you are no different than Drake."

For a moment he didn't reply, then said, "I suppose."

An awkward silence filled the room, and no one felt it more than she. "My apology. I don't mean to judge. You all have been sterling gentlemen."

Dominic inclined his head. Because of his day-long moodiness, he found her censure grating. "We appreciate your compliment, but we live as we do because the world is neither a fair nor a just place, as you well know."

Her lips tightened. "Touché, Captain."

He inclined his head again and drained his wine. "Gentlemen, we still have much to do before dark. Let's leave Clare to her reading."

They all bowed her way and exited. No one looked back.

On their way back to the hold, Gaspar said to Dominic, "You were pretty harsh with her, *mon frere.*"

Dominic sighed. "Maybe."

James corrected him, "Certainly."

Esteban added, "Now, if you do not want her, just say so. The only reason I've not swept her off her feet already is out of respect for you."

Dominic rolled his eyes. "She thinks we're thieves and plunderers."

"And we're not?" Gaspar asked. "We have loot from how many ships in our hold? None of it was given to us out of charity. We stole it."

James said, "In much the same way you stole her."

"Thank you for the reminder. Would you all feel better if I apologized?"

"Yes," they said in unison.

He sighed again. "Fine. I will apologize. Who knew a woman could divide us."

Gaspar tossed back, "Who knew we'd meet a woman like Clare."

They were interrupted by the arrival of the fiddler, Pierre Tait. "Captain, I have composed an ode to Miss Clare. Do you think she would care to hear it?"

"An ode?" Dominic wondered if the irritation he felt towards Tait was jealousy.

"Yes, sir."

Esteban chuckled. "Add one more man to the crew of the Lady Clare."

Tait inclined his head.

Dominic said to him, "Give me time to catch up with the inventory here, and I'll go ask her."

"Aye."

"An ode?" Clare asked, confusion in her face. "To me?"

"You're the only Clare on board," Dominic told her. "He'd like for you to come up and listen."

Clare was astounded by the tribute. Never in her life had she imagined there'd be a musical composition dedicated to her, a slave woman. "I'd be honored."

"Before we go, I'd like to apologize for my harsh remark earlier."

"Only if I may offer one in exchange for my judgmental reply."

"I am what I am, *petite*."

"I know, and I have not suffered under your care in any way."

Dominic knew his reply had been out of proportion but he had no idea why he'd responded the way he had, other than his surly mood. Was he suddenly ashamed of how he lived his life? Did he wish to be seen differently through her eyes? "My crew is very taken with you."

"And I with them."

Dominic found himself bewitched by all that she was. From her short-cut hair to her small stature and regal bearing, she was nothing like the women who usually drew his eye. "Come. If I stand here a moment longer I'll be kissing you, and Tait's ode be damned."

In response, she lowered her eyes away from his smoldering gaze, but it was that unexpected innocence that she exuded that fed his desire as well.

"I'll get my cloak."

Up on deck, the men greeted her with nods. Once everyone was positioned, Tait began. Clare had been expecting a seaman's tune, a simple, merry piece of music similar to the others she'd heard him play before, but instead he'd composed a slow sweet composition fit for a queen. The pace, the soaring notes, and the sheer expressiveness showed him to be an exquisite musician. "He plays so beautifully," she whispered to Dominic.

The music soared, floating on the evening breeze. Everyone standing around listening stared mesmerized as he plied the bow over the strings with grace and skill. As the tune came to its end, enthusiastic applause and whistles of appreciation filled the deck.

Holding his instrument, Tait looked embarrassed by the praise. After bowing graciously in Clare's direction, he and his fiddle departed. The rest of the crew slowly peeled away until Clare and Dominic were left standing alone.

Dusk had fallen, and the *Marie*'s bell sounded to give the time and the shift change. Clare looked out over the horizon where the darkening sky met the sea and knew this was an experience she would never forget. Who knew she would take part in a voyage as memorable as the slaver that took her from Africa, but in an entirely different and wonderful way. "I'll always remember this, Captain."

"As will I."

Her awareness of him flared. She directed her attention back to the dark sky and saw the first star peek out. Other small twinkles joined it and glittered overhead.

"If I were home, I'd be fetching Violet's nightclothes and slippers, or maybe building the fire in her bedroom grate, or bringing her warm cocoa so she'd sleep. I would never be allowed to simply stand in the dark and watch the stars."

"To be able to take a moment and visually enjoy

God's creation without the fear of reprisal is one of the small treasures of freedom."

"So I am learning," she said, turning back to him.

"Would you like to have a picnic under the moon?"

The low-toned question made her glitter like the stars.

"Then take a stroll down the beach hand in hand?" He reached out and dragged a slow finger down her cheek.

The contact was dizzying. "Yes," she whispered.

"I'll feed you mangoes and guavas, and place blooms behind your ear that are more fragrant than any perfume. You won't have to worry about fetching slippers or fires or cocoa unless it is for your own benefit." And then, tossing away his vow to distance himself, he gently raised her chin and stared down into her shadow-shrouded face. He didn't need light to know how beautiful she was. Her features had burned themselves into his mind, and because they had, he kissed the mouth that fit so perfectly against his own, then languidly drew back to press his lips against her eyes, her brow, the lobe of her ear, then recaptured her mouth. "I can't wait to get you home," he breathed. She was as sweet as the warm evening breeze.

Clare couldn't wait, either. Although her experience with men could fit inside a thimble, she knew he would teach her all she would need, and she planned to be a diligent student. As now. With each passing moment she grew bolder and moved her mouth temptingly over his. He gathered her in, deepening the kiss, and a soft moan slid from her in response.

Somewhere from behind them, someone loudly cleared his throat.

Dominic lifted his head, "What?"

Gaspar turned his back to spare Clare any embarrassment. "It's time for the disciplinary hearing. The men are waiting."

Dominic sighed with frustration, while beside him Clare fought to find her way out of the fog of desire. "Let me escort Clare back to my quarters and I'll be right there."

"Today, Dominic," the quartermaster warned with humor.

"*Au revoir*, Gaspar."

The smiling quartermaster departed, and Dominic turned his attention to Clare. "I must leave you."

Her whole body seemed to be sparkling like the stars overhead. "You are the captain, Dominic. Go attend to your duties, I know my way back."

"Are you sure you don't want me to escort you, *bien-aimée*."

No man had ever called her sweetheart. She reached up and touched his cheek. "I am sure."

He turned her palm to his lips, placed a gentle kiss of farewell in the warm center, then left her shimmering and breathless and alone.

The last thing Dominic wanted to do was to leave Clare and preside over a disciplinary hearing. Even as he eyed the men involved, the tantalizing lure of her resonated. "Hugo Watkins, you are accused of stealing from Washington Julian. What say you?"

"He's lying, sir," the carpenter declared.

The Cherokee Julian barked a curse and had to be restrained by the men nearby. "Bloody bastard! You're the liar here!"

Watkins smiled smugly. He was known to be a cheat at everything from cards to dice. The only reason he was still on board was his position as carpenter, and he thought himself impervious to retribution because of it, but as noted before, Dominic didn't care for the man any more than the crew. With the *Marie* so near home, the crew could afford to do without him now. Dominic just hoped Julian had proof to back up his accusation. "Mr. Julian, what was stolen?"

"An ivory fan I purchased for my wife. It has been in my trunk, but was missing when I came off watch this morning."

"Why accuse Mr. Watkins?"

"Because he's been wanting me to sell it to him, and I've refused."

Dominic eyed the short, squat Watkins. "And you say you know nothing about this fan."

"Nothing, sir."

Dominic didn't believe him for a moment, but without solid evidence there could be no punishment. "Can anyone corroborate either guilt or innocence?"

Richmond Spelling stepped forward. "Have someone check the bore of cannon five," he said firmly. "I saw Mr. Watkins slip something inside during this morning's watch change. He didn't notice my approach until I asked what he was doing. He said he was checking the fuse, and for me to go on about my damn business."

"Really?"

Watkins no longer looked so smug.

"Mr. Spelling, did you notice the color of this something?"

"It appeared to be white, sir."

Julian snarled, "I knew it!"

The accused carpenter shot daggers at the young powder monkey. Dominic noticed Gaspar slip quietly from the room.

"I was checking fuses!" Watkins countered, staring hotly at Spelling. "Boy's obviously had too much grog."

Dominic ignored that. "Thank you, Mr. Spelling."

His face set sternly, Spelling stepped back into the group of seamen crowded around.

Dominic addressed the assemblage. "We all know that thievery from your fellows is one of the sailing's most heinous crimes. The *Marie*'s articles state that anyone convicted of such will be immediately banished."

Watkins tossed back with a sneer, "But there has to be solid proof, and all you have are the lies of a dirty Indian and a boy."

Julian erupted furiously and had to be restrained once more. Gaspar entered the room and stepped over to the table where Dominic was seated. He tossed the fan onto the table.

Watkins's eyes went wide as dinner plates.

"Where'd you find it?" Dominic asked the quartermaster.

"Exactly where Mr. Spelling said it might be."

The crew members closest to Watkins grabbed his arms. He struggled to free himself but they held fast.

Dominic called out, "At sunrise, Mr. Watkins will be put in a canoe, given oars, food, and water, and left behind. What say ye?"

The crew roared their support.

"Tie him up and put him in the hold," Dominic instructed. "Mr. Julian, your fan."

After Julian retrieved his property and Watkins was dragged away, Dominic said to the remaining seamen, "Gentlemen, we are done."

The next morning, as dictated by the captain's decree, the sullen-faced carpenter climbed down the rope ladder to the canoe bobbing on the ocean's surface. In the gray fog of dawn he and the small boat could barely be seen, but his curses rang loud. "A curse on you, LeVeq! I curse your crew and the *Marie*!"

The crew responded by tossing down rotting fruit and vehement curses of their own; some in French, some in Spanish, and some in fervent Italian. The loudest of all was a death curse chanted in the ancestral tongue of the Cherokee.

As always, Clare awakened before dawn. Hugging herself against the chill in the room, she padded over to the dying fire, poked at it in an effort to bring it back to life, then headed over to the basin and splashed some water on her face. She would have given anything for a bath but knew fresh water was a luxury on a ship, so she did the best she could with the small amount of water available. Moving behind the Cathay screen, she removed the nightshirt and donned her same blue dress. It, like her body, could use a good cleaning but there was nothing she could do about it, either.

Upon hearing a cacophony of noise that sounded like cursing she hurried over to the porthole in hopes of finding the cause. She didn't see another ship moored nearby, but she could only view the side of the *Marie* the porthole faced and not the other. She prayed they weren't preparing for another battle.

A knock on the door grabbed her attention. "Yes?"

"It's Dominic."

Surprised, she hurried to the door and opened it. He was holding her breakfast tray, another surprise. "Come in."

"Good morning," he said as he entered. "Did you sleep well?"

"Yes, I did. What is happening up on the deck?"

He set the tray on the table. "We had to banish a man for stealing. He put a curse on the ship."

She stared.

"So the crew cursed him in return."

"Ah."

"Shall we eat?"

"I thought you considered me too much of a distraction."

"You are, but I've decided to stop fighting a battle I will only lose."

The words were heady ones. It pleased her to know that he wanted her company, yet she forced herself to remember that no matter the course of their relationship they were destined to part ways, and it was best that she not let her heart become involved. She was certain his wouldn't be and that as soon as he left her in Savannah he'd be on to the next conquest. As a slave woman destined to remain loveless, however, this was her only chance to be desired and she planned to take it. That settled, they sat and shared another tureen of turtle soup.

Chapter 6

Two days later, Clare was up on deck talking with Richmond Spelling when the lookout in the rigging shouted, "Land ho!"

The crew greeted the call with a mighty yell.

"Finally!" Spelling cried, showing a white-toothed smile. "Finally home, miss!"

Men rushed to the side, eager for a first glimpse of the home they hadn't seen in months. Their elation was so contagious she found herself brimming with excitement as well. Although she had no ties to the place, the knowledge that she might soon be returning to Savannah and her children held its own joy.

The imminent homecoming had the deck of the *Marie* awash in celebration. The big cast-iron bell tolled madly. Tait was happily sawing away on his fiddle while gleeful crewmen danced arm in arm. Clare watched the French flag being hauled down and the Spanish colors run up in its stead. The number of different flags flown by the ship continued to confound and amuse. Dominic walked into view and she watched him be greeted with fervent handshakes and pats on his back. If the smile on his face was any indication, he was enjoying the lookout's news as much as his men.

Then he noticed her, and the noise around Clare faded away. Such a fine specimen of a man, she noted inwardly. It didn't matter that his loose-fitting white shirt and dark breeches weren't the cleanest. Nor did she care that his boots were scuffed and worn. The intensity in his gaze seemed capable of stopping time, all the while reminding her of the pleasures they'd shared and the ones he'd promised once they reached his home.

The spell broke when Gaspar approached him and he turned away. Only then did she realize she'd been holding her breath. Richmond was still at her side, and he must have been watching because he gave her a knowing smile before turning his attention back to the ocean.

A short while later with cannons booming to signal her arrival, the *Marie* entered its azure blue home harbor. A flotilla of small boats, canoes, and makeshift rafts came out to meet her, and each vessel was filled with waving and smiling men, women, and children. Most bore the kiss of Mother Africa on their skin, but a few were of other races. Clare, standing beside James, had never seen anything quite like it. One large canoe carried two drummers who were pounding out a syncopated greeting. Infected by the happiness she saw on all the faces, she asked, "Who are they?"

"Family, friends, children, sweethearts."

Some of the crewmen, spotting loved ones, dove off the side into the water and swam to meet them.

Watching the crewmen reach the boats and be hauled up, only to be covered with hugs and kisses, increased her smile. More and more small vessels came alongside, and the crewmen lining the rail waved and shouted greetings in reply. While the celebratory homecoming continued, Clare took in the stately palm trees dotting the edges of the beach and, off in the distance, the verdant mountain standing against the cloudless sky. "So this is Cuba?"

"One of its islands, yes."

"And unofficially?"

"It belongs to us."

Another surprise. Clare turned to face him.

"Dominic will explain."

The enigmatic response let her know there was more to this place than met the eye so she would take his suggestion and save her questions for Dominic, who was presently below decks preparing the cargo for unloading. The fleeting glimpse she'd had of him earlier had been her only one.

A long train of wagons, drawn by oxen, horses, and mules, making its way up the beach, caught her eye. Upon each vehicle and animal were more people, and even more individuals were walking beside the wagons. They appeared to be heading for the welcoming celebration as well.

Amazed by the sheer numbers on land and in the water, she asked, "How many people live here?" By then, there were so many vessels in the water, she wondered how Esteban would pilot the *Marie* the remaining short distance without accidentally sailing into them.

"About five hundred."

It was a small number when compared to the populations of the larger cities of Europe or even the colonies, but this place with its fragrant air and warm breeze appeared so wild and untamed it was hard to imagine it having any people at all. "Where do they live?"

"About ten miles inland."

"And there is a town?"

Chuckling, he nodded. "A small one."

Clare had difficulty containing her questions. She had at least a hundred if not more, and she wanted to ask them, but rather than pester the doctor she held on to them until she could get the answers from Dominic.

When they finally reached the dock, the anchor was dropped and the cheers of the *Marie*'s crew were drowned out by the thunderous cheers of the throngs awaiting them on the beach.

"Oh, sweet Mary!" James whispered in a mixture of awe and excitement.

"What's the matter?"

"My wife! There in the yellow dress! See her?"

Clare followed his pointing finger and saw a tall, black-skinned woman jumping up and down and waving frantically. James was doing the same.

Dominic appeared and James grabbed him. "Look at Cinda. She's carrying! Look at her belly!"

Before the grinning Dominic could respond, James ran for the plank that had been lowered to facilitate the departure. Clare watched the doctor quickly make his way through the press until he reached the woman in the yellow dress and matching headscarf and caught her up for a kiss that she returned passionately and without shame. "How long have they been married?"

"Almost two years."

In the colonies such unions between races were frowned upon, and in many places were downright unlawful, but here there seemed to be no such restraints. It was easy to see that James and his wife were very happy.

"Are you ready?" Dominic asked, interrupting her thoughts.

"Yes."

"I usually stay aboard until all the cargo has been unloaded, but the quartermaster has granted me special dispensation so that I may escort you home."

Clare found herself looking forward to his company very much. "Remind me to thank him."

He extended his arm and she took it gladly.

As they reached the lip of the plank Clare was not prepared for what happened next, though in retrospect, she should have anticipated it. The moment the crowd spotted Dominic it became quite apparent that they'd saved their loudest cheers of welcome for him. The ovation seemed to shake the harbor. He bowed graciously and gracefully. The roar continued and continued. Out in the crowd, she spotted the fiddler Tait applauding happily beside a blond woman with bright blue eyes. Hooting and clapping beside them were Richmond Spelling and, beside him, an older woman who resembled him so much, she had to be his mother or grandmother. To their left stood a smiling Washington Julian, who handed a white fan to a strikingly beautiful woman with skin the color of gold. Sprinkled throughout the crowd now chanting, "LeVeq! LeVeq!" were the men of the *Marie*, men who'd taken a slave woman into their midst and treated her with a deference and respect no one had ever shown her before. She'd never forget them.

Their captain finally put up a silencing hand. In response a hush fell over the adoring assemblage. "*Merci*," he said in an emotional-sounding voice.

Clare saw the same depth of feeling on his face.

Speaking in French he continued, "It is always good to come home."

The crowd let loose with another boisterous round of cheers.

"I have returned to you your husbands, fathers, sons, and cousins. Those of you who wanted them eaten by leviathans, my apologies. Maybe on the next voyage."

Laughter greeted that.

"We also returned with a guest. This lovely lady is Clare Sullivan. She'll be here for a short while and then sail home."

Friendly calls of welcome rang out, and she nodded in pleased response.

"Gaspar will be in charge of the unloading, and I'll see everyone at the feast tonight."

It took him and Clare a while to make their way through the crowd of well-wishers because he kept stopping to shake hands, give hugs, and greet small children who looked up at him with adoration and love in their eyes, but once he was done, he escorted her to a waiting wooden wagon. Seated on the bench with the reins in hand was the woman who favored Richmond Spelling. He was seated beside her.

Dominic made the introductions. "Clare, this is Anna Spelling, Richmond's grandmother. She's my housekeeper and cook. Anna, Clare Sullivan."

"Pleased to meet you, Anna."

"I'm pleased to meet you as well. You two get in and we'll head home."

Dominic undid the leather ties on the edge of the wagon's gate and swung it open. Before Clare had a chance to react, he placed his large hands on her waist and picked her up, then set her down gently inside the bed. While she fought to recover, he climbed in and reclosed the gate. Once the ties were secured, Anna called to the mules and they were under way.

Clare was seated with her back to the slats, and he scooted over until their bodies touched. He then draped an arm behind her. "The road can bounce you around a bit, want to make sure you arrive in one piece."

The feel of his body against hers was so overwhelming she feared she'd melt and arrive as a puddle. Conscious of Richmond and Anna's presence, she did her best to remain unmoved and nonchalant but it was extremely difficult. The heat of him, the scents of him, and her own rising need for him were doing their best to undermine her control.

"How has the place fared since we've been away, Anna?" he asked.

"Very well. Six new babies were born. The cane is in the fields and the weather has blessed us."

Richmond said, "First thing I want to do is sleep and then eat anything that isn't turtle soup."

Anna glanced over at her grandson and smiled. "The hunters brought in some boars for the feast tonight and they are roasting even as we ride."

"Very good. We've had nothing but turtle the past few months. I was afraid I'd wake up each morning with flippers instead of feet."

"How long were you and the crew away?" Clare asked Dominic.

"We sailed in November after the storm season, so five and a half months."

She now understood why their arrival had garnered such a celebratory response. The *Marie* and her crew had been gone a long good while. For their families it probably felt like a lifetime. Thoughts of family brought to mind her own children. It seemed like a lifetime since she'd seen them last. Aware that thinking of them would only serve to make her sad, she focused on the beautiful surroundings instead. "You were right," she said to Dominic. "This is a paradise."

The lush green land was awash with both color and fragrance, and everywhere she looked she saw beauty. The road they were traveling took them away from the beach and into a forest of tall trees. Birds of all hues and sizes flew overhead calling to their neighbors to alert them to the wagon's passage.

As they rode along, Dominic asked Anna about people in the community, but Clare didn't know them so she passed the time soaking in the sights and sounds of her surroundings instead. While he and Anna and Richmond conversed, he absently slid a bent knuckle over the skin of her neck in a seemingly unconscious way, but she was very conscious of the warm touch and her reaction to it.

"Oh, by the way," Anna said, "Sylvie is here."

His hand froze. "Oh, by the way?" he asked pointedly.

Anna shrugged. "I've been trying to pretend she's elsewhere. You can't blame me for wanting to put her out of mind."

Clare wondered who this Sylvie might be, and why Anna's news had garnered the reaction it had.

"How long has she been here?" he asked tightly.

"Since March. Apparently her husband asked that she leave. She said she had no place else to go."

"Couldn't convince anyone else to take her in."

"Is that any wonder?" Anna replied, her sarcasm plain. "She spent the first two days here making demands and ordering me to do her bidding, all of which I ignored."

Dominic sighed inwardly. It had been his hope that he and Clare would be able to settle in and enjoy each other until the time came for her to sail home, but now he had to remove the snake from paradise first. Sylvie had once been his mistress, but her faithless, lying nature caused him to send her packing. She was a vixen in bed. Out of bed he learned not to trust a word she uttered. It was a given she wouldn't leave his house quietly or willingly, but she would go. He refused to have her sully

Clare's small taste of freedom. He looked down into her dark eyes and ran his eyes over the features he'd remember always. "Are you comfortable?" he asked quietly.

"I am."

"Good. Plan on being so for your entire stay."

Her shy nod pleased him.

"How long have you lived in this place?" she asked.

"Four years."

"That's not very long."

"No, but with each passing year our roots grow deeper, more children are born, and our harvests increase." For a world that he and the others created, the colony's success was a remarkable achievement.

Travel was slow but it gave him the opportunity to point out the rivers and the wealth of fruit trees that later in the year would be thick with bounty like bananas and mangoes, both of which were foreign to her.

Clare couldn't believe how many different kinds of birds there were. "I've never seen such a variety."

"At one time this was called Isla de Cotorras."

Clare made the Spanish translation. "Parrot Island?"

"Yes, it's also been called Isla de Tesoros."

"Treasure Island?"

"Yes. During the age of Blackbeard and Bellamy when piracy ruled, ships regularly stopped here to take on fresh water or hunt for food. Legend has it that some also buried treasure."

"Has any been found?"

"Not as far as I know."

Clare didn't know what to say about this adventure she was on. Her previous life had been so narrow and colorless, she felt like an emerging hermit staring directly up into the sun. Pirates, sea battles, and musical compositions bearing her name. Who knew existence could be so rich? Having accompanied the Sullivans all over Europe, she thought she knew how people lived, yet this was something different entirely, and it was threatening to take her breath away. The moment Dominic carried her off the frigate and onto the *Marie* a new woman arose, one who walked freely, thought freely, and watched sunsets at her leisure. One who'd been kissed by a man and given tastes of passion and desire. It was all so heady Clare was surprised she was still upright. She stole a quick glance over at his face. He caught the look and gave her a smile that made her insides melt. The day he abducted her from the frigate, it never occurred to her that in the end she might be thankful, but at that moment she was, very.

A short while later they entered an area that had been cleared of trees. The open land, now fields, stretched for seemingly miles. A sea of bright green shoots dotted the rich black soil. "What crop is that?"

"Sugarcane, the life's blood of the Caribbean."

A settlement of small wooden houses flanked the fields, and behind it stood a tall stone wall that hid from view whatever might be on the other side.

"Welcome to Liberté," he said, picking up her hand and pressing the tips of her fingers to his lips in a gesture one part formal and a hundred parts sensual.

Freedom, she thought, translating the word and trying to remain unmoved by the sensations flaring from his eyes to hers. "Thank you."

"I hope you will enjoy my hospitality."

"And if I do not?"

"Then I shall try harder to please you."

That took her breath away.

As the wagon rolled closer she saw people in the fields and near the houses, many of whom came running at their approach, calling Dominic's name. Anna halted the mules so he could speak with them. They were as happy to see him as the crowd down by the water had been and were of African descent as well. They stared at Clare curiously and he made the introductions. When he was done, Clare looked at all the faces. She was certain she wouldn't remember many of the names but they greeted her warmly.

Anna got the mules moving again and the wagon rumbled its way through the large arch opening in the wall. They entered an enormous stone plaza that was surrounded by what could only be described as a small castle of Spanish design, complete with intricate ironwork over the windows and making up the many verandahs attached to the wall face. A few of the windows even had stained glass. The sand-colored structure looked old, as though aged by time and weather.

"This is your home?" she asked, turning his way.

He chuckled at the surprise on her face and threading her voice. "Yes. It was built by the Spanish at the close of the last century."

In spite of the age and worn condition the building was spacious and beautiful.

"The Spanish king required that all of their colonies erect a church, along with a building to conduct crown business and a mansion for the governor. The people here only got around to building the mansion before abandoning the island."

As Anna drew the mules to a halt, Clare viewed the tunnellike alcoves leading from the plaza into the house. A weathered bell hung in a battered stone tower rising from one of the cone-shaped roofs.

"Christopher Columbus was the first European to drop anchor here." He undid the wagon gate and stepped out. "Spain enslaved the native population but lost them all to the diseases the Spanish brought with them."

Once again he placed his hands on her waist and gently swung her out and onto her feet. "They abandoned this outpost a half century ago."

Clare stood on suddenly wobbly legs. From past voyages she knew this was to be expected after so much time aboard ship and that it might take a day or so for her body to accustom itself to walking on solid ground again.

He seemed to be cognizant of what was going on with her and so scooped her up into his strong arms.

"Put me down!" she said, scandalized. Richmond was viewing them with humor, but his grandmother's face was closed.

"Put me down, Dominic! I can manage on my own." Although Clare didn't know a thing about Richmond's grandmother, something inside made her wish for the woman not to think her weak and in need of coddling.

Clare was just about to restate her demand when a tall, brown-skinned woman dressed in an expensive-looking green gown swept into view. Her stomacher and petticoats were of high quality, and the lace at her wrists flowed elegantly. Beneath her lacy cap, the features of her face were too sharp to be considered truly beautiful, but she had a regal bearing and appeared to be well endowed.

The sight of Clare in Dominic's arms brought her to an abrupt stop. Viewing Clare up and down as if she were an ugly insect she asked him coolly, "Your latest plaything?"

He slowly lowered Clare back to her feet. "Anna, will you escort Clare in, please."

Anna, shooting daggers at the woman, replied to him with a terse nod, while her grandson looked on coldly.

Before they departed, Dominic took a moment to gently raise Clare's chin. "I'll join you in a moment, *petite.*"

Accepting his words without comment, she followed the Spellings towards the house.

Chapter 7

alking with Clare and Richmond by her side, Anna sniffed, "With any luck, she'll be on a boat back to Jamaica by sunset."

"Lord willing," Richmond replied.

Anna had already given Clare the impression that she didn't care for the woman and this was further proof. As much as Clare wanted to know the extent of their relationship with Sylvie, she didn't ask. Being a servant herself, she knew gossip was frowned upon, and she didn't wish to put Anna in an awkward position.

"Miss Clare, I'll be leaving you now, but I shall see you this evening," Richmond said, favoring her with a bow very much reminiscent of his captain.

"Thank you, Richmond. You've been very kind."

After placing a kiss on his grandmother's cheek and receiving a strong hug in response, he left them to seek what Clare supposed were his own quarters.

"He's a fine young man, Anna."

"I've done my best to honor my daughter, his mother, with his raising." She didn't say more, so any questions Clare might have had about the powder monkey's personal life went unspoken.

A few short steps later, Anna pulled open a large iron grille that led them into a quiet courtyard awash with tropical blooms that scented the air. From her travels with the Sullivans, Clare knew that in Spain such places were known as piazzas. Stone benches flanked a reflecting pool built into the marble plaza. The enclosure had a peaceful, restful atmosphere that was almost palpable.

"This is beautiful."

"Yes it is. The captain sits out here to relax, and when he needs to think over things."

Clare wondered if this was the same piazza he'd made mention of on the *Marie* when he'd whispered his desire to have her stand nude in the sunlight. The scandalous thought scalded her cheeks. Hastily setting it aside, she focused on following Anna across the marble-paved way of the stone-capped breezeway. She couldn't help but wonder about what Dominic and the Sylvie woman might be discussing, though. What if he decided he'd rather entertain her instead of Clare? Yet another thought she put aside because she didn't wish to dwell on it or the possible ramifications.

They entered the house through another intricately worked iron gate. The interior with its soaring curved ceilings was many degrees cooler than it had been outdoors, and was filled with diffused light from the windows. To her left she saw an elegantly furnished sitting room, anchored by an enormous fireplace with fine Turkish rugs spread across the marble floors. She and Anna climbed a stone stairway to an upper floor and then walked down an expansive hall. Every few feet there were elegantly carved wall niches that might have held statuary at one time but now stood empty. At the hallway's end stood another decorative grille, and behind it an imposing, heavy wood door with aged brass fittings.

Inside Clare's eyes were caught first by the wealth of hanging panels of gold-toned netting flowing about the entrance, and as she advanced farther, by the view through the wide pane-free windows of the sparkling blue Caribbean off in the distance. Only then did she see the bed. The area around it was draped in the same fine-gauge netting, and it appeared to be even larger than his bed on the ship. The highly polished wood and the gilt-edged headboard with its monogrammed inset could have easily come from Versailles. "Is this the captain's quarters?"

"It is," Anna replied.

"Might there be another room for me to use?"

Anna studied her for a silent moment. "You don't wish to be in here with him?"

"If he needs privacy, I'd like to spare myself the embarrassment of having to move elsewhere." Clare had always been a realist and in spite of Dominic's promises to her on the *Marie*, she had no idea what would really happen between him and the tall and elegant Sylvie. If he chose to entertain her instead, Clare didn't want to be in the way.

"Are you certain?"

"Yes."

"Then come."

They left the room, and Anna led her back down to the other end of the hall and around a corner. The room they entered next also looked out on the water, but was smaller, as was the bed.

"I'll have to get bedding," Anna explained.

Clare could see the bare mattress. "If you bring it to me I can place it on the bed."

Anna stared again.

"Is something the matter?"

"I'm not sure." For a few more moments she evaluated Clare silently, then shook her head. "You are certainly nothing like the others he's brought here."

Clare didn't say anything but Anna must have seen something in her eyes because she added, "I like you. Settle yourself in and I will return with bedding. Is Gaspar bringing your trunks?"

"I have none."

"No? The others usually arrive with trunks bursting with gowns and make straight for his bed. You undoubtedly have an interesting story to tell."

Clare's eyes lit with humor but she didn't respond further.

"I will bring the bedding and send someone up with water so you may bathe."

The idea that she would soon get to bathe made Clare want to kiss the woman. "Thank you, Anna."

"You are welcome, miss. I'll return shortly."

Downstairs in the courtyard, Dominic was eager to join Clare but had to rid himself of Sylvie first.

She was trying to make the process difficult.

"But Dominic, where will I go?" she asked, pouting.

"Back to Jamaica and your husband."

"He's forbidden me to return. I told you the old fart caught me with one of the grooms. It was very embarrassing but what's a woman like me supposed to do for pleasure? I certainly don't find any with him, and besides," she said, sidling closer and draping her arms sinuously around his neck, "we both know I can warm your bed better than that one who is with you. I doubt she'll consent to any of the things I know you'll want her to do."

A muscle tightened angrily in Dominic's jaw as he gently but firmly removed her arms. "If you have nowhere to go you should have considered that before being mounted by one of Lord Kinney's stable hands." Her husband, Lord Kinney, was a retired Jamaican official. He was well up in age, and although she'd known that when they married last summer, at the time her desires had centered solely on having unlimited access to his gold. "Either remove yourself and your belongings, or I'll have placed them out by the road."

"But Dominic—" she whined pitifully.

"Good day, Sylvie." He bowed with icy formality and strode off.

Dominic entered his room, and the familiar sight of his sanctuary coupled with the idea of sharing it with Clare put a smile on his face. Now that he no longer had to contend with Sylvie, Clare filled his mind. He walked farther into the room expecting to find her there, but was met by echoing silence. Perplexed, he did a quick search of the rooms that led off his suite of rooms. No Clare. Thinking she must be somewhere with Anna, he strode back to the stairs. Anna was ascending, her arms laden with bedding. "Where's Clare?"

"In the blue room."

"Why?"

"That is the room she chose. She wants to give you privacy in case you need it."

Dominic didn't understand.

"She's not like the others you've brought to the island."

"I agree, and it's those differences that make her so special."

"I like her."

That pleased him. Anna was very special to him as well, even if she did tend to be abrasive more often than not. "Why would she think I'd need privacy?"

"Sylvie, maybe?"

"That's ridiculous."

"Maybe to you. To her, maybe not."

Dominic sighed. "I'll just have to move her back."

"That is her decision."

"Then I'll have to change her mind. Give us some time alone before you come up."

Anna nodded.

*   *   *

While waiting for Anna to return, Clare stepped out onto the verandah connected to the small room and looked out towards the water. They'd sailed in from the south, so the windows were facing north. She could see the southern coastline of Cuba's main island. Somewhere beyond it and the glistening sea were the colonies and home. She wondered how the war was faring. Had the rebels surrendered, or were the crown's forces on the run? Were the patriots still holding Savannah, or had the British invaded and restored the city to the crown? There was no way of knowing. Being on the *Marie* and now here had distanced her so much from the everyday events on the continent that her former life might as well have been imaginary. It wasn't, of course, and neither were her children, but at the moment she felt as if she were living inside a dream.

Her musings were interrupted by the sounds of footsteps in the room. She glanced in, and there stood Dominic. Her heart skipped. As he joined her out on the verandah he focused his gaze on the sea.

"Beautiful view, isn't it?" he asked, looking down at her.

"Spectacular."

Because he was gazing at her so intently, she set her eyes back on the panoramic view.

"Anna tells me you have chosen this room. May I ask why?"

She offered a tiny shrug. "I assume you and Sylvie were once together and I didn't wish to be an impediment if you decided to take up with her again."

He asked her softly, "Did I give you any indication that I might?"

"No, you didn't, but truthfully, I haven't much experience with men. However, I watched Violet's intended pursue her for nearly two years with pretty words and promises, only to not show himself at the church on the day they were to marry."

"I see. So you were trying to spare yourself and your feelings just in case."

"Yes. I may not know men but I know that I will not share you, Dominic, no matter how short the time we spend together."

The honesty in her eyes was plain. "May I be truthful with you?"

"Please."

Dominic wasn't certain how this small unique woman had worked her way into the fabric of his being in so short a time, but he would feed himself to the sharks before causing her even a second of pain. "Showing you the truth may be better than words. . . ."

Placing his hands around her waist, he eased her in against his length and raised her chin so he could feast visually on the lips he had come to crave from sunset to sunrise. Bringing his mouth down to hers, he whispered, "I've chosen you, *petite*. No other."

He kissed her, slowly, passionately, intensely. "You, Clare," he murmured. "Only you . . ."

Shaken by the power flowing from him, Clare returned the kiss and mapped her hands blindly up and down the muscled lengths of his hard arms, pressing herself closer. His lips traveled over the edge of her trembling throat and then drank from the soft skin covering her jaw.

"And I will not share you, either, *bien-aimée*," he pledged. "Ever. Never . . ."

Clare's world was spinning. Every press of his lips sank her deeper into the maelstrom fed by his touch and the seductively whispered promises.

He husked out against her ear, "Do you really wish to be in here where I can't kiss you . . . or touch you . . . this way . . . ?"

He circled his palm lazily over her breast. As the tip blossomed, hardened, and pleaded for more, a moan rose from deep in her throat.

"Do you wish to be alone . . . or with me, Clare?"

He bent and gently nipped her throbbing nipple. When he transferred his erotic attention to her other breast, her world exploded. Arching bonelessly, she cried out in a soft raw voice, "You, Dominic. With you . . ."

Knowing an orgasm when he heard one, Dominic picked her up and carried her from the room.

His boots sounded loud against the marble floor and his long strides made short work of the lengthy distance down the niche-lined corridor. In his arms, Clare was so overcome she didn't know if she was on land or sea. Only he mattered. Held against his heart, she pulsed everywhere, from her lips and breasts to the shadowy place between her thighs. His masterful caresses had made her body shatter, and she was certain she'd still be trying to find pieces of herself come sunrise.

As they approached his door, the sight of Gaspar and Esteban posed beside it narrowed Dominic's eyes. "What?"

Gaspar shrugged, keeping his gaze away from Clare. "Sorry. Levine wants to see you. He's trying to change the price on the guns."

"Can't you two handle it?"

Esteban shook his head. "Says he'll only negotiate with you."

Dominic wanted to lean back and roar with frustration. "Meet me downstairs."

They nodded and complied.

Dominic entered his suite and set Clare on her feet. Viewing her passion-swollen lips and thinking of the pleasure he'd hoped to continue, the last thing he wanted to do was to leave her. Tracing that same mouth with a light finger, he bent and kissed it softly. "I must go and handle this."

Clare's world was still hazy but not so much that she didn't feel the regret. "I understand."

They spent the next few moments sharing a reluctant kiss-filled farewell. "I'll send Anna up," he breathed against her ear.

She watched him remove a clean change of clothing from his armoire and depart. She and her pulsing desire were left in the room alone.

Downstairs, Gaspar and Esteban were waiting as he'd asked. After he conferred a moment with Anna, the three men left the house, but Dominic's angry strides took him in the opposite direction.

Gaspar and Esteban shared a confused look.

"Where are you going!"

"To the waterfalls for a cold shower! I'll meet you at Levine's shortly."

The two friends smiled.

In addition to owning one of the most fabled taverns in the Caribbean, Moses Levine was a prominent weapons merchant and smuggler. It was he who would make the arrangements for the selling and the shipment north of the muskets Dominic and his crew had taken from the British frigate, but the price he'd quoted Gaspar and Esteban was far below the price he'd contracted with Dominic. He was a mousy little man of about fifty years of age who couldn't see his hand in front of his face without his thick-lensed spectacles. "Ah, LeVeq," he voiced warmly as the freshly washed and clothed Dominic, flanked by Gaspar and Esteban, walked into his office above the tavern. "So glad the winds brought you and the *Marie* home safely."

Dominic inclined his head in greeting. "*Merci.* Just don't take all of my crew's gold in one evening."

Levine gave him a yellow-toothed smile, "That will be up to them and the girls, I'm afraid. Have a seat please."

Dominic knew that Levine's outwardly sunny disposition had nothing to do with the shark's heart that beat within, but he took a seat. The shabby office was piled high with papers and crates. It was a windowless space and smelled heavily of mildew, bodies, and rum. "My friends tell me there is an issue over payment for the guns."

"I'm afraid so. It has become increasingly difficult to run the blockade. The smugglers are demanding more, thus forcing me to cut what I can offer to pay good clients like yourself."

"And without my goods you make no profit at all, am I correct?"

Levine studied him for a long moment. "Aye."

"Then I suppose we'll just run the blockade ourselves. No sense in your people risking the danger if they are not up to the challenge." With that, Dominic stood. Clare was waiting. He had neither the time nor the inclination to dicker with greedy little businessmen. At least pirates kept their word.

"No! Wait, LeVeq."

"Will you pay me the agreed-upon price?"

"I can't, not and balance the books."

Dominic bowed and looked to Gaspar and Esteban. "Gentlemen, let's leave Mr. Levine to his books, shall we?"

Without further word, they exited.

Levine ran to the door. "Wait! LeVeq! Please! Let's discuss this!" but they didn't break stride.

Outside the noisy tavern, Dominic asked, "Esteban, do you think your cousin in Florida can get us a fair price?"

"If he can't, he'll know someone who can." Esteban's cousin Ferdinand lived on one of the Key Islands of Spanish Florida and was a well-known smuggler whose tentacles reached from Canada to Jamaica.

"Good. Gaspar, when can we sail again?"

"Between the careening and obtaining supplies, a month at least." Careening involved scraping the *Marie*'s hull free of the barnacles, seaweed, and other debris that might have attached itself during the long sea voyage. It was a long and arduous process because the ship had to be hauled onto the beach and turned over on its side.

"What if we take the *Liberté*?" Dominic asked. The *Liberté*, named for their home, was the sloop they employed for short runs to the islands in the area.

"Two weeks, give or take a few days."

"We'll sail her then. She's faster and we won't need as large a crew. We can also see Clare back to Savannah, so let's give ourselves a few days' rest, and you time with your ladies, then begin the necessary preparations."

They spent a few more minutes discussing the distribution of the remaining haul from the *Marie*'s hold. Some items, like the grain and gold, would stay with the people of the island, but the rest, from dry goods to casks of wine, would be sold to other Caribbean contacts.

Their talk now done, Dominic mounted his horse, Louis, and turned the white stallion's head towards home.

As he rode, he did his best to throw off the weariness. Exhaustion held him in so strong a grip he was surprised he hadn't already tumbled from Louis's saddle. As he cast his mind back in an effort to remember the last time he'd had a full night's sleep,

Clare's face rose to remind him that it had been the night before he brought her on board. Feisty, intelligent, beautiful Clare. She could speak four languages from lips headier than the finest wine. Thinking of her presented him with his other major problem. Arousal. Touching her and kissing her left him in a constant state of need. He was going to have trouble walking upright if he didn't get some relief soon. Just thinking about her made his manhood swell, and he found himself shifting in his seat in order to remain comfortable. Were it not for the gathering this evening, he'd spend the night teaching her the ins and outs of passion; however, the homecoming feast was a tradition, and he wanted to be there.

So for the time being, sleep would have to wait. Once his duties were done, though, he planned to sleep uninterrupted; preferably with the nude and sexually exhausted Clare Sullivan by his side.

Unaware of how long Dominic might be away, and rather than sitting in his room twiddling her thumbs, Clare opted to accompany Anna back to the beach to help with the feast. She was tired but not enough to take to her bed as Violet would have. They were riding along in the wagon as it bumped its way along the uneven tract that served as a road and she was again mesmerized by the island's lush beauty. "How long have you lived here, Anna?"

"Long enough to know that this is heaven on earth."

Clare wondered if the housekeeper was being purposefully enigmatic. "It is a very beautiful place."

Loaded in the wagon's bed were a number of large torches, old quilts, crocks of rice and beans, along with an assortment of tin plates, cutlery, and mugs. The sun was setting. "How long does the feast usually last?"

"Sometimes days."

"Really."

"Depends on how long the dancing goes and how much rum the men drink. One year after a particularly long voyage we celebrated for nearly a week."

"There's dancing?"

"And drumming and weddings."

Clare turned to her with surprise.

"There are no ministers on the island, so Dominic presides over them instead."

It was yet something else Clare didn't know about her pirate captain. "How many weddings will there be this time?"

"Just one. Gaspar and Suzette."

Another surprise. Clare had had no idea the quartermaster had an intended. She wondered if he'd had the chance to reunite with his Suzette since dropping anchor, or if he was still busy with tasks tied to the *Marie*.

The wagon rolled past a short stone building perched on a hill a short distance above the road. By its architecture it appeared to be another structure abandoned by the Spanish, although this one lacked the grandeur of the governor's mansion. Loitering outside its door were a number of men and women drinking from the mugs in their hands. They appeared to be having a good time. Rousing fiddle music drifted to her ears from inside the place, along with the sounds of laughter and raised voices.

"That's Levine's tavern. It was once a Spanish garrison. Now it's all doxies, ale, and gambling. He's going to do good business the next few days."

They'd almost passed the establishment when Clare noticed a wagon pull up to the tavern's door and then saw the familiar face of a woman being handed down by a short man wearing spectacles.

"I see Sylvie's found her a new home," Anna cracked. "The man with her is Levine."

Clare watched him gesturing to some of the male loiterers to unload what must be Sylvie's trunks before he escorted the woman inside.

"They'll do well until they turn on each other like vipers do."

Clare didn't know what to say to that prediction, so she stayed silent.

Anxious to get Clare in his arms, Dominic took the steps to the upper floor two at a time. Entering his room he was met by silence and no one. Again! Biting down on his frustration he went back down the staircase calling for her and Anna, but found only a note from Anna instructing him to meet them at the feast. Certain that the fates were bent upon keeping him from his prize, he remounted Louis and rode off.

The setting sun was like a ball of fire melting into the ocean and Clare paused to take in the magnificent sight. Who knew sunsets could be so moving or so brilliant? Over the past week, she'd seen more sunsets than she'd ever seen in all her life as a captive, and each held its own unique and distinct beauty. When she returned to Savannah there'd be no more stopping to watch the day's radiant end, but she vowed to remember the vistas and store the memories of them in her heart along with all the other wonderful experiences she'd tucked away in order to offset the silent gray existence awaiting her back home.

"Miss Clare?"

It was Anna, and she was viewing Clare with concern. "Are you unwell?"

"No, I'm fine," she replied. "Just musing on the beauty of the sunset." She hoped she'd successfully masked the melancholy that had suddenly washed over her.

She hadn't. Anna studied her for a moment more. "All right. Will you place this platter on that table there?" She was indicating the last of the three long trestle tables laden with food. "Careful, it's hot."

Clare worked her hands onto the pads Anna was carrying the crock with and walked it slowly over to the table, and set it down among the many other crocks and groaning platters of meat, fruits, and yams.

As she walked back to the women setting up the tables, Clare was glad she'd come along. She hoped helping out would let the women know she was willing to be a productive member of their island community and use this as an opportunity to meet more of the people.

Areas on and above the beach were buzzing with activity. Children were playing in the water, and those who weren't were running all over the place, having their own version of a good time. Stacks of felled trees hauled in on wagons were being set up in a circle down on the sand while other trees were dropped off in groups near the area where the food tables were.

"What are the logs for?" she asked Anna, who was coming out with yet another crock, this one filled with crowder peas and rice.

"Seating," she explained, handing the crock over to Clare.

Drumming suddenly filled the air, and Clare looked up to see a group of men on the hill above pounding the skins of beautifully painted instruments both short and tall. The hypnotic rhythms had everyone swaying and the little children dancing to the beats of Africa. Down near the water, a dozen big boars were roasting on spits over fire pits dug out of the sand. The men tending to them were sipping from mugs of rum and seemed to be having their own good time.

Called by the drums, more people arrived and immediately began to assist with the preparations. Clare saw the familiar faces of the *Marie*'s crew and people she'd met when the ship docked. Others were not known to her but all had ready smiles and a good word to pass along after Anna made the introductions. The women Clare was working beside seemed to accept her presence without issue and expressed gratitude for her help. Most spoke French, but a few were able to converse in French-accented English. When they found out she could speak French as well, the English was dropped and all conversation flowed in their native tongue. However, Clare soon realized that her tutor-taught command of the language was woefully inadequate in an everyday situation. Some of the words and phrases she understood fully, others caused her to struggle, but the women were patient with her even if they did chuckle at her Savannah-accented voice.

For her next task, Clare was seated on an over-turned bucket cutting up fruit to go into something Anna called sangria.

"It's a drink made out of wine and fruits," explained the woman beside her. Her name was Odessa. She was about Clare's age.

Clare was about to ask a question, but glancing up she saw Dominic moving through the gathering astride a beautiful white stallion and she went still. Everything on him was clean, from the snow white, long-sleeved shirt to his gleaming hair to the snug breeches that showed off the hard lines of his thighs above the white stockings and straight soled shoes. He sat the horse as regally as any king, and the people around, young and old, flocked to him as if he truly were their regent. When he bent down and took a young boy up onto the saddle in front of him, she smiled. She could see the boy's wide grin and that Dominic wore one as well.

"What a marvelous example of God's work," Odessa said in French. "He is a joy to look upon, is he not?"

The mesmerized Clare could only nod.

"You are a lucky woman that he has turned his eyes to you, Clare Sullivan."

Clare agreed, especially when those eyes found hers. His smile broadened, and he very gently placed the boy back on the ground before reining the powerful horse in her direction. As if she were already feeling his heated touch and magical kisses, her body blossomed with anticipation.

Odessa's laughing voice broke into her musings. "Clare?"

Clare shook herself free.

Odessa held out her hand. "Give me the knife before you hurt yourself."

Clare looked down at the loose hold she had on the large knife, and realized she'd no idea when she'd risen to her feet. Chagrined, she surrendered the blade and reset her focus on Dominic.

"Now, go to him. You've helped us more than a guest should today. Your tasks are done."

Being a well-mannered woman, Clare knew she should protest such largesse, but manners had nothing to do with the reality of how much she wanted to be with him. "Thank you, Odessa."

"Go," her new friend responded kindly. "I will see you later."

Walking to meet him was one of the boldest things she'd ever done; women were not supposed to be so forward as to approach a man this way, but since meeting him she'd done many bold things and doubted this would be the last of them.

"I've been searching for you," he said quietly as he pulled up beside her.

"And now that you have found me?" she asked softly, playfully.

He bent down so only she could hear, "There are a dozen things I'd like to do to you, sweet Clare, all of them scandalous."

Her knees turned to sand and she fought to regain her equilibrium. "I doubt the parents here would appreciate such a display."

"Which is why we'll save the displays for after the feast." Upright in the saddle again, he said, "Let me take Louis over to the pen." He patted the stallion's neck affectionately. "This is Louis. He is named for the French kings. Louis, meet Clare."

The horse turned black liquid eyes her way.

"He's very handsome," she said, but it was Louis's even more handsome rider who had her at sixes and sevens.

As if sensing her sensual distress, he asked wryly, his eyes as wicked as his smile, "Are you going to be all right?"

"Just go," she told him with mock impatience.

"As you wish, but when I return, plan on me being by your side for the rest of the evening. I've had a bellyful of chasing people around today when you were the only one I wanted to catch."

"You caught me earlier," she tossed back; another bold move. The memory of his mouth on her breasts set off its own inner fire.

"But unfortunately I had to let you go. There will be no such interruptions tonight. The first person to disturb us will get a musket ball right between the eyes."

She shook her head with amusement and watched him and Louis gallop away.

Chapter 8

Clare enjoyed the feast. There was wonderful food, there was dancing rooted in the African tradition, and, true to his word, Dominic never left her side. However, he had to excuse himself from her when it came time for the wedding. Guided by the burning torches set up along the way, everyone filed down to the beach and took seats on the logs while Dominic, Gaspar, and the tall, willowy, brown-skinned Suzette stood in the center of a torch-lit circle outlined by rocks.

Dominic waited until everyone was settled. When it became silent enough to hear the water meeting the shore, he asked in an affection-laden voice, "Suzette, are you certain you wish to do this? I've known Gaspar since we were both boys and I wouldn't take a king's ransom to marry him."

Everyone laughed.

In response, she smiled up at the solemn-looking quartermaster decked out in all his finery and placed a tender palm against his dark cheek. "More certain than I've ever been about anything."

"Then let's hurry this along before you change your mind."

More laughter.

When it faded, he asked solemnly, "Do you, Suzette, take my brother Gaspar as your one true love in fair winds and storm, in feast and in famine, in poverty and wealth, for the rest of your days?"

"I do."

Dominic asked the same question of Gaspar, and his answer echoed Suzette's.

"Then by the power invested in me as your captain, I pronounce you legally wed. May the sun shine on your marriage always."

Gaspar took Suzette in his arms, gave her a long kiss, and a rousing cheer went up from the crowd.

After toasts were given by *Marie* mates Dominic, Esteban, and the doctor James Early, the cake was eaten, the drumming resumed at a feverish pitch, and the revelers rose to their feet to dance as the true celebration began.

"Shall we sneak away?" Dominic asked after a while.

In the torch-lit darkness, Clare gazed up into his powerful face. His proposal flooded her senses with warm excitement. "Your duties are done?"

"Here, yes."

The implication made her tremble with anticipation. "Then I am ready."

After offering good-byes and collecting Louis from the makeshift pen, Dominic mounted, then set Clare in the saddle ahead of him. They rode slowly to keep Louis from injuring himself in the moonlit darkness. "Quite the day," Dominic said softly.

The sounds of the drumming could still be heard echoing against the night. "I agree."

"Didn't think I'd ever get you alone again."

She leaned in against his strong shoulder, content. "I've missed you as well."

"When we get home, we'll make up for lost time."

And it was another promise she couldn't wait for him to keep.

Unsaddling Louis and leaving him in his stall, Dominic draped an arm around Clare's waist and walked her up to the dark house. The breeze flowing in off the water had lifted the afternoon's oppressive heat, and replaced it with air that was cool and sweet. Unable to hold off any longer, Dominic stopped and lifted her face to the moonlight and his hungry eyes. Time stood still as he gazed down at her, and at the end of that timeless moment he kissed her gently and then gently again. For the next little while he took tiny sips from her tempting lips, feeding his passion and hers until they both craved more. Their embrace tightened, and the kisses deepened. Finally they parted so they could breathe.

"I want you, *petite*."

And she wanted him. Clare felt her body opening and calling. His kisses set her on fire. The lips now traveling over her jaw and throat made her lean back so she could offer him more. When he centered his mouth on the hollow of her throat and flicked his tongue against the soft skin, she moaned, then moaned again in response to the knowing hand moving over her breasts in a lazy erotic rhythm. Off in the distance laughter and drums could be heard, but Clare was more aware of the drum beating sensually between her thighs.

"If we stay here one more moment I'm going to take you right here on the grass," he confessed in a husky voice, "so let's go inside."

He picked her up and carried her into the dark house and up the staircase to his suite of rooms. Inside he walked through the darkness and the netting that was fluttering in the breeze flowing in through the open windows, and set her down in the center of the enormous bed.

He left her there for a moment to light a small oil lamp on the far side of the room, and Clare realized she was more nervous than she'd ever been before in life. Her past experiences with coitus had not been pleasant. In fact, if left up to her she'd never be a participant again, but Dominic had earned her trust; if he promised being with him would be different, she was ready and willing to be shown.

Framed by the low glow of the lamp he returned and joined her on the bed.

"Nervous?"

"Yes."

He placed a reverent kiss on her brow. "Don't be. Your pleasure is all that will matter."

Kissing her until she was supine, he continued to slowly learn her body with his hands; cupping curves, sliding his palms over planes, tracing the lines of her neck with trailing fingers. Clare already knew that being with him was wonderful but this unhurried, uninterrupted exploration was beyond words.

He sat up and gently undid the drawstring at the neck of her blouse and drew it out until the loosened fabric exposed her collarbone and the caps of her shoulders. He welcomed the satin skin with kisses and caressing hands. "Let's take this off . . ." he whispered.

Seconds later the borrowed blouse she'd been given by Anna was removed, revealing the thin white shift she wore beneath the tightly bound stays. The sleeveless shift gave him his first look at her bare arms, and he gifted each inner elbow with a tender kiss. His mouth roamed, and she wondered if there were any parts of her body he could not set aflame.

Moving up, he brushed his lips over the soft tops of her breasts covered by the shift and mounded above her stays, then began unlacing her with a deliberate, kiss-punctuated slowness that made her moans rise against the silence. The soft rhythm was between her legs again, a prelude to a new sensual dance.

The stays vanished and she was left wearing the shift that bore the wrinkles and creases of being bound up. For Dominic it was quite an erotic sight. She was lying beneath him like a painting. The taut nipples straining against the wrinkled garment made his desire swell, so he played with them for a moment until she groaned and her hips rose. Holding the bud between his fingers he ran his free hand over the dark skirt to caress her legs and thighs. She was slowly twisting now, her body arching, her lips parted as he continued to tantalize her with his touch. Brushing the halves of the shift aside he filled his hand with her breast and then brought the tight tip to his mouth.

Release crackled over Clare like lightning on the ocean and she crooned and cried and felt herself shattering into a hundred pieces. Above her, Dominic smiled malely. His manhood was hard as a ship's mast, and Poseidon knew he wanted to raise her skirts and push his way into paradise but he forced himself to hold off. It wasn't time yet. He'd spent days waiting to see her just this way and he had all night.

"Are orgasms always so powerful?" she asked finally, her voice hushed. Every part of her being felt full and hot.

He kissed her gently, "Yes, which is why the French call it *le petit morte*."

"The little death?"

He nodded.

"Dying can't be that spectacular, can it?" In retrospect, all the orgasms he'd brought her to previously had been magnificent enough to break the bonds of heaven. "My lord." She hadn't experienced any of this when her children were conceived.

Tempted by the softness of her skin, he trailed a finger over the edges of her exposed breast and circled the tight brown tip. "I told you it would be different. Are you ready for more?"

"Oh yes."

So he gave her more; more kisses, more tugs on her pleading nipples with his warm lips, followed by more wandering hands above and underneath her skirt and petticoat as he removed them both. Wearing only her opened shift, stockings, and drawers, she was a heady sight for his adoring eyes. Her stocking-covered legs were soft yet firm from working, serving, and walking two dozen miles each Sunday to see her children, and Dominic ran his hands over them as if they were pirate gold. He untied the ribbons holding up the stockings, rid her legs of them, then kissed his way up the trembling inner planes. When his hand began gliding over her loose-fitting drawers, her breath caught in her throat. He touched her in the damp shadowy place that had never been pleasured before, and all she could do was groan with delight and part her legs so he could play. He leaned up to recapture her lips but his fingers continued to dally and pluck until she breathed hoarsely, "Dominic . . ."

"Yes, *ma chère*?"

"I think I'm about to die again."

"Then let's make it memorable. . . ." To that end, he gently eased two long-boned fingers into the dewy swollen channel, and she screamed even before he cleared the gate.

Watching her ride out her passion almost forced Dominic into a little death of his own, so to keep himself in one piece he dropped his head to gently bite her breasts and give her more pleasure.

He withdrew from her, and while she lay there pulsing and panting and undulating seductively, he reached into the drawer of the nightstand. He found what he was after and closed the drawer. Standing now, he undressed as his eyes burned over her.

Clare finally regained the ability to open her eyes. Seeing him naked widened them. He was so glorious he brought to mind the Michelangelo statue of David she'd seen in Italy on Violet's Grand Tour. Violet had been so overcome by the height, breadth, and beauty of the male form, she'd fainted away. Dominic was so magnificently made that Clare could have easily fainted as well, but then she'd miss the erotic finale he'd promised. It occurred to her that she was staring, so she dropped her eyes, hoping he hadn't seen.

Dominic had. "It's all right for you to look, *petite*. This is my tribute of my desire. Impossible for a man to hide."

He moved back onto the bed. Kissing her on the curve of her shoulder, he confessed with soft humor, "If we don't consummate this soon, I'm going to be crippled or dead or both come sunrise."

She ran her hand down his strong dark chest. "And we can't have that, now can we?"

The humid kisses began again, followed by roaming hands and whispered words. Dominic was near bursting. He'd held himself in check for days now, and in a few more moments he was going to explode. "Open your legs for me, *petite*, so that I may put in the sponge."

She was so hazy with desire she wasn't sure if she'd heard him correctly. Glancing down, she saw the small object he was holding out for her to see.

There were two thin ribbons trailing from it. "What is it?"

"A sea sponge."

She looked so surprised yet confused, he chuckled softly. "It catches a man's seed. No responsible lover should be without one. Now open your legs, *bien-aimée*."

She complied and purred as he pushed the object over the swollen lush flesh and gently inside. She offered such a sumptuous view he leaned down and flicked his tongue over the small jewel and she crooned to that and the finger he trailed over it. Clare never imagined a man would love her there, but Dominic seemed to specialize in the unimaginable, and she fought hard not to let the little death shatter her again.

When he entered her, her body stretched to accommodate him. He was big and the power of him filled her until her breath caught. Only then did he begin his rhythm. The strokes were subdued at first; coaxing, inviting, and beckoning, enticing her to rise and fall. When they began to move in tandem, the pace increased, his strokes lengthened, becoming firmer and more urgent. Soon all caution was thrown to the wind, and they rose and fell together in a hot, tempestuous duet old as man.

Teetering on the precipice of orgasm, Dominic pulled her flush against him and rode her like a ship in a storm. Tossing his head back and gritting his teeth, he filled his hands with her hips and began to pump like a man gone mad. Beneath him she screamed her release, her body arching, the channel sheathing him pulsing and throbbing and clutching him even tighter. Then he exploded, growling, pumping, and calling her name as the little death finally swept him away.

Later, the night breeze teased the netting, and made the flame of the lone lamp flicker and dance in the shadowy room. On the bed, the two lovers lay still entwined, their breathing just beginning to calm. Afraid he was crushing her, Dominic withdrew from the shelter of her body and fell over on his back. Who knew she would be so uninhibited? Even sated and exhausted he wanted her again. He rolled his head so he could see her, and her eyes were waiting. Reaching out, he trailed a finger down her satiny cheek. There were no words to describe how he felt at the prospect of never seeing her again once she returned to Savannah.

"What are you thinking?" she asked quietly.

"How much I want you again."

A smile came over her face. "I want you again, as well. Although a proper woman should probably never admit to something so scandalous."

He reached out and slid her closer so that her back was against his chest. He then wrapped her in his arms. He placed a soft kiss against the curve of her neck. "Scandalous Clare Sullivan."

"Only because of you, my randy pirate captain."

"Am I yours?"

She turned to see his face. "For now." They both knew what she'd left unsaid. Clare didn't want to face or talk about leaving, at least not then. At the moment all she wanted to do was to be held by him and pretend there would be no end. Turning back so she could mask whatever he might see in her eyes, she made herself comfortable again and enjoyed the feel of his strong arms enfolding her.

They lay there in the silence for a long time, each mining his or her own thoughts while the breeze and silence flowed around them. "Should I remove this sponge?" she asked.

"Yes. I've plenty."

She looked up into his face. "Plenty?"

He shrugged, then grinned. "I won't lie. I enjoy women, and they enjoy me, so I try and be as protective as I can. They seem to appreciate it."

"The insertion's not a bad thing, either."

"You enjoyed it?"

"I did."

"Would you like a fresh one, m'lady?"

She felt him rise to the occasion against her hips. "You seem to have answered for me."

He looked amused and impressed. "You truly are scandalous, Clare Sullivan."

Reaching up, she laid a palm against his strong bearded cheek. "Only for you."

The sun arrived at dawn, coloring the fading night with stripes of purples and pinks. Down on the beach the drums were finally silent. In the governor's mansion, Dominic removed the fourth and final sponge from between her pulsing thighs and fit himself against her back. And just as he'd hoped earlier in the day, he fell asleep with a sexually exhausted and nude Clare Sullivan in his arms.

They slept well into midday. No one bothered them; his people knew better. They also knew that having just returned from a long voyage, he needed to sleep.

The heat of the day was just rising in the room when Dominic awakened. The first thing he saw was Clare, nude as an African sea nymph and sleeping soundly. He smiled. What a night they'd had. He'd expected her to be more reserved but instead she'd been an eager, tempting treat and he couldn't wait to have her again. She was probably sore, though, and only a brute would disregard his lover's well-being, so he'd give her a day or so before inviting her to take another amorous journey. That didn't mean he planned to be a eunuch with her; there were many ways to bring on *la petite mort*, and having spent his fair share of nights in some of the best brothels in the world, he knew more than he'd ever need. But just the thought of gifting her with all that made his manhood throb to life. Deciding he needed to leave the bed before he forgot his vow to let her rest, he did so with as much stealth as he could muster, then grabbed a robe to cover his nakedness and quietly exited the room. He hoped Anna had prepared something to eat because he was as ravenously hungry as a fully grown tiger shark.

When he returned bearing a tray with an assortment of dishes for them to eat, Clare was stirring awake. Seeing him, she smiled sleepily and dragged the sheet up to cover herself.

"Good morning," he said to her.

She could see that he'd bathed. He was dressed

in yet another white shirt and trim dark breeches. "And to you as well." With his hair tied back and his pirate-dangerous face, she found him terribly dashing.

"How do you feel?" he asked, observing her easily.

"Content."

A pleased smile claimed his dark features. "I've filled a tub with water. Would you like to bathe or eat first?"

"Bathe, please." She was clammy from the heat and sheets.

To her surprise, the tub was out on the verandah, and it was not the small traditional stand-in tub she was accustomed to using. This one with its raised claw feet was large and oval and designed to sit in, something she'd never done before, but it was the sight of the bright red blossoms floating on the water's surface that made her go still. The simple, quiet beauty of the fragrant blooms, coupled with the knowledge that never in her life would she have imagined something so luxurious would be intended for someone like her, made her eyes wet.

"What's wrong?"

"I know it's only water and flowers but it's beautiful," she whispered. "No one's ever prepared a bath for me—ever."

"Then let me show you another joy. Simply step in and sit."

Although she was unsure, she let him assist her in, then sank slowly down until the water covered her above the waist. The temperature was cool, but not too much that it was uncomfortable.

"And your verdict?" he asked, looking down on her with eyes that took her back to last night's many pleasures.

"It's very soothing," she admitted, having now gotten past the novelty of being immersed to the waist in cool fragrant water.

Hunkering down, he picked up a blossom and fit the stem behind her ear. "I didn't get my good morning kiss."

"Is that a prerequisite for beginning the day?"

"Yes," he murmured, his lips already teasing hers to come play.

A very familiar heat slowly spread its way through her veins. Placing a hand behind his sleek head, she raised her lips to meet his and gave him his morning due.

She didn't mind that he was circling handfuls of the cool scented water over her breasts because her nipples bloomed at his touch. Nor did she mind when he bent his head and took a damp bud into his mouth and rolled his tongue around it slowly while she crooned. When his caressing fingers slipped beneath the water and then between her thighs, she bowed back and let him feast and dally.

Dominic thought she had such a sumptuous little body. Every brown inch seemed made for his lips and hands. The feel of her nipples in his mouth, the throbbing little nubbin he was plying between her thighs, all added up to a woman he found himself now wanting night and day. "Let's give you the day's first pleasuring."

True to his word, he spent the next few moments making her hips rise, her nipples plead, and her legs spread wide. Only when her moans began spiraling did his mouth and fingers send her soaring into paradise.

She slid down into the water as boneless as a jellyfish and heard him whisper heatedly, "Enjoy your bath, *petite*."

After his departure, Dominic walked back inside and then outside to stand on the verandah attached to the opposite side of his rooms. He gazed out over the lush countryside. Touching and kissing her had left his manhood in an uproar again, but he was enjoying being with her. That such a small thing as a tub of water had the ability to move her so intensely made him want to purchase the world and set it at her feet. Basic comforts that other women like Sylvie and Violet might take for granted, like a soft bed or a drawn bath, were neither basic nor expected by Clare. She'd never been waited on or pampered. The thought of her returning to a life that measured her value only by forced servitude made him ache inside. His dealings with the softer sex had always been of a casual nature. Over his lifetime he'd had his share of mistresses, but none had ever inspired him to want to include her in his future. Clare did. Her beauty, intelligence, and wit were unparalleled. She was like a mermaid he'd accidentally found that he'd eventually have to return to the sea, and he was loath to do so. It occurred to him that if he could successfully rescue three hundred of his father's people from the clutches of his evil brother, doing the same for one woman and her two children had to be simple. All he needed was a solid plan. Back on the *Marie* he'd vowed to put all ideas for solving her dilemma aside out of respect for her wishes, but now the time had arrived to revisit the matter. He'd find a way to free her and her children; he had to, or lose her forever.

"Dominic?"

He turned to see her standing in the middle of the room. The scarlet bloom was still behind her ear and she was wrapped in a long drying sheet that clung revealingly to her damp body. Viewing the shadowy points of her breasts poking against the nearly transparent fabric aroused him all over again. "Did you enjoy your bath?" She was temptation on two small feet.

"Very much. It will be one of the many memories I shall treasure when I return to Savannah. Thank you."

He apparently didn't hide his reaction quickly enough.

"I know the prospect displeases you. It does me as well, but I must return, so let's enjoy the time we've been given."

He inclined his head graciously but kept his quest to secure her freedom to himself. "As you wish."

She walked over to him. Rising up on her toes, she offered him a short poignant kiss before saying, "You have been kinder to me than anyone ever before. I will remember you always."

Leaving him with his heart full, she slipped behind the screen to get dressed.

Behind the screen, Clare found her freshly laundered shift and drawers and sent Anna a mental thanks for the clean garments. Slipping into them, she put her stays on over the shift. "Dominic, can you lace me, please?"

"No," came his reply.

Sticking her head around the screen, she glanced over at him seated at the table where he waited for her to join him for the morning meal. "Did you say no?"

"I did. You don't need stays, Clare."

"No proper woman goes without her stays, Captain."

"Here a properly laced woman can keel over in the heat."

Clare had never considered walking around without the requisite undergarments.

Dominic grinned. "I'll admit there is nothing more sensual than unlacing a woman, but not when she is gasping on the ground. Consider going without. Most of the women here do."

"Really?"

He nodded.

Clare didn't mind trading her heavy gown with all the petticoats for the simple blouse and skirt Anna had provided, but no stays?

"Trust me, *petite*. You'll breathe better."

The summers in Savannah were stifling, and being constricted by stays made the soaring temperatures all the more stifling, but she'd never gone without them. "All right, I'll take your advice and leave them off, but I'll not feel properly dressed."

"You'll be fine."

Clare stepped back behind the screen and added the blouse, the thin petticoat, and the skirt. After donning the clean stockings and tying them in place with strips of ribbon, she put on her slippers and joined him at the table.

"You look lovely."

"I feel half dressed."

He didn't comment, but chuckling inward, he passed her a plate.

The meal consisted of fruit, rice, and slices of the meat left over from last night's celebration. As they ate silently, the looks that passed between them carried their minds back to their own celebration, and the memories of the fiery little deaths they'd shared.

Dominic asked, "Are you sore?"

"A bit."

"Then we will let you recover today."

The look of disappointment on her face was endearing. "You're new at this, my scandalous Clare. I don't wish for you to be injured and unable to enjoy yourself in days to come."

"I suppose." Clare knew he was only looking out for her health and she appreciated it immensely, but her need for more of his loving was immense as well. Another scandalous thought.

"We will make up for the delay, I promise."

Her smile met his and they finished the meal.

Chapter 9

He wanted to show her the island, so for the remainder of the morning, they rode Louis over the countryside. One of the places they stopped was the large log home owned by James Early and his tall Akan wife, Lucinda. After they dismounted, Lucinda met them on the wide porch. She greeted Dominic with a strong hug and Clare with a ready smile. They'd been introduced last night at the feast.

"James is away seeing to Irma's sick baby boy," Lucinda explained when Dominic inquired about the doctor's whereabouts.

"Is it something serious?" he asked, concerned.

"I'm hoping no, but we will find out when he returns. Would you like to come in?"

Dominic shook his head, "I'm giving Clare a quick tour of the island. We just stopped by to show her where you live."

"And it is paradise," Lucinda added, gesturing at the beautiful surroundings.

Clare took in the tall trees and the bright colors

of the grasses and tropical flowers blooming wild everywhere and agreed.

Lucinda was saying, "I was hoping to have James home for at least a few days before his duty called, but . . ." She shrugged. "The gods bless us with his presence and knowledge."

"Having a doctor here is indeed a blessing," Dominic agreed. "When does your babe arrive?"

"End of summer, and I hope my husband will be by my side and not sailing on the *Marie*, Captain."

Clare grinned at the pointed amusement on Cinda's face.

Dominic held up his hands in surrender. "I will do my best. With the storm season coming, I doubt we'll sail again before the autumn."

"Good. Anna is an excellent midwife, but I want my husband to catch my child."

Clare understood the sentiment and thought how wonderful it must feel to give birth to a child that no one could spirit away and sell.

Cinda, as if sensing her mood, asked quietly, "Do you have children?"

"I do. Two."

"Are they here with you?"

Clare shook her head. "No, they are captives."

"Oh, I am so sorry. Forgive my blunder."

"No need to apologize. You didn't know."

"The captain will fix it," Cinda declared. "He's very good at fixing things."

Clare gave her a soft smile.

"He is. Just wait and see." She skewered Dominic with her dark eyes. "You are going to help her?"

"Yes, Cinda. Soon as I can. I promise."

"Then Clare, set your mind at ease."

Clare nodded.

He asked, "Are there any more tasks for me besides freeing Clare's children and making sure James is present to catch his child?"

"No." She laughed. "But I expect Clare and her children to be here for the christening."

"Aye, sir."

Eyes shining with amusement, she said to Clare, "Enjoy the remainder of the tour."

"I will, and thank you for your kindness."

"Godspeed."

With that they mounted Louis and rode away.

"I like her," she said to Dominic as they headed up another tract carved through the thick foliage.

"She's a fine woman and James is a lucky man."

"You said on the ride over that she was Akan?"

"Yes. They are a tribe in central Africa known for their exquisite gold work."

"Where did they meet?"

"Jamaica. She was living in a maroon settlement up in the Clarendon mountains. He'd gone there to treat someone." Dominic could tell by the confusion on her face that she was unfamiliar with the word. "Maroons are fugitive slaves. The word comes from the Spanish, *cimarrones*."

"Which means?"

"Wild, unruly, fugitive. Originally it described cattle gone wild after escaping."

"Then it was applied to escaped slaves."

"Correct."

"Are there many maroons in Jamaica?"

"Yes, and they began fighting the British some fifty-odd years before the turn of the century."

"Really?"

He went on to explain how after the British invasion of Spanish Jamaica in the mid–seventeenth century, many of the wealthy Spanish residents fled to Cuba ahead of the conquerors and left their slaves behind. "The slaves took to the mountains, established villages, and terrorized the British. Wherever there is slavery in this part of the world there are maroon communities: here in the Indies, Brazil, the colonies."

Clare had heard whispers of towns established by fugitives in Georgia and in other places like the swamps of Virginia and Carolina from Teddy and some of the Sullivan guests. She got the impression that the slave owners were as afraid of the communities as they were of their own slaves revolting. "Are the maroons still fighting the British?"

"Some have signed treaties and were given land and limited freedom. Others are still at war and may be forever unless given the true freedom to plot their own destiny."

"What about the rest of the people here?"

They rode past more small, black-soiled fields, homes, and crews of men felling trees and clearing away the brush with long-blade machetes.

"Most worked for my father on the island of Martinique. He'd freed them, but after his death my brother planned to enslave them."

Surprise filled her face. "You said planned to. Did something change his mind?"

"Yes. I sailed to the island, put them all on boats, and we sailed here. He couldn't enslave people he did not possess."

She was impressed by his ingenuity and remembered Cinda's boasting of his ability to fix things. "He must have been very angry at you."

"No angrier than I, so his feelings didn't much matter. I found his plan appalling, as my father would have had he been alive."

"So that is one of the reasons you and your brother are at odds?"

"That and the fact that my father held him and my stepmother responsible for my mother's death."

She remembered the terrible story told to her about his mother's poisoning. "Will your stepmother ever be punished by the authorities?"

"Doesn't appear so, so I've punished their purse by taking their workers and making certain Eduard wouldn't be able to resurrect the plantation easily."

"How long ago did you bring the people here?"

"Four years."

"You've accomplished much in such a short time."

"We have, but there is much more to do. I'd like to build a school and a hospital where James can treat his patients. I'd like for us to begin harvesting the hardwood for exportation so we won't have to toil so hard in the cane fields, or take on letters of marque so we can all eat. I've many dreams, but my mother always reminded me that if I don't have dreams they can't come true."

"I've never heard that before."

He didn't doubt that; it was the rare slave owner who encouraged his captives to dream. Dominic wondered about her own dreams. Freedom for herself and her children were obvious ones, but as he'd mused back on the *Marie*, what dreams did she harbor for herself?

They rode west to look in on the fiddler Pierre Tait and his beautiful blond wife, Dani, whose log home was reminiscent of the small home of Cinda and the doctor. After they paid their respects and were once again riding away, Clare asked, "How did he lose his eye?"

"A duel with one of the king's guards."

She remembered him telling her of Tait's employment at the royal court. "What were they dueling over, has he ever told you?"

"Yes. Dani. She was one of the king's many mistresses but had the gall to fall in love with the royal musician, so the king sent the guardsman to challenge him, hoping Tait would be killed. He took a ball to the eye but it didn't kill him. He attributed it to his thick skull."

He paused to share her smile. "He and Dani fled to London. Gaspar and I met them months later at an alehouse in London where he was playing. We enjoyed his music, and after sitting with him and hearing his story we offered him a position on the *Marie*. His only condition was that Dani be allowed to come along. We agreed, and they sailed here and built their home."

She could still hear the pure, soaring notes of the composition he'd written for her. His skill was extraordinary. "And Gaspar? You said last night that you'd known each other since you were boys."

He smiled. "Yes. My father found him in an alley in Marseilles scavenging for food. He was ten years of age and had run away from his master. My father brought him home to Martinique. He was raised by my parents with as much love as they gave me. After her death, my father's grief made him return to the sea, and he took both of us with him. Although Gaspar and I are not blood we are brothers in every other sense."

"What about Esteban?"

"Have known him for many years. His father and mine were good friends. When I sailed to Martinique to rescue my father's people, Esteban's father loaned us his ship just in case we needed more room, and Esteban was its captain."

"He has no sweetheart here?"

"He has too many sweethearts, which is why Odessa will not give him the time of the day, let alone her hand."

"Odessa, whom I was with yesterday at the feast?"

"Yes. He's harbored feelings for her for some time, but until he stops hopping from bed to bed she won't have anything to do with him. He pretends that he doesn't care but in his heart he does."

Clare was stunned. "Esteban and Odessa."

"Love is blind, *petite*, what more can I say."

They rode back to his house to escape the oppressive afternoon heat, and she found the cool shade inside a welcome relief. Anna brought them a plate of fruit and rice.

Clare stood. "How may I help?"

"By retaking your seat."

"Surely I can—?"

"You can sit, miss."

Dominic watched the silent play. He already knew who would win, and was certain Clare would figure that out soon enough as well.

Anna set down the plate. "You are a guest here. Do you know what that means?"

Clare swallowed.

"It means that you are to let me do what I am being paid to do, which is to make your stay here a pleasant one, but that won't be possible if you jump to your feet every time I appear. Do you understand?"

She nodded like a scolded child.

"Then sit and enjoy your luncheon. I'll return with the beverage shortly."

After her exit, the still-standing Clare said, "I suppose she put me in my place."

"Sounded that way. I know better than to offer any assistance of any kind. I may be the captain of the *Marie*, but around here a powder monkey commands more status."

Chuckling, Clare took her seat.

They were almost done eating when Anna reappeared. Walking behind her were Sylvie and Levine. Sylvie's light blue gown looked so crisp and fresh it might have come straight from a seamstress shop.

The stomacher appeared to be of excellent quality. The petticoats peeking out from between the open face of the skirt were snow white and banded with strips of lace that matched the elaborate ruffles hanging from her sleeves. Levine, on the other hand, was wearing a grimy coat, a yellowed shirt, and stockings badly in need of laundering.

Anna said to Dominic, "I tried to make them wait until you were done, but they insisted on coming to you."

"Thank you, Anna."

Clare stood, intending to follow Anna inside in order to give Dominic the privacy he might need, but he stopped her. "You may stay, Clare. They won't be long."

Sylvie's chin rose with displeasure and Levine focused his spectacled eyes Clare's way. "So this is the lovely Miss Clare your crewmen have all been talking about. My pleasure, madam."

Clare nodded.

Sylvie sniffed. "It's said you are a slave from the colonies."

Clare didn't respond.

" 'Twould be terrible if your masters were to learn your whereabouts, wouldn't it?"

A muscle twitched in Dominic's jaw, and he said in an ice-cold voice, " 'Twould be terrible for you as well. Should anything happen to Clare while she's here, you'll be on the block in Martinique so fast you won't have time to change your gown."

She jumped.

"Think how many years you'd spend trying to

prove you were born free, Sylvie. It might take the rest of your life."

Levine uttered an uncomfortable-sounding little laugh, "She meant nothing, LeVeq. It was just an innocent question."

Because he knew Sylvie well, Dominic had no doubts that the question hadn't been an innocent one at all, so after letting Sylvie see the serious threat in his eyes, he turned to Levine. "Why are you here?"

"I've come to tell you I can give you your asking price for the guns."

"We found another buyer, so I won't need your help getting them to the colonies."

His mouth dropped. "But—"

"Is there anything else you wish to discuss?" Had Sylvie not threatened Clare, he might have done business with the man, but not now. He was too angry. "And Sylvie?"

Her hard eyes met his.

"No one threatens the freedom of anyone under my care. No one. For your own safety, remember that."

She flashed around. "Let's go, Levine."

The tight-lipped Levine gave Clare and Dominic a nod, turned, and followed Sylvie back the way they'd come.

When Clare and Dominic were alone again, she asked, "Was she serious?"

"As a viper, but then so was I. Should she cause you harm, I will place her on the block personally."

"No one should suffer that fate, Dominic."

"Agreed. Which is why she should have thought more carefully about the consequences before intimating what she did."

Clare could see the fury still sparking in him. He was not a man to cross, which he proved so well on the afternoon he ordered his crew to sink Vanweldt's *Amsterdam*. That Sylvie might alert the Sullivans to her whereabouts evoked a lingering sense of unease. Clare was planning to return to Savannah of her own accord, but if she was forced to do so by the authorities it might not bode well for her, or for Sarah or Ben. "Could she actually do what she implied?"

"Anything is possible. However, she may have burned too many bridges for anyone to care enough to act on the information."

"I hope you're right."

"For her sake, I do, too."

Dominic could see that the encounter had left her unsettled, and that alone made him want to maroon Sylvie. Clare's time on the island was supposed to be a worry-free respite, not one filled with anxiety.

Still worried, Clare asked, "In the colonies there are slave catchers. Are there individuals like that here, too?"

"There are men who hunt escaped slaves for profit all over the Indies. Even some of the Jamaican maroons are now collecting British bounties on fugitives. But not in Liberté. We are all fugitives of one type or another, and any outsider foolish enough to hunt here will die here."

Clare believed him.

"So, let's go back to enjoying each other. Where were we?" But Dominic planned to have Sylvie watched. Pirates were ofttimes called wolves of the sea, so he knew how to hunt as well.

He was just about to ask if she wished to join him for siesta when the sound of drums rolled in from the beach. They both looked up.

"More celebrating?" Clare asked.

"No. That's an alert." He went silent, listening to the cadence. "There's a ship approaching. Come, I need to get a spyglass."

He hurried inside and returned a few moments later with the tubelike instrument in hand. She followed him out through the large gates that marked the entrance to the mansion and waited as he used the glass to survey the water. All work in the surrounding fields stopped as people watched and looked to him for an explanation. Richmond Spelling came to his side. Clare hadn't seen him since last night's feast.

"Friend or foe, Captain?"

"Looks like a French man-of-war. About fifty guns." With its three masts and large bulk it was to him a beautiful sight, but he knew beautiful things could also be deadly.

"I wonder what they're after?" Richmond asked.

Dominic shrugged and pulled down the glass. "Let's go find out." He turned to Clare. "Stay here with Anna and we'll return shortly."

She nodded and watched him run back inside the gate. A few moments later, he galloped past her on

Louis. Richmond, astride a brown horse, rode hot on his heels.

Down on the beach, Dominic dismounted and pulled out his glass. The drummers were still sounding their coded warning. High up on the hills above the beach stood a small army made up of the men of the village. In their hands were machetes, clubs, and muskets. Closer to the beach, other men were hastily uncovering the cannons hidden by the brush and taking up their positions in case the intruders warranted firing upon. For now, everyone waited tensely.

Through his glass, Dominic watched a long-boat being rowed to the beach by a crew of men wearing the blue uniforms of the French marines. Among them in captain's attire was his cousin, Gabriel. Dominic grinned. He was the eldest son of his mother's sister Margarite, and a proud member of the French fleet. "It's Gabriel."

"Should I tell the drummers to sound a stand down?"

"Yes."

Richmond rode off, and Dominic waved both arms at the men on the hills and the ones behind the cannons. The two-handed signal denoted that all was well. The men relaxed and many drifted back to the fields and others towards home.

Soon the drummers were relaying the all-clear to the rest of the island, and Dominic walked to the edge of the beach to greet the members of the long-boat. His cousin Gabriel got out and embraced him.

"I could hear the drums as soon as we got within

sight of the island," Gabriel said with a grin on his handsome face. He was not as tall as Dominic but held more muscle mass.

"First line of defense. How are you, and what the hell are you doing so far from Paris?"

"Just came from Haiti and am on my way to the colonies to be a part of the French fleet helping the upstart Americans. France has sided with them, you know?"

"I do, but I didn't know Louis had authorized a fleet."

"Yes. We're to meet the admiral, Comte d'Estaing, off the coast of Delaware."

"How many ships?"

"Twelve, with eight hundred and thirty guns combined, and four thousand marines."

Dominic was impressed. "Louis is serious then."

"He is, but anything to poke a finger in the eye of the British."

"How long can you stay?"

"Nightfall, then we must push off."

"Then come up to the house and get a meal, and you can bring me up to speed on what else you know."

Gabriel nodded. He took a moment to coordinate the time when he wanted the longboat to return for him, and the oarsmen rowed back out to the waiting man-of-war. When Richmond returned a few moments later, Dominic borrowed his horse for Gabriel. The two cousins, pleased to see each other, rode slowly away from the beach.

"So how've you been?" Dominic asked as they rode side by side.

"I'm well."

"And Tante Margarite?" She was his late mother's youngest sister.

"Still feisty."

Dominic grinned.

"I come bearing news."

"Good or bad?"

"I'm not sure, but it will be surprising if nothing else." Gabe reached into his coat and withdrew a tied-up sheaf of papers and handed it over to Dominic.

"What is this?"

"A copy of your father's true will."

Dominic pulled Louis to an abrupt halt.

"Yes. His solicitors in London sent it to Mother because they had no way of knowing where in the world you might be."

Dominic was so stunned he couldn't move.

"They said they looked for you for over a year after his death but couldn't locate you."

"That's because I was here. No one was supposed to know."

"And you and Gaspar hid your trail very well. I didn't even know you'd been to Martinique until the day Eduard showed up at my door demanding to know where you were, and accusing you of stealing his slaves. My ignorance only made him more furious. Had I not run into you on Gibraltar last year, Mother and I still wouldn't know where you'd gone to ground. I heard that after you stole *his* slaves that he and Nancine sailed there to oversee the reestablishment of the plantation. He also screamed at me about you having burned down almost every building on the property, including the sugar mill."

Dominic smiled, but the document in his hand was sobering.

"Will you open it please? I'm very curious."

Dominic untied the string around the leather pouch and took out the document inside. He spent a silent few moments reading the accompanying two-page letter from the solicitor, and when he finished he grinned and looked over at Gabe. "Listen to this: *Dear Mr. LeVeq . . .*"

When he was done with the reading, it was Gabe's turn to be stunned. "Eduard was not his son!"

"That is what is written here. Apparently Nancine came into the arranged marriage carrying another man's child, but Father chose to give Eduard his name and claim him as his own in order to save her family and his the embarrassment of a scandal."

"That's unbelievable."

"Considering it was Nancine, it's not. According to this, Father changed his will after my mother's death and instructed the solicitors not to reveal the truth until after his death."

"So the will giving Eduard the estate was voided."

"Apparently, but Nancine wasn't told of its existence."

"I wonder if they know now."

"The solicitors say they have approached the French courts, and for me to correspond with them as soon as I'm able."

The cousins stared at each other, and Gabe said,

"You may come out of this an extremely wealthy man, cousin."

"Maybe, but knowing Nancine and Eduard will not get to pick at Father's estate like crows on a corpse will be enough for me." And it was. They'd hated him and his mother, and he'd not cared one whit for them, either. Now his father was speaking from the grave to offer his true feeling as well. Nancine would probably never be brought to trial for his mother's death, but for Dominic this would suffice. Still stunned by the implications, though, the cousins rode on.

"Why were you in Haiti?" Dominic asked as he offered Gabe a seat at one of the wrought-iron tables in the quiet, sheltered inner courtyard. He couldn't wait for Gaspar's return so he could tell him about the will. "Has there been another uprising?"

"No. There were rumors that some of the island's *gens d'couleur* wished to fight alongside the French on behalf of the Americans. I was asked to investigate. Since Marquis de Lafayette's arrival there has become so publicized, everyone in France seems to have come down with American fever. Droves of young Frenchmen are signing up to help. Some say the Haitians are volunteering to prove that they, too, are true sons of France."

"So the rumors are true?"

"Yes. They have over two hundred volunteers on the rolls now and they assured me they could easily muster in another two hundred given a few more months."

"Quite impressive, but will the Americans let

them fight? General Washington and the Congress can't quite seem to make up their minds whether they want Blacks bearing arms or not. One moment it is yes, next it is no."

Gabe shrugged. As most followers of the conflict knew, during the early skirmishes at Boston, and the first true battles of the war waged at Lexington and Concord, many patriots of African ancestry fought proudly and bravely beside their White counterparts in nonsegregated units. Some men like Peter Salem and Salem Poor had played pivotal roles and were widely recognized for their bravery. However, when the Continental Army was officially commissioned in April 1775 under the command of Washington, Black soldiers, both slave and free, were banned from the ranks. Presently they were being welcomed back on a limited basis, but some factions in the Congress, mostly the slave owners, were still unhappy with the decision.

The question about whether the Haitians would be allowed to fight on behalf of the American rebels was never answered because Clare appeared carrying a tray holding a platter of fruit and some bread. Both men rose to their feet and Gabriel turned to his cousin with delight and approval in his eyes.

Clare said, "I don't mean to intrude, but Anna is gone to visit with a friend. When I heard the voices I thought you might want something to eat while you talk."

Dominic did the introductions. "Clare Sullivan, my cousin, Captain Gabriel Tunis. Gabe, my guest, Clare Sullivan."

Gabriel bowed gracefully. "*Enchanté, mademoiselle.*"

"It's a pleasure to meet you, Captain," she said, inclining her head. "I take it you were on the ship that just arrived?"

"Yes."

"I will let you resume your visit," she said, turning to leave.

But Dominic countered her words. "Stay and join us please. There's nothing being discussed that you can't be party to."

"Are you certain?"

Gabriel nodded. "Please, no Frenchman ever turns down an opportunity to sit with a beautiful woman, especially when he's been sailing with a ship of men for the past three months."

"I see the blarney runs in the family."

Both men chuckled.

She took a seat.

Dominic said to her, "We're discussing the war between the rebels and the crown."

"Do you know how things are faring?" she asked Gabe.

He told her about the French fleet.

"Any news from the southern colonies, Savannah in particular?"

"It's rumored the British may try and recapture the city, but as far as I know nothing's come of it as of yet."

Rumor or not, Clare didn't consider it good news. Although the rebels had their supporters and now controlled the city, loyalist sympathies were still strong. She didn't want to return to a city under siege.

Gabe placed slices of mango on his plate. "By your speech, I take it you are from the southern colonies?"

"Yes. Savannah."

"Are you planning to return after the war?"

"I'll be returning as soon as Dominic can sail me there."

"I am on my way there now. I don't know what my cousin's schedule is but I'd be honored to take you back to the colonies if you wish to leave this evening."

Dominic shot his cousin a look. "I don't think Clare—"

"And I think," she responded quietly, cutting him off, "that Clare can speak for herself."

Dominic's lips tightened and he offered her a terse nod of acquiescence.

"You said you will be meeting the French fleet in Delaware?"

"Yes," Gabriel replied while masking his amusement at the sour look on his cousin's face.

"I doubt the British Navy will let a French man-of-war just sail into the Savannah River unchallenged, and I wouldn't want to be the cause of you missing your rendezvous, so I will wait for Dominic."

Dominic's mood brightened.

"I understand," Gabriel said to her.

Clare rose to her feet, and the cousins stood as well. Having men stand whenever she entered or prepared to exit was still taking some getting accustomed to. "I will leave you gentlemen now. Captain Tunis, it was a pleasure meeting you."

He bowed.

"Dominic, I'll be inside."

"I'll join you later."

After her departure, Gabe cracked, "I must say, she seems much too ladylike to be with an old sea barnacle like you, Dominic, so tell me her story."

Upstairs, Clare took a seat on the bedroom's verandah and wondered if she'd made the right decision in turning down Captain Tunis's offer. As she'd stated, the British Navy would certainly not allow a French ship to enter Georgia's coastal waters, and the ship was far too large to do so secretly. The only other alternative would be to sail with them up to Delaware hundreds of miles north of home, then face the daunting task of making her way back south. With both the rebel and crown forces jockeying for control of the eastern coastline, and having no papers on her person to verify her ownership, she could end up captured and sold again. She longed to see her children, but journeying home with Dominic's cousin was not a feasible solution, so she would stay on the island and go home with Dominic when the time came.

The afternoon lengthened into early evening. Anna returned, bringing Clare food and relaying an invitation from Odessa to visit her when Clare had time. Clare thanked Anna and made a mental note to ask Dominic if he could ride her over to wherever Odessa lived. In the meantime, she ate her dinner and settled into a seat out on the verandah to read *A Midsummer Night's Dream* by William Shakespeare from the folio she'd found in Dominic's library. In her opinion it was one of the Bard's best comedic works.

She'd just started act two when she noticed the sun setting. Closing the book and setting it aside, she walked to the railing and looked out. She was so engrossed in the beauty of the reds and oranges that she didn't notice Dominic standing in the doorway behind her, but she somehow sensed him and so turned and met his eyes. "Did you enjoy your cousin's visit?"

"Very much. It's been over a year since I saw him last."

"So, he's going to join the fight."

"He is."

"I wish him Godspeed."

"As do I. My mother was from a large family and I have many cousins, but Gaspar and I are closest to Gabriel." He stepped out to join her. "Are you angry with me?"

"For what?"

"For being so presumptuous as to speak for you."

She gave him a soft smile. "No. I am not. I was a tad piqued when it happened, but not angry by any means."

"*Bien.*" He sounded relieved. "I was concerned."

"There's no need."

"My wanting to answer for you was purely selfish. I didn't want you to accept Gabriel's offer. We haven't had nearly enough time together."

"I know, but I will have to leave eventually."

"I know." He fit himself against her back and wrapped his arms loosely around her waist. After placing a kiss on her brow, he stood with her, and together they watched the sun until it slipped below the horizon.

Chapter 10

Later, after darkness spread over the island, they took a walk on the beach. It was yet another experience she'd never had. The moon was fat and full and gave them all the illumination they needed to find a spot beneath a palm and to sit close together and enjoy the sounds of the sea as it lapped against the shore. The stars were out overhead. A soft cool breeze rustled the leaves and the silence.

Dominic sat with his back against the trunk and Clare in his arms. There were other sweethearts taking advantage of the velvet night, but each couple sought privacy in secluded places a distance away.

"This is so peaceful," she said to him.

"It is indeed." It was a peace he wished he could gift her with forever. The idea that she might be caught up in the struggles of the war when she returned to Savannah and maybe come to harm as a result did not sit well. Again he wanted to ask her to let him go and get her children, but broaching the subject might lead to a disagreement, and he didn't want to ruin their idyllic evening, so he stayed quiet on the matter, choosing to cherish her company instead.

"Did Gaspar and his new wife go somewhere special for their honeymoon?" she asked, eyeing the dark shadow of the *Marie* sitting at the dock.

"They're at the abandoned lookout station up in the mountains. It's the closest thing we have here to a wedding suite. I expect they will rejoin us sometime tomorrow or the day after." And as soon as they returned he planned on taking Clare up there for a few secluded days alone.

Clare savored her contentment. For as long as she could remember, every day of her captive life had been spent working from sunup to sundown. Being with Dominic and his people on their island refreshed her, soothed her, and let her live life on her own terms. "It will be hard leaving all this behind."

"Then don't. Let me rescue your children."

He felt her tense, but when she didn't respond verbally, he continued softly. "Think how much they'd enjoy running up and down the beach looking for shells with the other children. Think how much fun they'd have learning to sail and swim. Think of them never having to be afraid again. Let me help you, *petite*."

His voice held such tenderness and urgency her heart ached with longing for the future he'd described, but should the rescue fail, the consequences would be too dear to even contemplate. "I can't risk it, Dominic." Turning to look up into his face, she whispered again, "I can't."

"You don't believe I can do it?"

She placed her palm against his cheek. "Being here with you has me so muddled inside, I don't know what I believe, but I do know that I will take my own life before letting my fantasies trigger their being sold deeper into slavery."

"There are no guarantees in life, Clare."

"Maybe in yours, but the auction block is a guarantee in my world and in theirs, too."

"Touché."

She sensed his distance and tried not to let it make her angry. "You are a strong, brave man, Dominic; you've proven that to me in many ways."

"But."

Her lips tightened. "But if I lose my children I will be paralyzed." Emotion filled her and her voice with pain. "They are the only precious things this slave woman has in this whole ugly world, so please, can we not talk about this anymore?"

Dominic's heart broke and he pulled her close and held her tight. "I'm sorry. I will honor your love for them and do as you ask. Please don't cry." He wanted to flay himself for causing her such distress. It came to him that he was in love with her; masts, sails, and anchor. He lifted her chin and placed solemn, regret-filled kisses on the tears he'd caused her to shed. "I'm arrogant and selfish. Arrogant enough to think I can save all those who need it, and selfish because I want to hold you against my heart until the end of time."

Clare had never been one to lose her composure but she couldn't help it. All she wanted to do was cry for herself, for her children, and for what would never be. Her tears were also for this strong, wonderful man who cared enough to place flowers in her bath and treat her as if she were cherished. She loved him. Raising her eyes to his in the darkness, she held his intense gaze. "I'm glad you came into my life, Dominic LeVeq—more than I can ever say."

"I feel the same, so let's just enjoy this time and allow the fates to worry about tomorrow. Agreed?"

"Agreed."

And because he wanted to make her smile, Dominic asked, "Have I shown you the advantages of not wearing stays?"

She chuckled. "No, but I'm looking forward to a demonstration."

Pleased by the brightening of her mood, he traced her lips with an adoring finger, then grazed his mouth against them fleetingly. "First, I can do this . . ." His hand and kisses began to meander in such a way that after only a few humid moments her nipples beneath her shift and blouse ripened in welcoming response. "And then this . . ." She was positioned sideways across his lap, her spine braced against his strong arm giving him unfettered access to the length and breadth of her small, perfect form, and he took full advantage . He undid the drawstring of her blouse, then spread it wide to expose the snug-fitting shift she wore beneath. His ardor was heightened by the feel of her breasts straining against the cotton and how hard the tips were against his circling palm. "Can you sit up for a moment?"

Her vision and sense of self were lost in the fog of passion but she complied, pulsing as he gently tugged the homespun blouse down her shoulders. Once her arms were freed, the garment was left to pool at her waist while he deftly undid the three small buttons on the placket fronting the shift; one at the neck, one at mid-breast, and the other near her waist. His warm hands moved the open halves aside baring her to the moon, the sounds of the surf, and his heated need.

He took her breast into his mouth and feasted silently. A hushed sigh slid from her lips in response to his sensual ministrations and to the bold moves beneath her rucked-up skirt. He skimmed over the velvety skin of her thighs, then eased his fingers up past the legs of her loose-fitting drawers to find her damp warmth.

The lush flesh was so wet and enticing he dallied, lingered, and moved a brazen finger in and out, treating her to a series of slow, tantalizing invitations that made her hips rise and his manhood harden like a length of African iron.

"I'm going to bring you to pleasure, *petite*, then take you home and finish this out on the verandah."

His voice alone was enough to send her into the arms of the little death, but she held on. He made her greedy, wanton, and so uninhibited that she didn't care how scandalously wide her legs were spread or that she was twisting and moaning. All that mattered were his hands, lips, and the little death that raced through her body with so much power she had to turn her face into his shoulder to muffle her elongated scream of joy.

Once again, Clare was disconnected from reality. She knew she was in the saddle on Louis's back but had no idea where they were or how long they'd been riding. Every time clarity did rise, she was sent back into the fog by Dominic's erotic magic. Next she knew, he was carrying her into his room and out onto the verandah.

They began again, a slow passionate duet that was as sweet as any song. On the *Marie* he'd promised to make love to her on a moonlit verandah, and he proved to be a man of his word. She offered no protests as he stripped her bare and began to worship her leisurely. His bold mouth savored the buds of her breasts like succulent bits of sugarcane. Backed up against the iron verandah, her fingers gripping the edge, she stood on trembling legs, as heat and sensation captured her once more.

His attention moved lower, wandering over the soft undercurve of her breast, tasting her, tempting her. Kneeling, he brushed a kiss against the nook of her navel, and his hand drifted between her legs, circling and teasing the little kernel of flesh until hoarse pleas rose from her throat and her stance widened. It was the only invitation he needed to fill his hands with her hips and pull her to him so he could gift her with something else she'd never experienced—the most carnal kiss of all. In response to the torrid licks and small sucks, orgasm shattered her almost immediately. Nothing had prepared her for such overpowering delight, and she rode the little death for what felt like a lifetime.

But before she could regain her sanity, he gently pushed the sponge inside, then slowly filled her with another form of delight that was hard and firm and stretched her so she could accommodate him comfortably. The pleasure made her gasp, and his opening strokes pushed her hips solidly against the railing. Not wanting her to be bruised he lifted her, and she instinctively wrapped her legs around his trim waist. The stroking continued, dazzling her, branding her, and making her grip his arms tightly as she held on. Soon they were both lost in the lust and heat and he was possessively guiding her back and forth in tandem with the escalating pace. For Clare, it soon became too much. Her third orgasm crackled over her and she cried out.

Watching her shatter and ride him so wantonly, the furiously pumping Dominic threw back his head and growled. Moments later he shuddered and joined her in the earth-moving arms of *le petit morte.*

Later, as they lay on his bed in the dark, he trailed a finger over the swell of her breast. "I wasn't supposed to make love to you today. You were supposed to be recovering from last night."

"I know."

"Yet you said nothing."

"Not a word."

"Did I injure you?"

"No."

He leaned over and kissed her softly. "Next on

the list. Love in the courtyard under the midday sun."

"I can't wait."

He smiled. After he fit himself against her and covered their bodies loosely with the thin sheet, his eyelids drifted closed. A heartbeat later, hers did as well.

The next morning, Dominic left her sleeping soundly while he went to take care of his needs. He had a long list of duties to attend to that on past voyages had been handled the morning after the feast. The distracting Clare Sullivan hadn't been on those journeys, though, so as a result he was a day behind.

When Clare opened her eyes she saw that he was dressed. "Good morning, Dominic."

He gave her his first smile of the day, "*Bonjour, petite.* How are you?"

"Sleepy."

"I've business to tackle this morning, and since you don't, there's no reason for you to leave the bed until you're ready. So go back to sleep. You had a very athletic evening if memory proves correct."

It was her turn to smile. "Indeed." She viewed his attire approvingly. The black waistcoat and breeches were of the finest quality, as were the snow white shirt and stockings. With his hair tied back and shining with cleanliness and oil, he looked like a well-turned-out gentleman. "One would think you were a colonial governor."

"I suppose I do play that role here." Taking one last look at himself in the standing mirror, he walked over and stood beside the bed that had once sheltered his parents. His eyes traveled over her hungrily, and his mind slid back to last night's erotic encounter on the beach and the verandah. He could have made love to her until winter rains and still would have wanted more. His manhood pulsed, and he had to fight off his desire to undress and climb back beneath the sheets so he could savor her sleep-warmed skin. "You make me ravenous."

"I'm finding you make me the same."

He sat on the bed's edge and traced a finger down her brown arm above the sheet. "No athletic contests for you today. We're going to let you rest."

"And if I prefer the contests?"

"Saucy woman." Leaning over, he placed a tender kiss on her brow. "I'll return later. Anna's downstairs if you need anything."

She nodded. Once he was gone, she snuggled back beneath the bedding and closed her eyes.

Dominic spent the morning riding across the island to consult with the farmers about their crops, the hunters who supplied the community with game, and Odessa, who headed up the women's council. Each brought him up to speed on the state of their areas, and any issues or new ideas that had arisen while he was away. As always there were neighbor disputes, a few new residents, deaths, and births.

"Do you think Clare might like to assist me with the school?" Odessa asked as they talked outside the small tin-roofed cabin that served as the school, and where she functioned as the headmistress for the island's large population of children.

"I will ask her, but she'll be returning to the colonies in a fortnight or so."

Confusion claimed her face. "She isn't going to be one of us?"

"No."

"But you care for her so very much."

He couldn't mask his surprise. "How do you know that?"

"It's obvious. All the women are talking about it."

"Really?"

"But in a good way. We're glad you've finally found someone for your heart. My grandfather would be very pleased."

Her grandfather, Martine Rousseau, the LeVeq family's old butler, had died a few months after their arrival on the island.

"I do care for her and would prefer that she remain, but her children are in the colonies as well and she doesn't want them left behind."

"Then bring them, too. We have a school, and are bound to have children their ages." Seeing the look on his face, she asked, "What's wrong?"

Because Dominic had known Odessa most of his life and knew she'd be discreet, he told her of Clare's dilemma.

"I understand now why she has to return to the colonies but surely you'll find a solution to her problem."

"She doesn't want me to. She's afraid my efforts will fail and that her children will pay the price."

"That is a concern, but you rescued over three hundred souls in Martinique, surely two small children will be simpler."

He shrugged. "The colonies are at war. British forces are in the area and that complicates matters, but I'm confident a good solid plan will work."

"Then go forward. If you are successful she will thank you."

"And if I'm not?"

"You will be. I've no doubt in my mind."

He pulled her into an embrace. "You're a good friend, Odessa. Your faith means much."

"It is well earned."

They stepped apart and Odessa said, "I will keep Clare's story to myself."

"Thank you, but according to Sylvie, Clare's status is already on the drum."

Odessa's lips thinned and she said with disgust, "Sylvie. She was a bad decision, *mon ami*."

He couldn't dispute that. He'd been thinking with his loins and not his brain.

"I'd hoped you'd feed her to the sharks when you came home, but Anna says Levine is her new confidant now."

"Yes." He took a moment to tell her of the visit he'd received from them and the supposedly innocent question Sylvie had posed to Clare.

"She is such an evil witch," Odessa declared, eyes stormy. "How dare she try and intimidate Clare. All the more reason to bring her and the children here. Out of our sight, who knows what that whore might be plotting."

"I know. I'm hoping Clare will change her mind, but I've promised Clare not to broach the subject again, and I plan to keep my word."

"And who says pirates have no honor."

They shared smiles, and he mounted Louis ahead of his departure. "My dinner for the crew is tomorrow evening. You're invited, of course."

"As is Esteban, I suppose?"

Dominic smiled. "Yes."

"I'll think on it."

"You'll do more than that. You'll attend."

"I'll think on it," she tossed back, but she was smiling.

He waved good-bye and rode off.

Clare didn't stay in bed too much longer after Dominic's departure because lying about was not something she was accustomed to, nor anything she aspired to. Once she returned to Savannah being a lazybones would not be tolerated, so there was no sense in fooling herself now. So, after washing up and dressing, she went downstairs.

Anna was outside in the kitchen. "Good morning, Clare."

"Good morning, Anna."

"Did you sleep well?"

"I did. Thank you." What little sleep Dominic had allowed her to have.

"Hungry?"

"Famished."

"Go sit inside, I'll bring you a plate in a moment."

Clare wanted to tell her that getting her own breakfast was something she was quite capable of managing, but when Anna's eyes narrowed as if reading her mind, Clare replied simply, "Yes, ma'am."

After a meal of fruit, plantains, and poached eggs, Clare's hunger had been banished.

"I have errands to do this morning," Anna said as she cleared the china and cutlery from the table. "Would you care to accompany me and see more of the island?"

"I would, thank you." Although she'd seen much of it with Dominic, she had a sense that seeing it with Anna would be different.

So, with Anna handling the reins from the raised seat of the rattling wagon, they and the old brown horse set out. The rough terrain made for slow going but Clare didn't mind. She doubted she'd ever tire of taking in the island's lush beauty and so fed her eyes on all that she could see and hear; like the green-breasted parrots overhead in the trees calling out warning, and the wild turkeys that made Anna stop the wagon to let a small flock cross the road. Anna gave her some of the names of the brilliantly colored flowers and the blooming trees they passed crowding both sides of the narrow road. Clare slapped at a biting insect trying to make a meal out of the back of her hand. The little terrors were the only complaint she had about Dominic's paradise.

Their first stop was a small thatch-roofed home whose owner was one of the women Clare met at the feast. Her name was Henrietta Marsden, and chickens of all colors and sizes roamed her front yard.

"Morning, Henrietta," Anna called out.

Henrietta was short, tent-shaped, and wore a brown head wrap that matched her skirt. Her skin was the color of cream. "Morning, Anna. Clare."

Clare nodded and smiled as she watched a few chicks come out from under the porch and begin scratching in the dirt.

"You have my eggs?" Anna asked.

"Sure do." Henrietta held up a basket for Anna to see. Inside were a dozen brown eggs loosely wrapped in a cloth.

"Can you place them inside that crate in the bed?"

Henrietta nodded.

After the eggs were positioned, Anna asked, "Anything you need me to take on?"

"Yes, a message to Elam. I need that churn he promised me."

Anna sighed. "Judgment Day will come before he's done, but I'll try and light a fire under him."

"Thank you. If he picked up his carpentry tools as often as that rum mug I'd have butter."

"We all would. I've been waiting going on three months now for the one he's supposed to make for me."

"Four months for me."

Clare wasn't sure if she'd met this Elam, but both women seemed very unhappy.

Anna said, "If yours is finished, I will bring it to you on our way back."

"Thank you." Henrietta turned her attention to Clare. "Welcome again to Liberté. I hope you will be with us for a very long time."

Rather than try and explain her situation, Clare acknowledged the sincere words with a heartfelt "Thank you."

Once again on the narrow road, Anna asked, "Are you going to stay?"

"No, I can't."

"But you love the captain, *non*?"

The housekeeper's assessment made Clare smile. "I do, but— Anna, it is so complicated."

"Sometimes things just appear that way. Explain what you mean."

Clare told her the story and her fears.

"You are right to be afraid. No mother wants her children placed on the block and maybe sold away from her life forever, but you don't think the captain can rescue them?"

"I don't know what to think."

"Things could go wrong," Anna said easily.

"And that's what terrifies me."

"Or things can go right, and you and your children can bask in the captain's love until the Spirits take you home." She looked Clare's way. "We are women, Clare. Life will hand us nothing, so sometimes we have to make life look up and acknowledge us by our deeds. From the little I know of you, you impress me as intelligent, so think on this. Do you wish to spend the rest of your days in captivity wondering what might have happened if you'd taken the rope the captain wants to throw you and your children? Suppose they are sold anyway through no fault of your own? Will you feel guilty for not having given them this chance?"

Clare thought that over. No, she wouldn't want to spend her remaining days wondering *what if*, any more than she wished to bear the guilt of knowing she might have denied Sarah and Ben what might possibly be their only chance at freedom. However, for all the sage advice being given to her by various people, no one was risking their own children; they were risking hers. "How long have you known the captain, Anna?"

"Since he was young, but I didn't become his housekeeper until after he rescued the three hundred of us from the island of Martinique four years ago. When we left there we had no idea where we might end up, but even if it turned out to be the bottom of the sea we knew it would be better than slavery."

For the rest of the morning they crisscrossed the island. Clare soon realized that they were doing not only Anna's errands but a number of other people's as well. They picked up a goat and her two kids needing transportation to their new owners, then two little girls who appeared to be about her daughter's age. They'd been visiting with their grandparents and now were heading home. Clare had to force herself not to look at them because they made her think of Sarah.

Anna and Clare spent hours transporting goods and holding conversations with all the people they encountered. By the time Anna finally headed the horse back to the governor's mansion, they'd picked up and delivered barrels of fish, mangoes, bales of grasses, an armoire, cooking pots, three cots, and a dog who spent the entire time aboard the wagon barking at the goats. They didn't get the churns, however. Elam wasn't at home.

"How often do you do this, Anna?"

"Two, sometimes three times a week. It's my way of taking the island's pulse. If a man is mistreating his wife, I want to know. If a child is sick, I want to know. If someone has died, I need to know. When the captain is away, I make sure our people are well, and this is how I accomplish that goal. My traveling also helps everyone remain in contact. We have the drummers to help with communicating, but personal matters can't be sent over the drum, so I often carry messages, too."

Clare was impressed. She was tired from assisting with all the loading and unloading, but impressed by Anna's novel methods nonetheless.

Before heading home for the day, Dominic paid a visit to Washington Julian and his wife, Lara. They ran a twice-a-day ferry service to Jamaica from the eastern tip of the island. The tall, beautiful Lara was a descendant of the area's original inhabitants. Columbus had termed them Indians and their numbers were decimated by the slavery and disease brought by the Europeans who followed him. There were still small pockets of her people on Liberté and high in the mountains of Jamaica, but they seemed destined for extinction with the passage of time.

· Dominic found the couple repairing fishing nets

and they both stood and smiled as he rode up. "How's business?"

"Slow, but it gives Lara and me a chance to enjoy ourselves."

"And get some work done," she pointed out, indicating the fishing nets.

Dominic saw that she was fanning away the heat with the ivory fan that had caused the controversy on the *Marie*. He told them about Sylvie's veiled threat to Clare. "I want to know if she leaves the island, or meets anyone that you ferry here."

"She left on the morning run," Julian said.

Lara added, "Had a mountain of trunks as if she were leaving for good."

Dominic was surprised. "Maybe she's come to her senses and has gone back to her husband."

They had no answers.

"Let me know if she returns. On a happier note, I've come to invite you both to dinner tomorrow evening."

"We'll be there," Washington replied. "How's Miss Clare?"

"Enjoying her time with us."

"Is she still set on returning to the colonies?"

Dominic nodded.

"Be nice if she made this her home."

"I agree, but we shall see. In the meantime, tomorrow evening."

With a wave to them, he turned Louis around and galloped down the beach towards home.

Chapter 11

Clare was seated in the courtyard reading when he returned. Her smile of greeting warmed him like sunshine on a chilly day. He gave her a kiss. "How's the day faring?"

"Fine, and yours?"

He took a seat beside her on the stone bench and they spent a few moments discussing their encounters. He told her about Sylvie leaving the island. "Hopefully that will be one less thing for us all to worry over."

"I agree."

"What are you reading?"

"*A Midsummer Night's Dream.*"

"Ah, Oberon and Titania."

"And Puck, and poor Bottom. It is one of my favorites."

She was his favorite. "I'm having a dinner here tomorrow evening for my officers and some of the crew, I'd like for you to act as my hostess."

"Sounds lofty."

"Will you do it?"

"I've no experience, but for you, I'll pretend."

"All you need do is smile and be gracious and beautiful—which you already do exceptionally well."

She bowed her head. "Thank you."

The desire that always seemed to flow between them whenever they were together rose like curling wisps of smoke, and he lifted her up and set her on his lap much to her laughing surprise.

"I haven't held you all day. I'm due." While she made herself comfortable against his shoulder, he filled his nostrils with the scents of the fragrant oils Anna had given her for her hair. "Now, I'm content."

Clare was, too. "Are your men bringing their wives?"

"Yes."

"I won't need formal wear, will I, because I have none."

"No, whatever your dress, it will suffice."

"Good. I don't wish to embarrass you."

"Never. Had I the time, we could have gone over to one of the Jamaican seamstress shops and purchased you something formal."

"Why waste good coin on something you've just admitted I didn't need?"

"Because there's something very stimulating about making love to a woman in a beautiful gown. I think it has to do with searching for treasure beneath all those petticoats."

She laughed. "You are incorrigible."

"I know." He hugged her close. Since he hadn't kissed her today, either, he remedied that by placing his lips against hers. "Sweet as ever," he murmured, and as the kiss deepened and desire expanded to capture them, no further words were necessary.

Except—

"Ahem," someone said loudly, clearing his throat.

Annoyed, Dominic glanced up. "Your timing is always impeccable, brother."

Gaspar grinned. "Perfection is a worthy goal. Good afternoon, Clare."

Beside him stood the smiling Suzette.

The embarrassed Clare tried to pretend she wasn't sitting in Dominic's lap or that her lips weren't kiss-swollen. "Good afternoon, Gaspar. Suzette." She made move to rise, but Dominic clamped a gentle hold on her waist to make her stay.

"I see she hasn't divorced you yet," Dominic pointed out.

Gaspar draped an arm lightly around his bride's waist. "The future is still uncertain."

Suzette asked Clare, "Are you enjoying your visit here?"

"I'm having a wonderful time."

"Good. Gaspar says you are a true lady, which Dominic is not always known for, so we look forward to having you with us for a long while."

Dominic stared at her with mock outrage.

Clare tried to muffle her mirth but failed.

Gaspar shook his head sadly. "Alas, brother, Suzette knows you well."

"Control your wife," he ordered teasingly. "Nothing worse than a headstrong female."

"I beg your pardon," Clare replied.

Gasper quipped, "Now you've done it, Dominic. You should have quit while you were ahead."

Pretending to seek amends, Dominic asked Clare, "Did I say there was nothing *better* than a head-strong woman, too."

She and Suzette rolled their eyes, and Suzette said with a humor-laden voice, "We'll leave you two. We just wanted you to know we'd returned."

"I'll be expecting you at the dinner tomorrow night."

They nodded and made their exit.

Dominic lifted Clare's chin. Looking down into her eyes, he asked, "Now, where were we?"

"You were kissing me."

"Excellent memory, Miss Sullivan."

Echoing Gaspar, she said softly, "Perfection is a worthy goal."

The next evening, Clare and Dominic stood in the torch-lit courtyard and greeted their guests. Gaspar and Suzette arrived first, followed by the Julians; the fiddler Tait and his wife, Dani. James and Lucinda Early arrived with Odessa, and over the next hour they were all joined by other crew members and their wives and sweethearts.

Richmond Spelling, dressed as finely as Clare had ever seen him, wove in and out of the crowd carrying a tray filled with appetizing bits of meat and fruit, then returned to offer beverage choices of sangria, fresh spring water, and rum.

They dined standing, eating from small plates

of LeVeq family china emblazoned with the house crest. The arrangement enabled everyone to mingle, hold conversations, and have a good time.

Dominic watched Clare moving about talking, smiling, and making sure everyone was enjoying themselves. He thought she made an excellent host-ess, and it was easy for him to imagine her in the role permanently. Again he wondered how he was ever going to let her go when the time came, but he chose not to think about it and took a swallow of his cognac instead.

After the dessert of a rum-soaked trifle, Esteban made his entrance. Clare, standing beside Dominic and Odessa, saw him make his way through the crowd. He shook hands, kissed the hands of the ladies, all the while moving in their direction. When he reached them, Odessa coolly excused herself and walked over to join James and Lucinda standing with a group nearby.

Esteban watched her move away and smiled knowingly.

"Finally made your way out of Levine's," Domi-nic remarked.

Esteban turned back. "Not my fault, I keep ex-plaining to you."

"I'm not the one needing an explanation, but Odessa may."

"I think this will be explanation enough." From within his fine waistcoat, he produced a sparkling gold ring that he placed on his palm for them to see.

"That is beautiful," Clare told him.

"Enough to earn forgiveness?" he asked her, dark eyes lit with humor.

"Depends on how deep the transgression."

Dominic cracked, "He's going to need a chest of those just to begin negotiations."

"Maybe for a Frenchman, but not for a son of Spain."

Dominic chuckled and shook his head. "Clare, you might want to stand behind me so that you'll be out of the line of fire."

Esteban rolled his eyes and walked over to Odessa.

Clare saw that the gathering had quieted. Everyone had their eyes focused on Esteban. James and Gaspar appeared to be in the midst of taking bets, and across the terrace, Richmond was shaking his head dubiously.

Esteban called out loudly, "My friends, I'd like for you to bear witness." Getting down on one knee, he held up the ring for Odessa to see, and said to her, "Odessa, I love you like the wind loves the sea."

Silent, she took the ring.

"Will you marry me?"

She gave him a smile, then picked up a pitcher of sangria from the small table and slowly poured the contents over his handsome head. "I'd sooner marry a boar!" she snapped angrily. "How dare you propose to me after spending three days with the whores at Levine's. Are you truly a lunatic!"

As if needing to make sure he understood the true depth of her anger, she stormed over to the edge of the paved terrace and threw the ring as far as she could out into the darkness.

"Dessa!"

She spun on him. "Come near me again and I will put a musket ball right between your philandering eyes!" Picking up her skirts, she hurried into the house.

Lucinda started after her, but paused for a moment to say to Esteban, "She's correct. You truly are a lunatic."

While Clare stood shocked, Dominic chuckled. "Told him he needed a chest."

Clare saw Gaspar and James collecting their money. Esteban was drying his face and hair with a cloth handed to him by Richmond.

"Women!" the Spaniard snarled. "Dominic, I'm sure you'll understand my need to depart. I'll be back in the morning to look for the ring."

"Of course. I'll see you then."

Esteban bowed over Clare's hand, gave his regrets, stormed past James and Gaspar, who appeared to be laughing hard enough to fall over, and disappeared.

Lara met Clare's stunned eyes and smiled. "Last time she broke a platter over his head. You'd think he would have learned by now, but they make for great entertainment, so we all thank you for the invitation."

"To Clare!" Lara's husband crowed.

The guests raised their glasses and roared merrily, "To Clare!"

All she could offer in response was a shake of her head and a smile.

Later, as everyone prepared to leave, Clare realized she'd had a wonderful time. It was yet another episode she'd place in her heart so she could use the memory to help her survive the years ahead. However, the conversation she'd had with Anna yesterday about freedom and her children continued to play on the edges of her mind. The longer she stayed on the island, the less she wanted to return to Savannah. Clare could admit that to herself now. After meeting the residents and receiving their good wishes and words encouraging her to remain, the urge to do so was gaining strength. Leaving her children behind was not something she was considering in any way, so the only solution would be to steal them from their owners, the Hamptons, and bring them back.

That night, after she and Dominic made love, she lay in his arms. "I want to stay here, Dominic."

He kissed the top of her head. "I'd like that very much."

"I mean, I want you to help us escape so that my children and I can live here."

He stilled and looked down at her in the candlelit darkness. "Are you certain?"

"Yes, I am."

"What changed your mind?"

"A conversation with Anna yesterday. She's very wise."

"That she is."

"So how will you accomplish it?"

He shrugged. "You haven't wanted me to think on it, but now that I can, I'll begin planning."

"Thank you."

"This is a very brave decision, *petite*."

"It doesn't feel that way. The idea terrifies me."

He kissed her hair. "We will be successful. Don't worry."

"Easier said than done, Captain."

He told her softly, "I know just the thing to rid you of all your concerns."

She rolled over onto her stomach and looked down at him in all his nude magnificence. "Do you, now? And what might that be?"

"We start with this. . . ." He slid a slow finger over her nipple and teased it until it hardened. "And then, I do this." He maneuvered her so that he could take the bud into his mouth.

Soon, one thing led to another and when it was over, the breathless, passion-filled Clare had not a worry in the world.

The next day, Dominic called a meeting of his war council. They convened at the table in the mansion's large dining hall. All his officers were there, as were crewmen Julian, Tait, and Richmond Spelling. When he explained the reason for the sudden meeting, they all turned to Clare seated in a chair at the head of the table and applauded. They then turned to the business at hand.

Dominic was on his feet and pacing as he spoke. "My plan is to go in and set us up as a crew of French smugglers. The rebels are still in charge of the city as far as we know and that will work to our advantage, because we have muskets they'll want to buy. We also have enough of a variety of goods in our stores that we can take with us to sell, which will give further credence to our masquerade. Clare gets to visit her children on Sundays."

He asked her, "Do you ever take them children away from the house when you visit?"

"Sometimes I take them for a walk on the docks so I can buy them sugared pecans as a treat, but rarely anywhere else."

"Are you allowed to do this alone?"

"Usually. I'm a very trusted captive."

"Then that will work to our advantage as well. You'll bring them to the dock, board the ship, and we will cast off."

"Sounds so simple."

"I've found that simple is always best."

Gaspar had a question. "Clare, is there anyone in the city you trust enough to carry messages between us in case it becomes necessary?"

She thought for a moment, but only one person came to mind as a possibility. "Violet's aunt, maybe. Her name is Theodora Sullivan. She's always spoken out against slavery, but I've no way of knowing whether she'll choose her principles over her family heritage if we asked her for her assistance. The penalties for aiding an escape are very serious ones."

"Then we'll have to come up with another solution, but don't worry, we will."

Esteban said, "I've never been to Savannah; it

would be helpful if I knew where the river and city meet."

"I can draw you a map. I'm not a good artist but it will show you the basic lay of the land."

He nodded. "Thank you." He was glum because his search of the grounds earlier had not discovered the ring Odessa had flung out into the night. Because of the thick vegetation it could be lost forever.

"Any other questions or concerns?" Dominic asked, glancing at the faces. No one had any. "We all have our assignments. Let's get to the task."

The meeting ended and the men left to begin the preparations. Parts of Clare were elated with her decision but other parts continued to harbor fears and doubts.

"I can see that you are worrying again," he said to her softly.

"True, but I'm also pleased that we are under way."

"What do you think of the plan?"

"As you said, it seems very simple and workable, but do you have a plan for me to return to the Sullivans?"

"I will escort you to the door, let your mistress know that I have tired of you and that she may have you back."

"And then?"

"I'll leave."

"That is all?"

"Would you prefer Violet know how deeply I care for you? I could kiss you fervently, thereby arousing her suspicions."

Her smile peeped out. "No."

"My words to you may be harsh when the time comes."

"I understand."

"But they will not be the words of my heart, *petite*."

He walked over and took her into his arms. "This is going to be a dangerous game and we'll need every piece to fall into place, which is why I wish to keep things simple. The less pieces in the puzzle, the easier it will be to complete."

She held on tight, her cheek against his strong chest. She couldn't wait for it all to be over. "Dominic, if things unravel and you have to make a choice, take my children. Bring them here. If I'm left behind it will be bearable if I know they are in your care."

Dominic had no intention of leaving her behind, no matter the circumstances.

She looked to him with eyes filled with serious emotion. "Promise me, Dominic."

He studied her for a long moment, then finally nodded. "I promise."

"Thank you."

For the next week Clare and Dominic spent their days apart. His attention was focused on preparing the small sloop for the sail to Savannah and determining which items in the stores might bring the most profit once he and his crew of smugglers arrived. He hoped to take advantage of the shortages caused by the British blockade by bringing in textiles and luxury items that appealed to the women: items like perfume, china, and fine wine; all things he and his people had accumulated through four years of privateering and piracy. Clare was often asleep by the time he returned home each night, and he didn't have the energy or the heart to awaken her.

He was also working on other tasks tied more directly to the island's future, like the careening of the *Marie*'s hull, clearing land for fields so more food could be grown, and holding negotiations with a Cuban company that wanted to begin harvesting some of the hardwood trees for exportation to Spain. He felt as if it had been months since he and Clare had had time alone, but he was too busy to remedy the situation.

Clare, on the other hand, spent her days with Anna traveling over the countryside and relishing the company of the island's women. She helped the women plant, a task rooted in their African traditions, and she helped out at the school. Odessa was still angry at Esteban, and no, the ring hadn't been found. Clare sorely missed Dominic's company, but she knew how much he was doing and that a good portion of it was being done on her behalf, so she didn't complain.

As the preparations for Savannah were finalized and a date for departure was chosen, Dominic wanted to spend some time alone with Clare, and he wanted it to be special because it would have to last them until they all returned to the island from Savannah. With that in mind, he loaded the wagon, and the two of them drove up to the abandoned lookout station Gaspar and Suzette had used for their honeymoon.

When she walked inside nothing about the place was romantic as far as Clare could see. It was a stone hut with a dirt floor. There was a grate where a fire could be built if needed. Two openings in the stone walls constituted windows. There was an alcove that led to what she supposed was a back room, a couple of cane chairs, and a rough-hewn table.

Dominic entered carrying some of the supplies they'd brought with them and set them down. "Pretty gloomy?"

"A bit."

"Step this way, please."

Curious, she followed him through the alcove. To her surprise it led outside to a covered stone platform. Nestled inside was a four-poster bed. Its size rivaled the one back at the mansion. Fine-gauge netting hung from rods in the stone roof and enclosed the bed in a way that appeared very romantic indeed.

"Better?" he asked with a smile.

"Oh yes, and the view is magnificent." They were high up on the mountain. A curved, waist-high stone wall circled the platform, offering a safe place to stand so one could look out over the beautiful blue sea and the surrounding tropical forest. It was yet another jewel in the Eden he called home. "Now I see why your island's sweethearts come here."

"It is a spectacular place. I wanted to spend a day

or two here before we head to Savannah. Give us a bit of time together."

"I'm glad we came."

"Good. Let's unload the rest of the wagon and then I want to show you something even more spectacular."

The something more spectacular turned out to be a waterfall. The rush of frothy water filled her ears as it poured over a cliff and down into a wide pool below. Clare was awed by its beauty. "I've never seen a waterfall before."

"Yet another reason why lovers come here." He sat on a fallen tree trunk and removed his shoes and then his stockings.

"What are you doing?"

"Undressing, and I encourage you to do the same."

"Why?"

"So we can wade in."

She stared at him blankly. He was by then pulling his shirt over his head to reveal his strong chest and powerful arms. After tossing it aside he set about undoing the buttons on his breeches, then shrugged them down. Nude as Adam in the Garden, he folded his breeches and shirt and laid them at his feet. Giving her a grin, he ran to the edge of the pool and dove in. He came up a few moments later, dragging his hands over his streaming face. He called out over the roaring water, "Come on in, *petite*!"

"But I can't swim!"

"The edges are shallow!"

Clare had done some fairly outrageous things

since meeting him, but stripping herself nude and walking around under the sun and sky was a bit more than she was ready for. "I don't know about this, Dominic," she said mostly to herself.

"No one will see you!"

Clare remained skeptical. The deepest water she'd ever been in was the bathing tub that he'd placed out on the verandah that day.

He called again, "It's no fun to play in the water alone! Come on! Please?"

While she debated inwardly she watched him swim back and forth, his long arms breaking the water fluidly. He looked as natural as if he'd been created for the sea.

Clare made up her mind. *Why not?* Taking a seat on the log, she removed her shoes and stockings and then her skirt, blouse, and drawers. Her shift, she left on. It was one thing to be fully nude in the darkness of his bedroom or in a dark spot on the beach, but it was another thing entirely to be nude outside in the middle of the day.

Dominic didn't chastise her for not removing her shift. She was a product of her colonial upbringing. In truth, he found her modesty sweetly arousing because beneath the prim exterior beat the heart of the very sensual and delightfully uninhibited woman he planned on making love to around the clock for the next two days. When they temporarily parted ways in Savannah he wanted her to remember that she was cherished.

Clare walked to the edge and he swam to meet her. When he reached the shallows he stood and

walked up out of the water with the graceful bearing
of an African sea deity. Of course her eyes strayed to
that part of his anatomy that brought her so much
joy, then catching herself staring, she quickly looked
up and found his smiling eyes waiting.

"It's the effect of the cold water," he explained.
"We'll put it to rights later."

Embarrassed to her toes she finally composed
herself enough to raise her gaze again.

"You are too bold, Captain."

He lifted her chin and fed his eyes on the soft
curves of her smile. "Yes, I am."

"Modest, too, I see."

"Also arrogant, and very selfish when it comes to
you." He pressed his mouth to hers. "Very selfish."

It was their first kiss in days and they reveled
in the familiar tastes of each other. "Ready?" he
asked.

"No." She laughed. "But I'm willing to try."

Holding her hand, he led her to the edge of the
water. "It's chilly, so be warned."

Clare waded in gingerly. The cold water lapped
over her ankles, then her knees, and delight came
over her even though she was scared half to death.
He led her slowly around the edge of the pool, and
the closer they moved to the cliff where the water
poured down, the louder the roar sounded in her
ears. There were rocks beneath her feet and the
water level now rode mid-thigh, dampening the
hem of her shift.

"You're doing well, Clare."

"Just don't let go of my hand."

By then they were standing to the left of the water cascading down. The spray and splash had turned her shift into a transparent second skin. Of all the new experiences she'd had, this had to be the most incredible. She was being soaked but didn't care. He stepped directly into the plummeting stream and she followed. The force made her scream but it was a scream of joy. Raising her arms above her head, she opened herself to the tumbling water and it obliged.

Dominic's love for her surged watching her play. There were so many things he wanted her to experience, feel, and see. Captivity had deprived her of so much that if she asked him for the moon and stars he'd find a way to obtain them. His heart and soul had been captured by a small, strong-minded slip of a woman who could curse at him in a variety of languages and read Shakespeare but had never slept in a bed, taken a bath, or been shown the tenderness and care she deserved for simply being alive. The idea that by month's end, she'd be in his life permanently filled him with an anticipation usually reserved for children on Christmas morning.

Since he doubted she could hear him over the falls, he took her hand again and pointed in the direction he wanted her to walk. She let him lead her and he took them through the downpour and into the cave behind the falls.

Startled by where they were, Clare looked around. "This is a cave."

"Yes. We call it Sweetheart Cave."

Clare wiped at the water on her face and stared

around. With no sun to warm her she was beginning to shiver.

"Come with me." Taking her by the hand again, he led her through the cave and out into the sunlight on the other side.

"Oh, thank you."

He gave her a quick kiss before disappearing back inside, and returned a few moments with a large sheet of muslin that she gratefully wrapped herself in. He wrapped himself in another one.

"Where'd this come from?" she asked, taking a seat on a sun-warmed boulder nearby. The roar of the waterfall could be heard but it was much quieter where they were.

"Chest inside. Couples use this place fairly regularly, so once a month Anna or one of her women comes up and restocks the chest."

"What a novel plan."

"Works well. You may want to strip off your shift and let it dry."

The idea was embarrassing but logical, so she dropped the muslin to her waist. She stood, and after removing the wet garment spread it out on a bush beside her. She made move to sit and cover herself again, but he gently stayed her hand.

"Let me look at you, *petite*."

Torn between self-consciousness and how reckless the heat in his voice made her feel, she let him have his wish.

"You are so gorgeously made." He ran a trailing finger from the base of her throat down to the hidden nook of her navel. When he slowly reversed the path, her eyes slid closed. Both hands joined in whispering over her breast to her waist, then skimming over the flare of her hips so he could gently urge her to come stand between the vee of his spread legs. A flick of his tongue against the already tightened buds of her breasts made her pulses pound and she placed her hands on his strong shoulders for support. He fed on her lustily, lingering and dallying while his large hand ardently circled up and down her spine. It dipped lower to map her hip, then lower still to treat the damp vent between her thighs to a series of elongated touches that made her croon, arch, and flow. Soon, all contact with time and place was lost; sensation became her world.

Having learned to pleasure him in return during the warm nights spent in his bed, she grasped the smooth hard shaft jutting between them in a knowing hold, and his eyes slid closed. Moving her hand over him with slow finesse, she smiled sultrily. Clare found that she loved the power her touch had over him because it matched the power he wielded over her. When she dropped to her knees and proceeded to show him more of what he'd taught her, he groaned, and she raised her head and whispered, "The pursuit of perfection is a worthy goal."

Chuckling, and feeling himself about to burst from the randy ministrations of the scandalous Clare Sullivan, he growled and picked her up. As he held her in the air above him, his hot eyes met hers. "Open your legs."

She did, and he eased her down onto the tip of the shaft she'd prepared so wantonly and pushed his way into paradise. She purred with pleasure. Hands filled with her hips, he began to stroke; guiding her up and down, back and forth, filling her and loving her until they were moving and gasping as one. The pace increased, the rhythm rose, and all she could do was ride. The glory of it had him gritting his teeth and tightening his hold to direct her faster and faster still. He felt himself teetering on the edge, his manhood demanding more. Seconds later she came, growling low in her throat, her body twisting. The sight of her and the feel of her sheath tightening and pulsing blew him apart like a grenade on a deck. He let out a yell loud as any waterfall and began to pump like a man gone mad because he had.

Later, as peace and quiet returned, she was seated on his lap with her arms wrapped loosely around his waist, her cheek against his still-pounding heart while he held her close. "That was very nice, Captain."

"I think we should start over to make sure we did everything correctly."

Humor in her voice, she asked, "You think so?"

"Maybe later when I can walk."

After a few more minutes of silence he kissed the top of her head. "My apologies though."

She looked up into his face. "Whatever for?"

"I left the sponges in the hut."

Their eyes held for a long moment, then she cuddled back against him. "Too late to go back."

"You're going to marry me when we return from Savannah anyway, so it won't much matter."

"I am?"

"Yes, scandalous Clare Sullivan, I'm going to make an honest woman of you."

"I suppose that will be all right."

"You suppose? You're supposed to say, 'Why Dominic, I'd be honored.'"

"Really? Is that an island precept? I've never been proposed to before so I wouldn't know."

"Sassy woman."

Looking up at him with love shining in her eyes, she whispered, "I'd be honored to marry you, Dominic."

"And I'd be honored to marry you, as well, *petite*."

Chapter 12

They spent the following two days, making love, playing in the waterfall pool, and storing up the joy they found in their love because the mission to Savannah was looming. On the last night together they lay in bed after another passionate interlude, cocooned by the netting and the night. "When we return from Savannah, I'm going to issue a royal decree declaring this place off limits to anyone but you and me."

She chuckled. "Your selfishness is showing again."

"I know, but that's to be expected from a man in love."

Hearing him declare his love for her filled her with emotion. They were words she never expected to be directed her way, especially not from a man as powerful and caring as he. Her time with him had been like a fairy tale filled with light and hope and most of all freedom. Returning to Savannah was a necessary chapter in that same tale, but she was not looking forward to it.

"After we return here and the storm season fades,

I must sail to London to meet with my father's so-licitors. There's been a new turn in the settlement of his estate."

"A good turn, I hope."

"I believe so." He told her the story relayed to him by his cousin Gabriel. "If all proves well, you could be married to a much wealthier man."

"Wealthy enough to forsake pirating?"

"That's a thought."

She looked up and met his smile in the dark. "You can't spend the rest of your life stealing from others, Dominic, no matter how noble your intentions."

"I have to feed my people, *petite*, so let us not argue. This is our last night, you can flay my moral shortcomings when we return from Savannah, but until then . . ." He ran a possessive hand down her nude body. "I think we can find other more pleasur-able ways to pass the time."

Her passion rose in response to his wandering caresses, and he proved to be quite correct.

They set sail in the late afternoon on Wednesday, June 3. The sloop was built for speed, and with a fair wind they reached the Key Islands off the coast of Florida just after dark. They dropped anchor, and leaving Clare, James Early, and the rest of the small crew aboard, Dominic, Gaspar, and Esteban rowed in to meet with Esteban's cousin Ferdinand. The Key Islands had been a haven for pirates, smug-glers, and other hunted men since the late 1500s. Sea powers like the British and the Spanish swept through periodically, hoping to clean out the nests of lawlessness, but the citizenry always returned.

Seated in the office of Ferdinand's raucous ale-house, Dominic and the others looked at the crude map Clare had drawn of the Savannah River and the adjacent city.

"This isn't going to be much help getting us from here to there," Dominic remarked. "Do you know a guide we can trust?"

"Yes, a man named Sam. He was born in the Carolinas, and for a price can guide you there and back."

"How long will it take for you to find him?"

"He's the barkeep. Let me get him."

Moments later, he returned with a short, thin Black man. Ferdinand made the introductions, and Dominic described what they needed him to do.

The man nodded, "I can guide you in and out."

They then talked about the blockade.

Ferdinand said, "Latest reports say the British fleet will begin moving south by summer's end. Right now they are concentrated near New York and Delaware. They have only a small presence here in the south and their brigs are too large to patrol close to the coastline without running aground."

"So if we can hug the coast?" his cousin asked.

"You should be able to arrive without much worry."

It was what Dominic had hoped to hear.

Sam asked, "So when do we sail?"

"It's a moonless night. Can you leave immediately?"

"Faster than that if your coin is good."

Dominic tossed him a small felt bag.

The man hefted it on his palm and by his smile seemed to approve of the weight. He gestured to the door. "After you, gentlemen. I'll fetch my belongings and we can depart."

Back on the sloop, Dominic introduced Sam to the others. Clare could see him eyeing her curiously, but she gave him a polite nod of welcome and went back to her spot by the stern. Under his guidance they sailed east and then north.

Clare was dressed as she'd been the day Dominic carried her away from the frigate and onto the *Marie*. She tried not to give in to the sadness threatening to overcome her at the reality of returning to captivity, but it was difficult. If the plan went awry, who knew what price she'd have to pay. On the other hand, if they were successful, she and her children would have a happy and free future, and she tried to buoy her mood with those positive thoughts, but fears that this rescue might not be as cut and dried as Dominic hoped continued to plague her. The one thing she was certain of was how good it would feel to see and embrace her children after being separated from them for what seemed an eternity.

Dominic made his way to the stern to see how Clare was faring. "How are you?" He took a seat beside her. Although he couldn't see her features clearly because of the darkness, he sensed her sadness.

"I'm well. A bit melancholy, but it's to be expected."

"True, but once we reach Savannah we'll do

what is needed and be back on Liberté before you know it."

"I pray you are right."

"I am, so rest easy."

She nodded. He placed a kiss on her lips, then departed, leaving her alone with her thoughts and the darkness.

They entered the Savannah River and sailed east into the city in the wee hours before dawn. The docks were more crowded with ships than they'd expected but they found a spot for the sloop and dropped anchor. Richmond Spelling scrambled off and tied the boat down and Clare looked around. The smells of the water were as familiar as her own heartbeat. There was little pedestrian activity as most of the city was sleeping, and the shanties and shops were either shuttered or covered with tarps. On the opposite side of the river lay the strip of land known as Hutchinson's Island; on this side of the river behind the docks lay the town and her destiny.

Georgia was the last of the thirteen colonies to be established by the crown. Named Georgia for King George II, it was founded by Member of Parliament James Oglethorpe, who, along with thirty-five English families, arrived at the mouth of the Savannah River in the spring of 1733. Oglethorpe established a settlement on a bluff looking out over the river and the waters of the Atlantic and called it Savannah after the river. Slavery and spirits were outlawed by the original charter, but in 1749 the restrictions were overturned. There were now fifty

thousand people in the city and surrounding countryside, half of them captives. It was Clare's hope
that that latter population would be reduced by
three when the sloop lifted anchor again and sailed
back out to sea.

Dominic made his way to her. "Richmond is
going to wake someone up so we can procure a
wagon, and then we'll head into town."

"Thank you."

As always, he sensed her mood. "We're not going
to let anything happen to you or your children,
petite. The three of you will be returning with us
even if I have to burn down the town to ensure it."

That made her smile.

"Your bravery astounds me. Not many people
would willingly walk back into slavery for any
reason, but by Sunday evening you will be owned
by no one, so keep that in your heart."

"I will."

He pulled her into his arms for their last embrace,
and he thought his heart would burst because of
how much he loved her. "Let me kiss you so you
can place that in your heart as well."

Clare knew that if she began to cry the tears
would flow forever, so she gave herself up to the
kiss instead and let her love for him add to the
strength she knew she would be needing to help her
through.

Richmond secured a wagon and brought back
with him the owner of the livery, a man by the
name of Calhoun, who was short and rotund. By

his disheveled clothing and the lopsided, dirty white wig, it was apparent that he'd just gotten out of bed. Calhoun looked at the finely dressed Dominic, flanked by Gaspar and James dressed in plainer fare, and stuck out his hand to Dominic. "Milton Calhoun."

"François deMille. Thank you for the wagon." It was an alias he'd used before.

"You're welcome. Just had to come make sure the boy was telling me the truth, didn't want to be participating in a slave escape or aiding the crown, you know."

Dominic didn't respond.

"You sound foreign. Where's your home?"

"France."

"Ah. They had a big celebration up in Boston a few weeks back when word came that your king's going to help us. Welcome to Savannah."

Dominic could see that the dock was coming awake. Men were rising from the tarps they'd slept beneath. From the looks of it, the place would be fairly busy shortly, and he wanted to get under way. "I have some business in town but would appreciate you spreading the word that I have goods to sell."

"What type of goods?"

"I'll return shortly and we can discuss it. How much for the wagon? I'd like to have it for the duration of our stay, if I may."

Calhoun looked at the men flanking him and seemed to see Clare standing beside James for the first time. "All these Blacks yours?"

"Your price for the wagon, monsieur."

His focus back where Dominic wanted it, Calhoun quoted him a price that Dominic knew was exorbitant, but he gave the man the coin anyway and helped Clare up to the bench. Once he and the others were aboard, Dominic inclined his head. "Thank you, and please let the others on the wharf know that the men remaining on my sloop are well armed, and will not look kindly on unwelcome visitors."

"Of course," he responded quickly.

Gaspar slapped the reins and turned the two-horse team towards town.

Once they cleared the docks, Gaspar asked, "Which way, Clare?"

"Straight. I want to stop at Teddy's first."

Dominic on the seat beside her asked, "Why there?"

"So I can ask about Ben and Sarah. Their owners are kin to her husband."

"Ah."

Because Theodora lived not far from the river, the journey was a short one. Her wooden home was larger and more distinctive than the others nearby, and its owner was by far the most eccentric woman in Savannah and maybe in the entire colony of Georgia.

Clare and Dominic went to the door and Dominic rapped on it with the head of his walking stick, a necessary accessory for every fine gentleman.

It took a moment for someone to answer the summons but the door was opened. The houseman, an African Clare knew to be named Prince, peered out sleepily.

"Mistress Sullivan, please," Dominic demanded haughtily.

Only then did Prince see Clare, and his eyes widened.

"Come in and wait here. I'll get her."

Moments later Prince returned, and the person entering the parlor behind him could have easily passed for a man. Tall, dressed in a man's nightshirt, robe, and slippers, and holding an oil lamp in her hand, Theodora looked quizzically at the two people standing in her parlor and then her eyes widened. "Clare!"

"Hello, Teddy."

"Oh, my word!" She turned and called back into the house, "Meggie, come quickly! It's our Clare!"

Clare was pleased by the reception. Teddy had always been fond of her.

"My god, girl. We thought you were gone from us forever."

"How are Ben and Sarah?"

"Perfectly fine. I saw Sarah yesterday. Ben's still out in the fields of course." Behind Teddy now stood a woman wearing much more feminine night attire. Her sleepy face was as lovely as a china doll. She took Clare's hands in hers. "Welcome home. We were so worried about you."

"Thank you, Meg."

Teddy turned her eyes on Dominic. "And you are, sir?"

"François deMille. You may tell Clare's mistress that I've returned her property." And he turned and strode out of the room and back outside to the wagon.

Clare closed her eyes for a breath of a moment to keep in the pain as Teddy asked with surprise in her voice, "He was the one who took you?"

"Yes."

The three women watched as the wagon rolled away, and once it disappeared, Teddy said soberly, "Are you well?"

And with those words, Clare became a legal captive once again.

She spent the next little while sitting in the parlor drinking the tea and nibbling on the biscuits Meg brought to her while answering the questions Teddy put to her about the abduction by the man calling himself François deMille.

"No, I've no idea where he took me. We've been at sea the entire time."

Meg said, "It must have been terrible."

"Yes," she lied.

Teddy asked gently, "Were you harmed?"

Clare knew what she was implying. "Yes."

Teddy shook her head sadly. "Well, it's all over now. I'll take you to Violet later this morning. Would you care to sleep for a while? You must be exhausted."

"I am."

Teddy added, "But I can't believe he simply walked up here bold as day and returned you the way he did."

"He'd grown tired of me, I believe."

"And you are fortunate he did and that he brought you here. He could have easily cut your throat and tossed you into the ocean."

Clare didn't speak to that. "The Sullivans made it home safely, I take it?"

"Oh yes. Violet ranted for the first few days about not being able to find someone suitable to replace you because of the importation ban, but she did, of course. The new girl's not nearly as talented as you, so I'm sure my niece will be happy to get you back."

Clare didn't speak to that, either. The importation of new African captives had been banned by one of the acts of the new American Congress, but the illicit trade continued to thrive in places like the neighboring Carolinas.

Teddy stood. "Come, we'll make you a pallet out in the kitchen."

Moments later, Clare bedded down on the pallet set on the rough-hewn timbers of the kitchen floor. Although Teddy frowned on slavery, she owned slaves she'd inherited from her father's estate, and she was a product of her upbringing. It never occurred to her to give Clare the bed in the extra bedroom or a place to sleep inside the house, and Clare didn't expect it. Meg brought her an old quilt to stave off the dawn's chill, and then she and Teddy retreated back to the house to resume their sleep in their fine feather beds. Alone, Clare fought off all the turmoil in her mind, then closed her eyes hoping sleep would carry her away, but it took a long time.

*   *   *

On the ride back to the riverfront, Dominic and the others were silent. They were all thinking of Clare.

Richmond said, "She's a very courageous lady."

They agreed.

"Let's hope we can get her back quickly." Dominic's heart still ached from having to leave her. "And if we can, we need to find out what her children look like. Clare said they are owned by a family named Hampton. If the plan falls apart and we have to take them by force, we don't want to rescue the wrong ones."

"Good point," voiced Gaspar. "Maybe we can come up with a solution once we learn the lay of the land here."

Dominic added, "And you and Richmond need to be extremely careful. We don't want you winding up on the block."

Richmond smiled. "Don't worry."

James hadn't said anything so Dominic looked back at him seated in the wagon bed with Richmond. "You've been awfully quiet, James."

"Just thinking about what Clare must be feeling, and what it would be like if it were my Cinda. We must get her out of there, Dominic, and without delay."

"I know," he responded. "And we will."

His heart was breaking. Having to leave her there was the hardest and most difficult thing he'd ever done. The memories of the fun they'd had together, although precious to him, would not be enough to sustain him through this. He was honest enough to admit that anything could happen in the few days until they planned to sail again, none of it good. What if she'd returned only to find she'd been sold? He had no idea how the Sullivans would treat her. From the stories Clare told him about Violet, he doubted there would be a celebration, more than likely she'd be put right back to work. It took all he had not to turn the wagon around, go back, and grab her and the children and sail away, but he had to wait. Not knowing how she was faring was going to be the worst part.

"Are you all right, *mon frere?*" Gaspar asked.

"No."

At about midday, Teddy, dressed in her breeches, waistcoat, and stockings, drove Clare to the house owned by Violet and Victor Sullivan. Because women were not allowed to own property, Victor's name was on the deed of the house in town, but he lived on the Sullivan rice plantation in a house that he also used as his medical office.

A young woman who appeared to be no older than Richmond answered the door. She was dressed in the plain black gown and full white apron of service. She curtsied to Teddy. "Good afternoon, Miss Sullivan."

Although Teddy's married name was Marks, she refused to use it, just as she'd refused to live under the same roof with the English husband her parents had arranged for her to marry in exchange for four hundred–odd acres of land when she was fifteen.

He now lived in England and had for many years. "Hello, Dot. Is your mistress at home?"

"Yes, ma'am. Come in. I'll fetch her."

Clare took a deep breath to steady herself and followed Teddy inside. The familiarity of the interior washed over her like waves on the sea. Her eyes took in the staircase that led to the second floor as they passed it on their way to the parlor. The furnishings were in the exact position they'd been in when she and the Sullivans sailed off to England. As far as the house was concerned, nothing had transpired between that day last spring and the present. Her adventures with Dominic could have easily been a fever dream.

Teddy took a seat on the settee and lit up her pipe, but Clare knew to remain standing.

Violet entered the parlor, and upon seeing Clare, stopped short and looked her up and down silently. "You're back." Her face was an unreadable mask. If she was pleased to see Clare again, it didn't show. "You don't look any worse for wear."

Teddy said, "We're grateful to have her with us again."

"Yes we are. Now I have someone competent to lay out my gowns and keep them clean."

Clare shot Dot a quick glance just in time to see anger flicker in the young woman's eyes before she lowered her gaze to the floor. No, Clare thought, nothing had changed.

"How did you get back?" Violet asked Clare.

Teddy answered, "Why, that scoundrel walked her right up to my door."

Violet's eyes narrowed, "He's here?"

"He most certainly was. Said to tell Clare's mistress he was returning her property, then he turned on his heel, got back on his wagon, and was driven away."

Violet studied Clare. "Why did he bring you back?"

"He was tired of me, I suppose."

"Then why not just drop you off at the nearest port?"

Teddy waved her pipe, "Who knows the mind of a man like that? When you add in that he's French, one's surprised he can think at all."

"Has he sailed?"

Clare shrugged. "I don't know."

"If he hasn't, I'm having Victor notify the authorities. I want him arrested."

"He's French, dear," Teddy explained. "Since Louis XVI signed the treaty with the Continental Congress the French are the rebels' darlings and mine. They'll not detain him, he's an ally. Besides, what crime are you accusing him of?"

"Slave theft, of course."

Teddy sighed loudly. "He's returned her, Violet. I doubt your case will go very far once that's learned."

Teddy had cut down all Violet's arguments, and it was plain to see that she wasn't happy. "Why are you still standing there?" she asked Clare. "Go change clothes and put that necklace and those ear bobs back in my chest. The gowns in need of pressing are hanging in my armoire. You'll know them

when you see them. Take that one with you and
train her," she added, indicating Dot. "Now that
you're here, I won't be needing her. If she can master
being a good lady's maid, she'll bring a better price
at the market in Charleston."

Clare kept her face blank when she met Dot's
eyes. "Come with me."

The servants' quarters, kitchen, and laundry were
located in the basement of the house. Although the
Sullivans employed two hundred captives in their
rice fields, only Clare, Birgit the cook, and now Dot
worked in Violet's house in town.

"How long have you been here?" Clare asked,
opening the armoire in Violet's room and going
through the gowns. She'd changed into the servant
uniform of black and white that matched Dot's.

"A fortnight."

"Where are you from?"

"Virginia."

Clare gave one armload of the gowns to Dot and
took the rest herself. Downstairs, Birgit greeted
Clare with a strong hug and tears in her eyes. "Oh,
miss. I'm so glad you're home. When Miss Sullivan
said you'd been taken by pirates I was so upset I
didn't know what to do."

Birgit was an indentured servant from England.
She'd been sentenced to London's Newgate prison
for petty theft and given the option of serving her
seven-year sentence in the colony. She'd been with
the Sullivans for the past three years after having
her contract bought out by Victor from a family
that had left Savannah to return to England. "It's so

good to have you home. Dot's been doing her best to fill your shoes, but we all know how impatient Miss Violet can be."

Clare knew, so she went straight to work. It took them most of the day to properly press Violet's many gowns, stomachers, and lace insets. She showed Dot how to heat the two flatirons in the fire Birgit kept burning day and night and then test the temperature. "Some people spit on the plate," she explained. "But I hold it close to my cheek and can tell the right temperature in that manner. Over time, you'll find a method that works best for you. And make sure there are no ashes on the plate when you begin. You don't want to iron ashes into the gown."

Dot watched the process closely and saw how Clare used the metal smoothers to do the linen insets.

The cellar had no windows and therefore very little air circulation. Between the kitchen stove and the fire, the heat rose to almost unbearable levels, but they had no choice but to work on. When the last gown was finally done, Clare wiped at the perspiration on her brow, and she and Dot carried the garments back up to Violet's room.

There were shoes to clean and linens to gather for the wash next week. Some of the shifts Violet had worn during her courses had spots of blood, so they needed to be soaked in lye to remove them. Using one of the kettles she'd designated for that purpose, Clare poured in the lye and put the shifts in. "Never ever run out of lye." The garments would need to

soak for twenty-four hours, then rinsed, and if the
spots remained, soaked again.

"Why not?"

"Because you don't want to be forced to use
chamber lye."

"What's chamber lye?"

"Urine."

Dot's eyes widened and then her nose wrinkled.

"It works well, believe it or not, but collecting it
from the chamber pots . . ." Her voice trailed off
and she shuddered.

The two women shared a smile.

They beat rugs, swept floors, and did everything
else Violet wanted done. By the time Clare finally
found a moment to eat supper and catch her breath,
night had fallen, and for the first time in weeks, the
sun had set without her.

Dominic spent the day thinking of Clare and
passing himself off as smuggler François deMille
to the good citizens of Savannah. He met with the
local rebel commander and negotiated a price for
the guns, then with a town merchant who purchased much of the fabric in the sloop's hold. Mr.
Calhoun let Dominic set up shop in the back of his
livery, and by evening word had spread about him
and his goods. Upon hearing that he had items like
fine ladies' stockings and French colognes, women
began coming around to investigate.

That afternoon, Theodora Sullivan entered the
livery. With her was the beautiful young woman he
knew to be named Meg. Teddy was dressed in a

pair of men's breeches, a jacket, and hose. Her arrival surprised him, but he hid it as he stood. "Good afternoon, Mistress Sullivan."

"Good afternoon, Mr. deMille. Meg and I are here because you are rumored to be selling quality goods."

Meg was looking through some of the items displayed on the trestle tables spread out around the small room.

"The rumors are true." He wondered if she had another purpose for coming.

Meg stopped at the ladies' stockings and held up a pair. "How much for a pair of these, sir?" She was a handsome woman with a good figure, dark hair, and green eyes, but couldn't hold a candle to Clare.

Dominic quoted the price.

"So much?"

"I'm a smuggler, mademoiselle. Our prices are always dear."

She smiled. "I suppose when one puts it that way . . ."

She resumed her perusing.

Teddy was eyeing him closely. "So, you tired of our Clare." She voiced the words as fact and not a question.

"I did, and returned her none the worse for wear as you witnessed," he responded as if the subject bored him.

"We are grateful."

"Did you come to buy, Mistress Sullivan, or simply to quiz me?"

"A bit of both, I'm thinking."

Meg was eyeing a tortoiseshell hairbrush and comb.

Teddy asked her, "Would you like those, Meg?"

"I would."

"Bring them here."

Dominic quoted the price, and Teddy took the coin from a change purse she withdrew from an inner pocket of her waistcoat. "Thank you, Mr. deMille."

"Thank you, mistress." He thought she and her companion made an odd but intriguing couple and wondered what the rumors were surrounding the relationship.

Teddy asked, "How long will you be in Savannah, Mr. deMille?"

"A fortnight. Maybe longer, maybe less."

"I am having a dinner tomorrow evening to celebrate the French and American alliance. I'd be honored if you and your companions would be my guests."

Dominic knew from speaking earlier with the rebel commander that news of the alliance had been cause for much celebration. Although Louis XVI had signed the treaty in February, the news didn't reach the colonies until May, after which General Washington had called for parties, parades, and prayer to mark the event. "What time and where?"

She gave him the particulars. "Clare may be there."

"Clare is no longer of interest to me."

"I see. I will see you there then?"

"Of course." And he bowed.

That said, Teddy and Meg departed.

Gaspar, who'd looked on silently during Teddy and Meg's visit, studied Dominic with seriousness in his eyes. "Are you really going to attend?"

"I am. It may help us learn more about the lay of the land, and I'll see Clare." The prospect somewhat lifted the black cloud that had encased his heart since returning her to her owners. He needed to see with his own eyes how she was faring. They'd been apart less than two days' time, but it felt like an eternity. He'd not be truly content until they were back out at sea and sailing home.

"We'll get her out of this," Gaspar promised.

"I know."

They counted up their sizable profits and were about to take the unsold merchandise back to the ship when a man Dominic vaguely recognized stormed in.

"So it is you?" the visitor voiced angrily.

"Good evening to you, too, sir. Have we met?"

"Yes, in the middle of the Atlantic. I'm Victor Sullivan."

"Ah yes, the slave owner," Dominic replied. "Have you come to buy some of my merchandise, too?"

"No, I've come to tell you that you are a French cad, and that Savannah doesn't want your sordid business."

"Really?" Dominic responded drolly. "Your neighbors seem to think otherwise. I made quite a profit today and hope to do the same tomorrow.

And besides, I fail to see why you are so upset. I returned her safe and sound."

"You had no business taking her from the outset." Sullivan was almost Dominic's height but lacked his muscle and bearing.

"It's what we pirates do, and she is just a slave, after all."

"She's not just a slave," he spat back in reply.

"And that means what, exactly?"

"She has feelings. She's intelligent."

"If she possesses so many sterling qualities, why is she being kept captive against her will? Why hasn't your family freed such a diamond of the first water?"

Sullivan snapped his mouth shut, and his eyes blazed. Without another word he stormed out.

"Too hard of a question, you think, *mon frere*?" Gaspar asked.

"Apparently." Dominic wanted to drag the slave owner back and beat him to a pulp, but knew that wouldn't help rescue Clare or her children. He'd been in a surly mood all day because of where Clare was, and he didn't need his morals flayed by the likes of Sullivan. "Let's get these items packed away and go find something to eat."

"Excellent idea."

After helping Violet prepare for bed, Clare changed into her nightclothes and waited for Violet to get into bed so she could douse the lights. Dot slept in the cellar with Birgit.

"Did he ravish you?" Violet asked.

Clare kept her face neutral. "Yes, Violet, he did."

"Are you breeding?"

"I don't know."

"If you are, it goes on the block in Charleston as soon as it's weaned. I'll not have pirate get in my house. You may douse the light now."

Clare extinguished the lamp and lay down on her pallet at the foot of the bed. In the darkness she wondered if she could be carrying Dominic's child. The answer was yes, of course. The idea of giving birth to a free child would be something to celebrate, if she herself were free, but because she wasn't, Violet's warning sent a chill through her blood.

Chapter 13

While Violet lay sleeping, Clare got up at dawn, dressed, and went down to the cellar to begin the day. Birgit was awake and stoking the fire for its own long day of work, while Dot was nursing a cup of tea. Grabbing two large buckets Clare walked hastily out to the pump and filled them. Dot ran out to help.

"You get that one," Clare instructed her.

Dot struggled with the heavy bucket, but managed to get it back to the kitchen without sloshing too much of the water away on the journey.

The water was poured into the big black kettles and set on the fire. The household would use it for its morning chores, like washing up and the cleaning of the china and cutlery after breakfast. The kettles would be refilled as needed, but one was kept full, hot, and at the ready all day.

Leaving Birgit to begin breakfast, Clare and Dot went outdoors and swept the porch and the brick path that led to the house. With that done, it was time for chamber pots to be emptied and replenished with fresh water. It was not Clare's favorite task.

After a thorough washing of their hands, they set the table for breakfast. According to Birgit, Victor would be joining his twin sister for the morning meal, so Clare and Dot set out plates and cutlery for them both. Once that was accomplished, Clare sent Dot down to the kitchen to eat and she went up to awaken Violet and help her dress. Clare and Violet had never been friends; Clare was her slave, after all, but in their early days together, she'd been kinder. Being left at the church's altar on what was supposed to be one of the happiest days of a woman's life, with all of Savannah's society looking on, had changed her. She became bitter, self-centered, and mean; no one else mattered, and the Ancestors forbid anyone be happy in her presence. Growing up, Clare also got the impression that Violet was jealous of Clare's quick mind. The wager that resulted in the two of them being educated together showed that Clare was not only bright, but considerably brighter than Violet.

Their morning routine rarely varied. Clare would wait for Violet to wash her face and such, then help her with her stays and then the gown. Hair would be done next, and after that Violet's day would officially begin.

Violet had just taken a seat at the head of the table when her brother arrived at the front door. Clare ushered him in.

"Good morning, Clare. We're pleased to have you back with us. Are you well?"

"I am."

He greeted Violet with a kiss on her cheek and

took his seat at the other end of the long table. Clare returned from the kitchen with a tray holding hominy, bacon, eggs, and biscuits. She set everything down as quietly and as quickly as she could.

"Clare, what would you do if you were free?" Victor asked.

She stopped.

Violet said dismissively, "Victor, what a ridiculous question."

"No, it isn't. I'd like to know if she's ever thought about it."

Violet, adding butter to her serving of hominy, scoffed. "Why would she think about something that will never happen?"

He looked at Clare. "Have you ever thought about it, Clare?"

"No," she lied. "Your sister is correct. Why think on something that will never be? May I get you anything else?"

They both shook their heads. As she turned to go she could feel Victor's eyes on her back but she didn't acknowledge him as she exited.

When Dominic awakened that morning it took him a moment to get his bearings. He and the crew had taken rooms at one of the local boardinghouses, and at first the unfamiliar surroundings were confusing until he remembered where he was. His first thoughts were of Clare, just as she'd been in his final thoughts before sleep claimed him last night. In his mind's eye he could see her beautiful smiling face, and he wondered how she'd fared her first day back in captivity. It was a given that no one had brought her breakfast, or drawn her a bath, or shown her how much she was loved. At the moment she was undoubtedly running from pillar to post in an attempt to complete all the tasks put to her by Violet Sullivan. Not having her by his side was like having a hole in his soul.

Around him the others were stirring awake. With all their goods now stored in the Calhoun livery, there was no need for anyone to stay with the ship. He nodded morning greetings to Richmond, Gaspar, Tait, and the rest, and once everyone was dressed and ready, headed downstairs to breakfast. The place was owned by a free Black woman named Jenny. According to her there was a small but vital group of free Blacks in the city of Savannah. Many of them were women and made their living doing laundry, cleaning homes, and offering other domestic services.

Downstairs she greeted them with a smile. She was tall and thin and wore a head wrap like many women of color, slave and free.

As she set the fare on the table she asked, "Will you be needing me for any more meals today, Captain?"

"Not if you have pressing business you need to take care of."

"I do. I have to help out with the church. We Blacks have our own place of worship in Savannah."

"Really? That's not very common."

"No it isn't, and we are especially proud. Right now we're allowed to worship on one of the local plantations but we plan to build a place soon with our own hands and using our own coin from folks both slave and free."

"Then we shall arrange for meals elsewhere."

"Thank you so much, Captain."

"Tell me though. Do you know a White family named Hampton?"

"Mrs. Hampton, the dressmaker?"

Dominic shrugged. "I'm not sure of her calling."

"She and her husband are the only ones I know with that name. They have a rice plantation about twelve miles from here."

"Can you draw us a map? I'm told she may be interested in some of my merchandise."

"Be glad to."

A few moments later the map was drawn and Dominic and his friends left the boardinghouse. They drove back to the docks to drop off Esteban, Richmond, and Washington Julian, who would oversee the day's selling, and left Tait with the sloop. Dominic, James, and Gaspar headed for the Hampton home.

Traveling by wagon down the poor excuse for a road, Dominic wondered if it was the same one Clare walked on Sundays to see her children. He could only imagine how tired she'd be after the journey there and back, but he was certain the weariness would be secondary to the joy generated by seeing her Sarah and Ben.

They found the house. Outside a little girl dressed in a black dress and white apron was sweeping the doorstep. When she looked up at the wagon's ap-

proach, Dominic's heart stopped. The small face
was an exact copy of Clare's.

James said quietly, "That has to be her, Captain.
She looks just like a miniature of Miss Clare."

"Aye," Gaspar added with a smile. "She's going
to grow up and be a beauty just like her *maman*."

Dominic continued to stare. The emotions filling him had no name. There stood Clare's daughter, a little girl destined to be raised as his own. As
she continued to look out at them from her side of
the road, Dominic's heart swelled. To keep himself
from jumping out of the wagon and carrying her
away, he said softly to Gaspar, "Drive on and head
back."

"What about the son?"

"We'll figure out something in the next few days.
I just wanted to make sure we knew the correct lo-
cation of the house."

As they drove away, the girl watched them for a
moment, then resumed her sweeping.

Clare and Dot spent the morning on their hands
and knees scrubbing floors. The lye and harsh soap
in the water immediately took its toll on Clare's
hands and turned them red and raw. They'd healed
up while she'd been on the island, but were now just
as rough as they'd been before. "So, Dot. How did
you wind up in Savannah?"

They were upstairs doing the floor in the hall.

"My parents went over to Dunmore two years
ago and died on his ship of the pox."

Lord Dunmore had been the royal governor of Virginia. In '75, when the crown became desperate for men to aid the loyalists against the rebels, he'd issued a decree promising to free any slaves who joined his forces. Colonial slave owners were outraged, and in the areas where the captive population outnumbered the Whites they were terrified by thoughts of massive slave insurrections. According to the newspaper accounts Clare read at Teddy's at the time, about eight hundred slaves officially answered the call. Three hundred were trained and outfitted in military uniforms with the words *Liberty to Slaves* inscribed over the breasts. They fought under the name of Lord Dunmore's Ethiopian Regiment. They had limited battle success, but because Dunmore had been forced to flee Virginia and was doing his governing offshore, on a ship in the British fleet, he had no land base to house the volunteers or his regulars. The ships were overcrowded, food and supplies were at a minimum, and smallpox spread through the vessels like wildfire.

"After my parents died, me and a few others decided to take our chances in the swamps, but we were caught and I was sold again, this time to a woman in Charleston."

"That didn't go well?"

"At first it did, I suppose. But then, one day, I dropped a china plate setting the table for dinner and she spat in my face. I slapped her. She sold me that next day."

Clare shook her head sadly and was about to comment when Violet called up to them. "Clare, leave the scrubbing to Dot. I'll need you to help me dress in a few moments."

It was almost dinnertime and she wondered why Violet needed to change her gown, but she did as she was told and went into Violet's room to await further instruction.

Violet entered the room saying, "Teddy is having a dinner this evening to celebrate the rebels' alliance with France. In order to continue the pretense of supporting the so-called patriots, Victor suggested I attend. Once I'm dressed, you get dressed, too."

Clare was confused, "Why?"

"I'll need someone to attend me while I'm there and because your Frenchman is supposed to be making an appearance as a representative of his country."

"But why subject me to his presence knowing what I suffered?"

She offered a cold smile. "Because I can, dear Clare. Because I can. Now, get the blue gown for me. You'll wear the green."

Outwardly Clare showed no emotion but inside her heart soared at the idea of being able to see Dominic. For the first time in her life Clare was happy that Violet prided herself on being so mean-spirited.

Down on the docks, Dominic and his men prepared to close shop for the day. They'd done well. There were still enough small items like spices, stockings, cologne, kegged wine, and sets of china to last a long while. Residents of nearby Charleston were also venturing into Calhoun's livery to buy from the Frenchmen.

In spite of the British ships looming off the coast, there were quite a few ships going in and out of the port. Most were loading up on rice, one of the area's biggest exports. Male captives both young and old lined the ship's ramps, moving the heavy bags along and dumping them into the holds.

Dominic was so busy watching the loading that he wasn't paying attention to where he was walking and was almost bowled over by a young male slave straining behind a wheelbarrow loaded with bags of rice. In his trying to avoid Dominic, the wheelbarrow tipped before the young man could get it upright and some of the bags tumbled onto the wharf.

Dominic and his men sprang to his aid, hastily helping him right the wheelbarrow and restacking the bags. "My apologies for not watching where I was going," Dominic offered genuinely.

The young man looked up into Dominic's face out of Clare's brown eyes, and Dominic's heart stopped for the second time that day.

"Thank you, sirs," the boy said.

Up ahead, a man standing on the ramp of one of the ships called out harshly, "Ben! Get a move on. This ship ain't gonna wait all day!"

Having the identity confirmed only added to Dominic's sense of shock. The boy set his feet and pushed the wheelbarrow down the dock.

Esteban said, "You look like you've seen a ghost."

"That was Clare's son."

"What?"

They all turned.

Dominic was visibly shaken, but now he knew the faces of both of Clare's children.

Teddy Sullivan had one of the largest homes in Savannah. Everyone knew where she stood on the war; she supported Washington and the rebels. Violet and Victor had been staunch loyalists during the crown's control of Savannah, but now that the patriots held the city, they, like many other planters, were pretending publicly to embrace the Americans' cause. Clare supposed it was a simple matter of survival since no one knew who would eventually win the war and everyone wanted to be on the side of the victors no matter the flag. So as she and Violet were driven up to the house by Victor, she saw the Black coachmen of most of Savannah's wealthier citizens dropping off their owners and moving the vehicles into a field nearby.

"Looks like everyone is here," Violet remarked.

"Seems that way," Victor added.

"And as always we're the only ones without a Black driver."

His lips tightened. "Right again, Vi."

Because of Victor's gambling and his lack of business acumen, the Sullivans weren't nearly half as wealthy as they once were. Since the death of their father five years ago, the rice plantation hadn't turned a profit; the reason there were only a few servants in the house. The voyage to England this past April had been undertaken because Violet had been told via correspondence that her father's late cousin had left her a bequest upon his death. And he had—a brooch. She'd been so furious she'd thrown the thing into the Thames. As it stood now, every bit of coin Victor didn't gamble away went to satisfy Violet's needs for gowns, silk stockings, and shoes, which left little for the plantation's necessities like more field slaves, feed, and seed.

On the other hand, Teddy was one of the richest women in the colony. Because she was forbidden by law to own or sell property, her absent husband's name was on the deed to her land, but it was she who oversaw her vast holdings, ran the day-to-day operations, and kept the ledgers. She also had over five hundred captives in her rice and indigo fields and a dozen or so working in her home. With so many servants about, Violet's claim that she needed Clare to attend her this evening was a sham. Making Clare accompany her was nothing more than Violet wanting to place Clare in what Violet thought would be an uncomfortable situation.

The two liveried footmen at the door were men Clare knew from their church out on the Brampton Plantation; they were members of the congregation as was she. Teddy paid her slaves a nominal wage and many of them contributed to the church's operations. Because the Sullivans paid her nothing, Clare contributed by secretly teaching the members to read.

"Good evening, Dr. Sullivan. Miss Sullivan. Clare. Welcome," the footman on the right said.

Victor said, "Thank you, Prince. How are you?"

"Well, sir. And you?"

"Victor, we are not here to talk to the slaves," Violet declared shortly. "Come along."

Clare glanced over at Prince, who rolled his eyes, and she had to hold in a giggle.

Inside, the large parlor was an inferno. Too many bodies and too little circulation of fresh air made it hard to breathe, even though there were slaves positioned all over the room with large fans made of imported palm fronds doing what they could to cool the air.

"I'll go out to the kitchen to see if Della needs help," Clare said. Della was Teddy's housekeeper.

"Della is a very competent slave. I'm sure she has everything under control. You just stay close. Ah, I see the receiving line. Come, Victor. Clare, you, too."

Victor looked over at Clare. "Are you comfortable with the Frenchman being here?"

"Of course not."

"Then why—"

She cut him off and told him with quiet frankness, "I'm a slave, Victor. I do what I am told."

He pursed his lips and followed his sister.

In the receiving line stood Teddy and Meg, and beside them Dominic. Teddy was outfitted in a fine blue waistcoat and matching breeches. Meg looked as beautiful as a European princess in her stunning gown of yellow silk. Next to them were Esteban, Gaspar, and James. Clare fought hard not to look Dominic's way, but when she did, his eyes were waiting. They twinkled just long enough for her to see it before becoming hooded and bored. Even as her heart pounded with her love for him, she kept her features masked and braced herself for whatever Violet might do or say.

Teddy said, "Violet. Victor. Hello, Clare dear."

Clare nodded. Gaspar and Esteban offered her kindly smiles that she met blankly.

"Let me introduce my guests."

"We're already acquainted, thank you," Violet said bitterly.

Teddy glanced over at Dominic, who took a sip from the drink in his hand, his eyes smiling coldly.

"Have either of you been down to the docks to see Mr. deMille's merchandise? Meg and I were surprised at the quality and the variety."

"No," Victor replied, shooting daggers Dominic's way. "We met him this past spring on the Atlantic, remember. He raided our ship, stole gold, guns, and took Clare from us."

Dominic held his eyes. "She was intriguing, but since I'm no longer interested, I've returned her to you."

Clare kept all emotion from her face.

Teddy looked into Clare's face as if trying to see beneath the mask. "Clare, I'm sorry if this has caused you any embarrassment. Violet, I hoped you would leave Clare at home but if you're uncomfortable as well, I'll understand if you choose to leave."

"We'll stay. Won't we, Clare."

Clare didn't reply.

Violet looked over at Dominic and said with a smile that didn't meet her eyes, "Be aware that if she's breeding, your get will go on the block."

He froze.

Meg gasped.

His hooded gaze brushed Clare before he replied drolly, "Thank you for that information, Miss Sullivan. Enjoy the evening."

It was apparent by the shock on the faces of some of the guests nearby that Violet had been overheard. Buzzing began among the people standing closest to her in the receiving line. A few even leaned out of the line to get a look at Clare. Keeping her mask in place, she ignored them. She was a slave, and that reality was far more painful than being the subject of slave owners' gossip. Inside, however, she was furious at this latest vicious attempt by Violet to break her spirit.

Echoing Dominic, Violet said, "Enjoy your evening."

Clare followed the Sullivans away from the receiving line. She knew Dominic was watching the departure; her sense of him was as strong as her angrily beating heart. She dearly wished to turn back and meet his eyes, but she kept her feet moving forward.

Victor viewed his sister disapprovingly, and once they were out of range he asked quietly, "Was that truly necessary?"

She took a glass of punch from a tray carried by a white-suited slave. "Of course it was. I want everyone to know that the man's a slave stealer."

He sighed. "Clare, I need some relief from this stifling heat. Would you care to accompany me?"

"She doesn't need air," Violet declared, voice

dripping with contempt. "She's African, she's accustomed to heat."

Victor countered, "Nevertheless, we'll return shortly." He gestured tersely to Clare. "After you."

Having little choice, she led him into the crowd. A discreet glance sent Dominic's way was met by eyes already waiting. In terms of length and time the connection lasted less than a breath, but it was long enough for her to see his fury. Breaking off the link, she focused her gaze ahead, and he seamlessly moved his attention back to the guests moving through the receiving line.

Once outside in the cooler night air she drew in a series of breaths. Her constricting stays prevented them from being very deep ones, but they were sufficient to gain some relief from the oppressive heat filling the parlor and to calm her pounding emotions.

There were other people out milling about, laughing, talking, and taking advantage of the food and drink being offered on the trays of the circulating slaves. Victor escorted her over to a quiet spot.

"Are you carrying?" he asked in a voice laden with concern.

She looked up at the stars and remembered viewing them at another time and in another place. "I don't know."

"If you are, and you wish to keep it with you, I'll see that you can. I promise."

Clare shook her head and expelled a soft, bitter chuckle. "And what is that promise worth, Victor? You've already sold both of my children."

"It was necessary, Clare, you know that. I had to pay the back tariffs on the land or lose it. I had no choice."

"And if a similar necessity arises again? What will your promise be worth to the child that may be growing in my womb?"

He looked out at the night and didn't reply for a moment, then said finally, quietly, "I wish things were different. If you weren't . . ." His words trailed off.

"If I weren't African?"

Their eyes met in the dark for a moment before his moved away. They were the same age and had been raised under the same roof: master and slave. Over the years he'd given her the impression that he had feelings for her, and had even kissed her once when they were adolescents, but that had been the extent of it. Unlike some slave owners, he'd never forced himself on her, or treated her with anything but respect. However, Clare had no tender feelings for him, at least not in that way; she wasn't foolish enough to even begin to imagine their relationship being anything but what it was: master and slave. Yes, he'd been kind to her, but the day he sold her children their relationship had been altered forever. Clare would never forgive him for as long as she drew breath. "Why did you ask me about being free?"

"When I confronted deMille on the waterfront the other day and told him how intelligent you were, and that you had feelings, he wanted to know why I hadn't freed you, if I thought so highly of you."

"And your reply?"

"I had none."

She sighed audibly. "I'm going back, Victor. I'll see you inside."

As she approached the door she saw Gaspar standing beside it with a drink in his hand. She assumed he'd come outside ostensibly to take in the night air, but in reality was watching over her. The knowledge filled her heart. When she passed by, he asked quietly, "You are well?"

Looking up into his kind eyes almost made hers fill with tears, but she nodded instead. "I am. Thank you." And she proceeded back into the hot, noisy parlor.

Teddy was standing just inside the door speaking with Abner Holloway, a staunch patriot and the owner of one of the largest rice plantations in the Carolinas. According to Teddy he had over a thousand captives in his fields. As soon as she saw Clare she excused herself from him and said, "I'd like to speak with you, if I may."

"Yes, ma'am."

Teddy stopped one of the servers, a young woman named Hallee, and asked that Violet be told that she and Clare would be speaking in the study for a moment. Hallee and Clare knew each other from the church. Halle's eyes brushed Clare before resettling on her mistress. "Yes, mistress."

Once they were inside the quiet book-lined study, Teddy said, "I won't keep you long, but I wanted to apologize for Violet's behavior and for my being responsible for putting you in such an embarrassing situation. DeMille may be French but he appears to be an unfeeling cad."

It pained Clare to have Dominic be thought of as malevolent when in reality all he'd shown her was care and love, but this was the game they were playing. "I appreciate your sympathy."

"And as for your mistress. All I can say is you deserve better. You are one of the most intelligent women in Savannah, slave or free. Were you mine I would have freed you long ago just as I've freed Della."

Clare stared. "Della is free?"

"As are Halle and her husband, Prince."

Expecting a trap, Clare studied her face. "Why tell me this?"

"One, because I know you will be discreet, and two, because I'm hoping to take them north to Boston come spring, war or no war, so they may live free as they deserve. I'd like for you and your children to come accompany us as well, but if my niece and nephew refuse to sell you again, I—"

Clare's heart raced. "Again?"

"Yes. Last autumn I offered good coin to buy you, but they refused."

Her eyes widened.

"I can see by your face that is the first you've heard. As your owners, them not telling you is their prerogative, of course."

Clare's knees were so weakened she thought she might fall down. "May I sit?"

"Of course."

There were so many emotions flowing through

her it was difficult to separate them all. "Did they give you the impression that I might be for sale?"

"They didn't, but it's common knowledge that Victor will lose the land by the end of summer if he doesn't sell something valuable to pay off this year's tariffs, and everyone knows that when you subtract the Sullivan land, their next most valuable property is you, Clare."

Her eyes closed at the thought of what the future might have held had she not already had Dominic in her life. Gathering herself, she stood once more. "Thank you for telling me this."

"So, do you wish for me to try and buy you and the children again so that you may travel with us to Boston, or have you made other arrangements for your future?"

Clare's eyes shot to hers and held.

Teddy said, "He's not the man he wants us to see, is he? I know you won't answer that, but I saw all I needed when Violet threatened to put your babe on the block. For a split second his mask slipped. He recovered quickly but I saw the pain. He's in love with you."

Clare stayed silent.

"I'm going to make the assumption that you came back for your children. I know I would, so if I can be of any assistance please let me know."

"Thank you for the apology," were the only words Clare allowed herself to say.

"You're welcome. Now, let's go back before that vicious niece of mine accuses your man of stealing you again."

Outside the door and standing a few feet away were Esteban and James Early. They appeared to be nonchalantly talking to each other, but Teddy didn't buy it. "She's fine, gentlemen, as you can see."

They didn't respond, but let the ladies pass them and reenter the parlor before they moved from their post and discreetly followed.

As Clare searched the noisy gathering crowd for the Sullivans her head was spinning from Teddy's revelations. Had anyone else seen through their charade, or was she the only one? The idea that she might have been sold added to the emotional whirlwind.

"Ah, there you are," Teddy said to Violet, Meg, and Victor as she escorted Clare back. When Clare's eyes met Victor's, guilt flashed over his face before he lowered his eyes to the glass in his hand.

"I must see to my guests. Come, Meg."

"What did she want with you?" Violet asked Clare suspiciously after Teddy and Meg were swallowed up by the crowd.

"To offer an apology, nothing more."

Violet was about to say something else when Teddy's voice rose over the din. "May I have your attention, please."

Everyone quieted. "It has come to my attention that Mr. deMille has with him a musician from the court of King Louis XVI who has graciously agreed to play a few selections. I'd like us to step outside where it is cooler so we may enjoy the music at our leisure."

Clare almost let a smile slip as she saw Tait, fiddle in hand, leading the way. She'd had no idea he'd accompanied Dominic and the others. She looked forward to hearing him and his fiddle. Teddy, Dominic, and the rest of the crew except for Gaspar fell in behind him. She nonchalantly glanced around the room searching for the quartermaster and found him positioned against a wall only a few feet away from her.

Violet sniffed, "Victor, go and get the carriage. Clare and I will meet you out by the road. We won't be staying."

He hissed in reply, "Yes, we are. You've embarrassed the Sullivan name quite enough for one evening, so act as if you have a modicum of decorum remaining and indulge Teddy."

Furious, she rose to her feet and walked stiffly into the crowd flowing slowly towards the door.

Tait played for nearly an hour, alternating between French folk songs, classical pieces, and Catholic and Anglican hymns. When he finished, and after the applause died down, he said in his French-accented English, "Now with your permission I will close the performance with a melody I composed for a beautiful woman of my acquaintance."

Clare sensed what he was about to play, and in the darkness the hairs stood up on her neck.

"It is called 'Ode to a Lovely Lady.' "

The familiar sweet notes rose against the night and she closed her eyes. The beautiful melody captured her and transported her back to the *Marie* and to Dominic and the island. Even though she'd been in captivity only a few short days, those wonderful times seemed to have been very long ago.

When the music faded away and the applause began, Clare felt a sadness wash over her, but there was happiness, too, in knowing he'd played the composition just for her. She guessed it was Tait's and Dominic's way of letting her know they cared. She'd needed buoying after such an emotional evening and being treated to "Ode to Clare" had helped immensely.

The applause finally ended and was followed by Teddy's farewell to her guests, "Thank you all for coming. *Vive la France!*"

The phrase was echoed again and again by the shouting crowd, and then everyone headed to their carriages and drivers for the journey home.

On the short ride back to the house, Violet said to Clare, "By the way, we're going to Charleston in the morning and taking the early ferry, so I'll need you to pack tonight and provide me with enough clothes for a few days. We'll return Monday, at the latest Tuesday."

"I wanted to see my children on Sunday, Violet. I haven't seem them since we sailed to England back in March."

"Maybe next week. Dot will be traveling with us. I wish to do some shopping and visit the slave market for an estimate on how much she may be worth. If the price is fair we'll leave her with the owners."

Clare felt sorry for Dot, but focused on pressing her own case. "I would prefer to remain here and see my children, Violet."

"I heard you the first time, Clare, but did you hear me?"

When Clare didn't respond, Violet asked again, "Did you?"

Clare responded tightly, "Yes."

"I thought you had."

While Teddy stood on the porch saying good night to the last of her guests, Dominic waited for her to step back inside so that he could thank her for the invitation and then make his own departure.

The news that Clare might be carrying his child filled his heart, and Violet's stated plan to put his progeny on the block made him want to strangle her on the spot, but he put her out of his mind and mused on Clare. Had they really created a child? Would he be holding a tiny baby girl or boy in his arms sometime in the near future? The prospect was thrilling and humbling. That neither of his parents was alive to help welcome their grandchild to the world sobered him a bit. Were they here, he knew they'd be pleased not only with the child but with the mother. He'd asked Tait to play Clare's signature tune as a token of his love and to let her know that she was supported and surrounded by those who loved her as well.

Teddy walked through the doors on the heels of that thought, and for a moment she simply studied him with an enigmatic smile. "Thank you for your attendance this evening, Captain."

"It's been my pleasure."

"Do things usually turn out the way you plan them?"

"Most times."

"They don't for me."

Since he had no way of knowing where this might be headed, he went ahead and took the bait. "What do you mean?"

"I think very highly of Clare. I made my niece and nephew an offer for her last fall."

"Which they refused, I assume, since she is still with them."

"Yes, but rumor has it that Victor is going under. He'll need to start selling things, and frankly she's the most valuable thing they own."

"Why reveal this to me?"

"In case you decide to take an interest in the child she may be bearing, you'll need to know her fate."

"My lack of feelings for Clare notwithstanding, no child of mine will be placed on the auction block."

"Victor might accept an offer from you."

Admittedly, it was an avenue Dominic had toyed with. "Then maybe I will take up the subject with him."

She nodded. "Good night, Captain."

He bowed and made move to leave, but before he could step out, she added, "And Captain, may the love that binds you and Clare be strong forever."

He stiffened and turned, but she was climbing the stairs and did not look back.

Chapter 14

Clare, Violet, and Dot arrived at the dock before dawn to catch the early ferry for Charleston. Because the place to board the small boat was at the far end of the dock, and away from where the larger craft were moored, she couldn't see Dominic's sloop. She needed to alert him that because she was going to Charleston the rescue would have to be delayed another week, but she had not means to do so. When it became time to depart their trunks were loaded and Violet took a seat up front, while Clare and Dot stood in the rear with the rest of the slaves.

Because of all the stops along the way to pick up other passengers, the ferry ride up the coast to Charleston got them to the city's docks a bit past midday. The weather was overcast and a bit windy, but only a hurricane would stop Violet from shopping, so they stepped off the ferry and waited for their luggage to be unloaded. Once that was done, Clare walked over to the cabs lined up for hire and made the arrangements to be driven into the city proper.

Violet had the cabdriver stop first at the boardinghouse she always stayed in when in the city, and after securing a room for herself and a place for Clare and Dot in the servant quarters out back, had him drive on to the small, exclusive dressmaker's shop she loved to frequent. Clare was still angry over not being able to see her children, but had no recourse but to go along.

Inside, the shop owner greeted Violet a bit coolly. "Miss Sullivan. How are you?"

"I'm well, Miss Dexter, and you?" Without bothering to wait for a reply, Violet passed the woman by and went over to view the ready-made gowns on the dress forms. "This is very lovely," she said, gently flaring the skirt of a brown sateen gown. "How long would it take for this to be fitted and sewn?"

"Less than a week for my clients with accounts that are not in arrears."

Violet turned.

Miss Dexter said plainly, "You have yet to send payment on the gowns you received last fall, Miss Sullivan, or the one delivered this past February. You assured me at the time that the matter would be resolved. Am I to assume that you are here to take care of the outstanding debt?"

Miss Dexter was known not only for her dressmaking but for being genteel and polite, so for her to publicly shame Violet this way in front of the other patrons milling about the shop spoke to how seriously she was taking the matter of Violet's unpaid bill.

Clare could tell by the tight set of Violet's jaw and her red face that she had not been prepared to have her dirty laundry aired for all to hear. Violet considered herself to be a wealthy pillar of society even if, in reality, that was no longer the case.

She trilled, "My brother must have forgotten. I will give him a piece of my mind on your behalf, I assure you, and you will receive the overdue funds by month's end. Now, as for this gown—"

But Miss Dexter cut her off. "I won't be offering you any further service until your bill is paid, Miss Sullivan. I run a business, not an almshouse."

Violet turned scarlet this time, and huffed with offense. "Well, I'll be sure to patronize someone else in the future. Come, Clare. Come, Dot," she snapped icily.

Clare and Dot followed her to the door, and as they exited and stepped out onto the street were nearly bowled over by a fair-skinned man and woman passing by. As both parties recovered, Clare froze upon recognizing them. The woman's eyes widened as she recognized Clare also.

A cold smile came across Sylvie's face. "Well, if it isn't our dear Clare. Is this your mistress?"

Violet scanned Sylvie up and down. "I am Violet Sullivan. And you are?"

"A former acquaintance of Clare and her lover LeVeq. Did he finally tire of you, little Clare?"

Violet turned to Clare, "LeVeq? Who is LeVeq!"

Clare's heart was racing. She saw a light of interest flare in the eyes of the man with Sylvie. She recognized him, too. It was Dominic and Gaspar's nemesis, Paul Vanweldt.

Sylvie answered helpfully, "Why, he's the privateer who stole her from her mistress, if the rumors are true."

"She was stolen from me, but by a man named deMille. He's in Savannah now."

Sylvie threw back her head and laughed. "It's an alias he's used in the past. You say he's in Savannah now?"

"Yes."

"Do you know why?"

"He returned Clare and is there selling smuggled goods. He said he'd tired of her."

Sylvie shook her head. "I doubt that to be truth, Miss Sullivan. He was very much smitten with your slave, and she with him. He wouldn't have returned her to you willingly. If he is still in Savannah he is there for a reason that is undoubtedly tied to her."

Violet turned to Clare. "Is this true? You are lovers!"

Clare didn't respond.

She grabbed Clare's arm, nails digging into the skin, "Answer me!" She slapped her. "Answer me, whore!"

Clare's hand flew to her burning cheek.

"Why is he still here!" Violet demanded.

Violet appeared to have an epiphany and stared at Clare with wide eyes. "It's those cubs of yours, isn't it. You came back for them! That's why he hasn't sailed! After all my family has done for you!"

She hauled off to slap her again, and Clare blocked the blow and pushed her back. Violet fell. "You struck me? I will sell you, right this minute, you lying whore!"

People were stopping to watch the spectacle along the traffic-heavy thoroughfare.

Vanweldt helped Violet to her feet and said kindly, "Mistress, if you mean what you say, I may be able to assist you. I am a trafficker. I hate LeVeq as much as I am sure you do now. I can arrange for the sale of this traitorous slave to a party in Martinique who would be overjoyed to gain custody of someone LeVeq cares for. In fact, I can pay you good coin for her now, and be reimbursed upon delivery."

Clare's whole world began to shake. "No!" she cried out in angry disbelief. "Violet!"

"Silence! How much!"

He whispered a sum into Violet's ear and she responded with wide eyes. "So much?"

"No, Violet! Don't do this!"

Vanweldt took a small bag from his pocket and gave it to Violet, and then clamped an iron hold on Clare's wrist while Sylvie looked on, pleased.

"Let me go!"

Clare wanted to fall to her knees and beg but knew it wouldn't change things.

The amused Sylvie told Clare, "Who knew that when Paul and I met in Jamaica and found we had a mutual dislike for your lover, that we'd both be able to extract our revenge on him through you? Now we can all sit back and laugh at the idea of him searching frantically for you, but not knowing where to look. I'll bet his bastard heart will break."

"Speaking of bastards, she may be breeding," Violet informed them while she placed the bag of gold in her small knit handbag.

As he scanned what he could see of Clare's still flat belly within her cloak, Vanweldt's eyes took on an evil glow. "Even better."

No one noticed Dot edging towards the road that ran by the front of the shop. Suddenly she bolted into the thick midday traffic, dodging wagons and carriages.

"Get back here!" Violet screamed and took off after her, but she was so angry and focused she didn't look first, and ran directly into the path of a fast-moving wagon being pulled by four thundering horses. The impact threw her up in the air and then under their powerful hooves. By the time the surprised driver pulled back on the reins it was too late. Passersby hurried to the scene. Sylvie reached her first. The numb Clare watched Sylvie kneel over Violet's broken corpse, ostensibly to check for vital signs, but in reality she was placing her handbag atop Violet's. She deftly picked up both, keeping Violet's smaller one hidden beneath her own. A man claiming to be a doctor came running up, and Sylvie quickly but smoothly backed free of the people now circling the kneeling doctor and the dead Violet.

When Sylvie was again by Vanweldt's side he said to her quietly, "You are a woman after my own heart."

"No sense in letting all that gold go to waste. What about the girl?"

"Forget her. By the time she makes her way back to Savannah, if that is indeed where she's heading, we'll be halfway to Martinique." With his hand still clamped on Clare's arm, he forced her to accompany them away from the scene.

They put her in a carriage driven by the giant dark-skinned mute Clare had last seen with Vanweldt on the deck of the *Amsterdam*. "Dominic will find me and he'll kill you. Save your lives and let me go."

"Be quiet," Vanweldt ordered shortly.

"He wanted to kill you the afternoon he sank the *Amsterdam*."

He turned to her sharply.

"Yes," she assured him. "I was there on the *Marie* that day. You and what was left of your crew were lucky he let you escape with your lives. I doubt he'll be so generous again."

"Quiet!" Sylvie snapped.

"And you, poor, poor Sylvie. Maybe he'll maroon you. Leave you all alone on a deserted island with only a pistol for comfort. You were his mistress. You know how deadly Dominic can be, especially if it involves someone he cares for, but he doesn't care for you anymore, does he?"

Clare was struck again, and blood oozed from her split lip, but she wasn't deterred. "When Dominic finds me, you'll both beg to be sent to hell."

The giant drove them through the city to the docks, where she was taken aboard a small ship. While Vanweldt and his crew members got them under way, Clare was below decks being bound hand and foot by the mute. Sylvie was holding a pistol on her, and once Clare was tied, Sylvie told the mute, "Force open her mouth."

Clare tried to keep her lips and teeth locked but

the powerful hand grabbed her by the jaw and the great pressure made her mouth open in response.

Sylvie smiled. "I doubt you can make trouble trussed up as you are, but just in case. This is something Vanweldt uses on difficult slaves." She poured the foul-tasting draught past her lips, and the struggling Clare had to swallow or choke.

Moments later the cabin began to spin, or was it her head, Clare couldn't tell, but before she could make sense of it, the world went dark.

A few hours past dark, Gaspar boarded the moored sloop followed by a young girl. The worried look he wore when he entered the cabin immediately grabbed Dominic's attention. "What's happened?"

"I'm not certain, but she is anxious to speak with you."

"Your name, my dear?"

"Dot. Please, sir, you have to help her!"

"Who?"

"Miss Clare. Miss Violet sold her. I tried to get here as fast as I could, but—"

"Sold her! When?" He looked to Gaspar. "Gather the others."

Dominic gestured her to a seat in his cabin. She had tears in her eyes.

"Now, start again and from the beginning."

Dot told him the story beginning with the early morning ferry ride to Charleston and ending with Clare's sale and Violet being struck by the horses. "I don't know how badly she was hurt. I ran. Once

I got back to the dock, I convinced a fishing boat going to Savannah that I'd gotten separated from my master and needed to get home, and they brought me, so then I came here."

"You did well, Dot." And she had. "You said the woman at the shop called the man with her Paul? Can you describe him?"

She did. "He claimed to be a trafficker. The woman with him, she never said her name but she said she knew you and Miss Clare, and that she and the man Paul had met in Jamaica."

"Sylvie and Vanweldt," Dominic spat. It had to have been they.

By then, the others had entered and Dominic hastily filled them in. Their faces were torn between concern and fury.

"Did he say where he might be taking her?" he asked.

"Martinique. He said he knew someone who'd enjoy owning someone that you cared for."

"Eduard," Gaspar bit out. "I'll bet my share it's him."

Dominic's tightened jaw throbbed with emotion.

Esteban said, "I'll ready the sloop."

"Good."

He hastened back up to the deck.

Dominic focused again on Dot. "We will find Miss Clare, but I don't wish to leave you here in Savannah unprotected. Do you wish to sail with us?"

"Will I be free?"

"Yes."

"Then yes. I'll sail."

"Richmond, you, Tait, and Sam stay here. Hide her well. Everyone else with me."

"Where are we going?" Gaspar asked.

"To get the children. Then home for the *Marie*."

"You should have killed Vanweldt when you had the chance."

"I've no time for hindsight, brother, but you are correct."

They hurried to the livery for horses.

Calhoun said, "You seem to be in an all-fired hurry, deMille."

"We are, but we'll be returning shortly."

Once the horses were saddled, Dominic, Esteban, James, and Washington Julian tore out for the Hampton home.

Dominic was sick inside. The woman he loved was in the hands of Vanweldt. He knew the Dutchman would take a perverse joy in inflicting whatever harm or terror he could as a means to strike back at him, and putting Clare in the clutches of his snake of a brother would be the ultimate revenge for both men, and for Sylvie. However, Dominic hoped they knew they would be paying for this perfidy with their lives because ultimately and eventually they would.

Arriving at the Hampton home they saw no lights inside. Either no one was home or they were sleeping. Dominic thought the latter. The house was located on the edge of the property; the fields and, he assumed, the slave quarters were situated in the back.

"Do we have a plan?" Gaspar asked.

"No," Dominic said, getting off his horse. "We

go in, put a pistol to their heads, and demand the children. We've no time for politeness."

Gaspar grinned. "Aye, sir."

A sharp rap on the door brought a sleepy, middle-aged slave to the threshold. He raised the candle boat in his hand in an effort to see the visitors. A pistol pointed at his face appeared out of the dark. His eyes widened and his hand holding the candle began to shake.

"Get your master. Now. Do not tell him we are armed or it will cost you and him your lives."

He nodded, appearing too afraid to speak.

Moments later the slave returned with a tall, aging White man.

"Hampton?"

His eyes widened. "Who are you? What is the meaning of this?"

"We're here for Ben and Sarah Sullivan. Where are they?"

"Please," the man voiced, trembling. "Take whatever you want, just don't kill us."

"Ben and Sarah!"

"Why?"

James quickly put the bore of his pistol against Hampton's temple and held it there. "Where are they?"

His wife appeared at the top of the stairs. "Harold, what's . . ." Her voice and words trailed off as she took in the men crowded in the foyer. "Oh!"

"Ma'am. Sarah Sullivan. Where is she?"

"Why, she's sleeping."

"Get her. Now."

Before she could make sense of what might be happening, Gasper took the stairs two at a time. "Show me."

They disappeared, but returned a few moments later. Mrs. Hampton held Sarah's hand.

"Now, Mr. Hampton, where's her brother?"

"Slave quarters."

Dominic nodded at James. "Go with him. And Mr. Hampton, please refrain from alerting your overseers or anyone else that will cause me to shoot your wife."

His eyes widened. "You would shoot a defenseless woman?"

"That's up to you."

James forced him towards the back of the house and they disappeared.

Dominic said softly, "Sarah, please come stand by me."

She looked up at the tearful Mrs. Hampton, who gave her a nod, and Sarah reluctantly walked over to Dominic.

"What do you want with me and Ben?" she asked in a scared voice that although younger in tone was reminiscent of her mother's.

"We'll talk once your brother gets here, but we're not going to hurt you or him." He could see she was afraid but holding up well.

Hampton and James returned with a sleepy-looking Ben. When he saw Dominic and the others his steps slowed. He studied Dominic as if attempting to remember if and where he'd seen him before. His eyes suddenly widened as if he'd solved the matter.

"Come stand by your sister, Ben, please."

He took a quick look back at the Hamptons, then crossed the foyer to comply.

Still holding his guns on the couple, Dominic nodded at Gaspar, who took a few lengths of rope from inside his coat and tied up the arms and wrists of Mr. Hampton. Mrs. Hampton was gestured to a chair and given the same binding, as was the slave. They were then all gagged and left in the dark.

Gaspar took Sarah up in the saddle with him and Dominic did the same for Ben, and lit out for the docks. They hoped it would take some time for the Hamptons to free themselves. The last thing they needed were the authorities holding up the departure of the sloop. Earlier, Dominic had ordered the remaining merchandise placed on board the sloop under the mistaken belief that they'd be raising anchor tomorrow as soon as Clare arrived with the children. Now they had the children, but no Clare. He prayed she wasn't suffering and that he'd get his hands on her abductors as soon as the fates allowed.

Once they were on board, they lifted anchor and sailed up the river and away from Savannah. Esteban then steered them south. Having to drop Sam the guide off in the Key Islands of Florida would further delay their reaching their home but it couldn't be helped. Luckily, Martinique was less than a day's sail from Liberté. The sloop had only a few guns and therefore would be useless in an assault, which meant more delay while they spent time readying the *Marie*.

Up on the deck of the sloop, the moon supplied light to the nocturnal sail, and the wind was fair, but Dominic, standing by the stern, wished for wings so he could make the journey faster. Esteban was steering them as swiftly as the winds allowed but not swiftly enough for Dominic. The children were below deck and hadn't said a word since coming on board. He supposed he should go down and see about them, but his concern for Clare had blinded him to all else. Suddenly, they were by his side.

"May we speak with you, sir?"

He looked down at Clare's children. "Of course."

"Where are you taking us?"

"To freedom."

The children exchanged looks.

"Freedom, sir?" Ben echoed.

"Yes. You won't be captives anymore after this night."

"But why?"

"Because that is your mother's wish."

"Our mother?"

"Yes, Ben. Your mother is very dear to everyone on the sloop and especially to me."

"Where is she?" Sarah asked.

"On an island called Martinique. We, the crew and I, will sail for her once you are safe at the place that will be home."

Ben then said, "My sister is very sleepy. Is there a place for her to lie down on the boat?"

Dominic nodded. He walked over and called below for Dot. When she appeared he asked if she would get Sarah settled, and she agreed with a smile.

Once they were gone, Ben asked, "Mama is in trouble, isn't she?"

Dominic didn't lie. "Yes, but we'll rescue her. Don't worry."

"I want to go with you."

Dominic studied him. "It might be better if you stayed with your sister."

"I can help."

"Can you climb the rigging, load a cannon, or even swim?"

"No sir, but I'm strong, I can follow instructions, and she is my mother. I promise, you will not regret the decision if you agree."

Dominic smiled inwardly. He was a boy of heart and courage just like his mother. Dominic knew that if his mother, Marie, had been the one taken, no one in the world would have been able to deny him the opportunity to help return her to those she loved. "You may come, but you'll do as I say or be chained in the hold, do you understand?"

"Aye, sir."

The brisk reply made him smile, and Ben did, too, before saying, "Tell me what has happened to her."

When he was finished, Ben looked out over the water. "These are bad people."

"Very bad."

"But we will get her back?"

"Yes, we will."

"I will hold you to that, sir."

"I expect nothing less."

There was silence for a moment.

"That day on the wharf, you knew me?" Ben asked.

"Not until you looked up and I saw your mother's eyes."

"What is your name?"

"Dominic LeVeq."

"Will that be our new name, Sarah and I?"

"If you wish, but I have to marry your mother first."

"Then I hope we can get her back soon. I believe I will enjoy being a LeVeq."

Dominic simply smiled, and they both went back to watching the sea.

When Clare awakened she had no idea if it was day or night, or where she might be. Her head ached and there was a terrible taste in her parched mouth. Heat seemed to be pressing down onto her from all sides and she fought to clear her mind. She sensed she was lying on a dirt floor. As she slowly became cognizant of the bindings on her wrists and ankles everything came rushing back: her sale, Violet's death, Dot running, and the rest. The fear made her whimper.

A man's voice asked, "Would you care for some water, Clare?"

Through her clouded vision she saw the outline of him standing over her.

"Yes," she croaked.

He helped her to sit upright, and soon cool fresh

water passed her lips. "Slowly now, my dear."

Her vision gradually cleared and she looked up into the brown eyes of a man she didn't know. "Hello, we've never met, but my name is Eduard LeVeq. Welcome to Martinique."

Because she knew who he was, tears filled her eyes and slid down her cheeks.

"Are those tears of joy, Clare?"

"Should they be?"

He shrugged. "It depends on what role you choose to play here, but we'll get you bathed and rested up before I present your options."

"Dominic will be coming for me."

He gave her a cold smile. "You say that with such conviction, but alas, he doesn't know where you are."

Clare knew he was wrong. Dot was a bright, resourceful young woman. Clare was certain she'd made it back to Savannah and Dominic, but she didn't reveal her thoughts to Eduard. It would be better if he thought himself invulnerable. Pride goeth before the fall.

"Bring her along, Yves."

For the first time she noticed the other man. It was Vanweldt's giant. He picked her up and they followed Eduard out into the hot night.

Chapter 15

The sloop reached Liberté in the wee hours before dawn. The island's night watchmen armed with torches and weapons came down from the hills to greet the returning ship.

Dominic told them, "Get a message to the drummers. Tell them I want all the men to meet me at the *Marie* as soon as possible."

"What has happened?" one of the men asked.

"Clare has been taken."

Gasps were heard. Several men ran to relay his orders to the drummers.

He told the rest, "Once everyone is here, I'll tell as much of the tale as we know, but until then, I want you back at your stations. Keep an eye out for any passing ships. If you see one alert me."

"Aye, sir."

As in Africa, the drummers were positioned at various points around the island and they began pounding out their coded cadences from station to station.

Dominic didn't think Vanweldt would be foolish enough to be seen in the area again, but it would be just like him to sail by the island just to gloat. "Richmond, borrow a horse from one of the night crew and take Sarah and Dot to Anna, then get back here quickly. Everyone else, to the *Marie*." He looked down to see Ben striding at his side. The determined set of the lad's face made Dominic look to Gaspar, who was flanking the boy. The two men shared a quick smile but it soon faded as they set their minds on the battle to come.

An hour later, all the men of the island, along with many of its women and children, too, were gathered by the *Marie*. In the moonlight the torches flickering in hands and others planted in the sand added just enough illumination for them all to see.

Dominic looked out at the concerned faces of those assembled and was reminded of how they'd all come to be on the island in the first place. "Four years ago, the men of the *Marie* and I, aided by Esteban and his crew, laid siege to Martinique because my brother, Eduard, decided to take charge of people he did not own. He has struck again."

"Oh no," he heard a woman cry.

"This time he and our old enemy Vanweldt have taken my Clare."

Everyone listening looked stunned.

"And I want her back!"

Shouts of revenge filled the air. He waited for that to fade, then told them the story of the abduction. "It is imperative that we get the *Marie* refitted as quickly as possible so we can bring Clare home. Are you with me!"

The roar of assent shook the beach. Although many of the men were former slaves, more of them were pirates. They were battle-tested and would follow their captain to the gates of hell should he ask, and they were ready.

At sunrise they began in earnest. The crew moved over the ship like ants, repairing rigging, outfitting the masts, and using the animals to aid in hauling everything on board from guns and cannons to food and shot. Muskets were cleaned, pistols, too. Down the beach a ways, Richmond was overseeing the making of grenades. He showed his helpers, who included Ben, Sarah, and Dot, just how much gunpowder to place inside the small hollowed-out iron balls, while some of the women cut cotton rags into strips to make the fuses.

When the *Marie* was docked after the last voyage, it had taken a day and a half to unload the forty old and inoperable cannons that rode beneath her hold as ship's ballast. Now they had to be put back again. Ballast gave her balance and weight, and even though the journey to Martinique would be less than a day's span, the ship still needed ballast to sail proud and upright the way she was supposed to.

As Dominic and Gaspar oversaw the replacement of the ballast, Dominic was getting more and more impatient. He knew he was being hard on everyone with his yelling and finding fault but he couldn't help it. Every minute they were confined to the dock was another minute Clare spent being held by his brother. He had no idea what Eduard might do to her, but any man who'd planned to enslave three hundred already free people was not someone Dominic wanted Clare to be held by. It had occurred to him that her abduction might be a trap to lure him back to Martinique and it was working, but he hoped Eduard, Sylvie, and Vanweldt were prepared to give their lives to keep Clare with them, because he was ready to give his to set her free.

Gaspar said, "The crew is going to be too angry to sail anywhere when the time comes if you don't stop telling everyone how to do their job."

"I know. I'm just anxious."

"As you should be, but the men know what they're doing, and doing it as fast as they humanly can."

"I know."

"I'm worried about Clare, too. Who knew that day you stole her from the frigate that she would steal your heart?"

"I told you at the time, I thought I was in love."

Gaspar laughed. "True. You did."

Esteban walked over to where they stood on the deck. He was ready to sail as well, and like everyone else had pitched in with the loading. "I say we cut Eduard into tiny little bleeding pieces and toss him into the sea."

"He may be too rank for the sharks," Dominic said. "But I like the idea." He'd spent the morning fantasizing myriad ways he could pay Eduard back for his sins; all unsuitable for the eyes or ears of children. "And I'm open to suggestions."

They were bantering, but they couldn't gloss over the seriousness of the situation. In truth, there was no guarantee Clare was still on Martinique. Eduard could have set sail for France or places unknown as soon as Vanweldt made delivery, which was why they were outfitting the *Marie* as if they were truly going to sea.

Esteban asked, "Why is Eduard even on Martinique? Didn't the copy of the will Gabe gave you specifically cut him out?"

Dominic had told them about the will previously. "Yes, it did. Maybe he doesn't know. I've no idea if the London solicitors have informed him or not. Would be nice if I get to tell him, though, don't you think?"

"I think it would be just. Be an awful way to learn that not only are you not your father's son but someone else's bastard."

Gaspar said sarcastically, "I know I'd want to learn that I'm a bastard from the man I've been sneering at as my father's bastard the bulk of my life."

They chuckled.

Dominic countered. "I want to see Nancine's face when I tell him. Being turned out penniless couldn't happen to a more saintly woman."

"Aye."

Clare was in a bedroom of the main house. It was hot, and the open windows looked out over the water and captives in the field working under the late morning sun. There were hundreds of them spanning all ages and genders. She assumed the three men on horseback were overseers. They were very free with the lash, bringing it down on the backs of those deemed slacking, but the punishments appeared to be indiscriminate, as if they were being whipped simply because the overseers had the authority to do so.

She turned away from the window and focused on her own fate. Her stomach no longer felt the queasiness brought on by the awful draught Sylvie had forced her to drink, and her head and vision were now totally clear. When Yves left her inside at whatever time it had been, she'd slept, then got up and bathed in the stand-up tub someone had filled and placed in the room. There were clothes, too; a simple blouse, a lightweight skirt, and rough cotton stockings.

Her musings were interrupted by the sound of a key scratching at the lock on the door. She tensed and waited. When it opened, a young African girl entered bearing a tray. She looked so surprised to see Clare she almost dropped it. Recovering, she set it down on top of the bed, then withdrew silently. The key sounded again, indicating she'd locked Clare in.

The breakfast fare was bread, fruit, and tea. The bread was moldy, the fruit overripe and bruised, but Clare ate what she could of it and washed it down with the tepid tea. She wondered how close Dominic was to arriving. In spite of Eduard's claim, Clare knew in her heart that he and his men were on their way. Thinking back on the happenings in Charleston, she knew that as a Christian-raised woman she should feel something in the face of Violet's untimely demise, but there was nothing. Pity perhaps that Violet had let her life be ruled by her inner personal pain, but nothing more. The woman had sold her on the street as if she were a bag of rice.

Clare placed her hand on her stomach and wondered if she was really carrying Dominic's child. If she was, she hoped it hadn't been affected by the draught or the anxiety. Taking her mind off that so as not to cause herself more distress, she waited to see what would happen next.

She didn't have to wait long. A few moments later the door was opened again and this time it was Eduard LeVeq.

"Good morning, *chérie*. Did you rest well?"

"I did."

He seemed mildly surprised by her easy manner, but Clare had no intention of letting him see her fear; she refused to give him that satisfaction. She also had no plans to trust him.

"Would you care for some fresh air, perhaps?"

"I would, thank you."

He gestured her out and she led him from the room.

The house was large and well furnished. The wealth of unshuttered windows let in the sea breeze. "This is a lovely house."

"My father built it. It was the only thing my bastard brother didn't burn when he raided the place four years ago and stole my slaves."

And Clare knew why. This was the home of Antoine and Marie. Dominic had been born here and had grown to an adolescent within its walls. She was certain that had he known Eduard would be taking up residence, he probably would have torched it as well.

"Come, let's see if Mother is ready."

Clare froze inside. This would be the woman that poisoned Dominic's mother. She drew in a steadying breath and followed him.

They stepped out onto a sheltered, ground-level verandah. Nancine LeVeq had just finished her morning meal. Clare wondered if her bread had been moldy and her fruit old and bruised.

"Mother, this is Clare."

She was dressed in a dated but fashionable gown. There was fraying around the collar and on the hems of the half sleeves, and the lace insets were yellowed and worn. The face might have been beautiful in her youth but the aging skin was dry and papery, as if the island's heat had drawn all the moisture from it. However, the dark eyes were sharp and focused. "Why is she in the house?"

"She's a guest."

"Africans are servants, Eduard. Not guests."

She could have easily been the resurrection of Violet.

"This one is a guest, for now."

Nancine evaluated Clare critically. "Why?"

"She's Dominic's mistress. I have need for her."

"And you have her in my home? Are you planning to debase yourself the way Antoine did with his African whore?"

"No, Mother. Are you ready for the morning ride?"

"Am I riding with that?" she asked, pointing at Clare.

"Yes."

"Then I'll decline."

He bowed. "As you wish."

"I wish to go riding," she countered coolly, "but not with that. You can take me out later, alone." She gave Clare a look shot through with displeasure and went back inside the house.

Tight-lipped, he said to Clare, "The carriage is this way."

To her surprise Yves was their driver. As she settled into the seat, she said, "I assumed Yves would have left with Vanweldt and Sylvie."

"You know Yves?"

"Not personally, no. I saw him with Vanweldt, the afternoon Dominic sank the *Amsterdam*."

"Yet another sin my brother must pay for. Part of the treasure on that ship was supposed to come to me. As for Yves, he has driven for me before. He and his master have visited numerous times in the past few years. Paul's new lady is uncomfortable around him, but I'm assuming they all will leave together when the time comes."

Another surprise. "He and Sylvie are still here?"

"I asked him to transport some troublesome slaves to the market in Antigua. They return this evening and sail for Africa in a few days. I need more slaves. They keep dying."

Clare turned away so he would not see her satisfaction with that news. Vanweldt hadn't had the good sense to sail to the other side of the world in advance of Dominic's wrath; now it would be three birds with one stone. Four, if Dominic chose to count the evil Nancine.

With Yves driving they toured his holdings. The island didn't appear to be as mountainous as Liberté, but that could have been because of how developed the land was on Martinique. Everywhere she looked there were Africans in cane fields and overseers on horseback, along with processing buildings and hutlike slave quarters. The LeVeq land was spread across the entire eastern side of the island. She noticed no defenses, however; no cannons, no stone walls that would impede an assault by raiders or storms bringing high seas, but maybe Eduard didn't feel he needed any, or maybe they were just well hidden. Either way, she doubted it would matter to Dominic.

At one of the fields they were flagged down by one of the overseers.

Eduard had Yves stop the carriage.

The man rode over, and she was surprised to see that he was a mulatto.

"Yes, Griggs?"

"Two of the Africans died during the night."

Eduard sighed angrily. "That's six this month and we haven't even gotten into the heat of summer. Give them more water and ten minutes away from the heat every two hours or so."

"All right."

"Have you disposed of the bodies?"

"We have."

"Good. I'll ride out and see you later this afternoon."

Clare could see Griggs fighting to keep his attention on Eduard but wanting to get a good look at her. "Very good, sir."

The man then slid his gaze over Clare. She smoothly turned her face away.

Eduard asked, "Is there anything else?"

"Uh, no sir."

"Then get back to work."

The overseer rode off, and Yves got the carriage moving again.

"May I ask where you bury your slaves?" Clare said. "Is there a cemetery?"

He laughed. "No. We toss the bodies into the sea. The sharks enjoy the meat."

Clare's eyes closed and her heart ached in response to such indignity.

"The sharks have come to rely on the meat so much, they circle the island regularly. They serve as a deterrent to any slaves foolish enough to try and escape by swimming."

So he did have a defense of sorts.

He looked her way. "I'm taking great joy in knowing my brother is frantic in mind and spirit wondering where you are. I'll be forever in Vanweldt's debt for presenting you to me."

"For what purpose?"

"I'm going to sell you, of course, and if there is a child, it, too. Dominic will be enraged but there's nothing he'll be able to do once I put you on the block. I hate him, you know. He and his whore of a mother stole my father's affection from Mother and me. My father left us and never returned. That Dominic will never see his child will also make up for that."

"The last person with designs on this child died beneath the heavy hooves of a team of horses. What will be your fate, Eduard?"

He slapped her with the back of his hand so forcefully she cried out involuntarily in pain. "How dare you mock me! You are in no position to be anything but respectful and obedient. Any more sass and I'll take a whip to you, child or no child." He grabbed her by the jaw and seethed, "Do you understand me!"

The mask of the slave remained firmly in place.

"Do you!"

"Yes."

He tossed her away. "Yves. Drive us back."

The giant turned his head around for a moment and looked at Clare just long enough for their gazes to connect, then drove them back the way they'd come.

Dominic felt as if he might burst into a hundred angry pieces if they didn't get under way soon. Because of the unrelenting way he'd been driving the men and himself, not only were they going to be too angry to sail, they were going to be too physically exhausted, but they knew why he was so on edge; they were in a hurry to rescue Clare, too, so, so far they hadn't let his sour mood deter them from their tasks.

It was two hours past midday. The ballast had been loaded in record time and he felt as if fate was finally smiling on him at last. The gunners were placing the last of the cannons into their slots while Richmond and the powder monkeys, who now included an apprentice named Ben Sullivan, distributed grapeshot, cannonballs, and grenades at each of the stations.

Gaspar came up out of the hold. "Everything's secure down below."

"Good. Thank you. I believe we're almost ready."

"Yes we are. Do you wish to talk strategy now?"

He nodded. "Tell everyone to meet me in my cabin as soon as possible."

Once everyone was gathered around the large map he'd unrolled on top of his desk, he used his finger to trace the course. "We'll head east and then northeast past Cuba and Haiti. East again and south past Antigua and Montserrat."

"So we'll come in on the eastern side of the island just like before," Esteban noted.

"Yes. The lands are on that side, and my cousin Gabe said the French are using the western side as a connection for ships ferrying guns and supplies to the colonies. Last thing we want is a battle with the French Navy before we can get to Clare. The western ports are always filled with slavers, too, as we all well know."

"When are we raising anchor? Day or night?" Gaspar asked.

"That I don't know. I'm open for suggestions because were it just me, I'd sail as soon as everything was in place and to hell with the time of day."

"Then I vote we do that," Esteban said.

Dominic looked to his childhood friend. "Your vote?"

"Now."

"James?"

"Yesterday."

He took in Washington Julian, Tait, and Richmond. They all voted to leave as soon as the *Marie* was ready.

A pleased Dominic nodded his thanks. "I'll go tell the crew."

Ninety minutes later to the sounds of battle drums and cheers from the people on shore, the *Marie* slipped out of the harbor and headed east.

Clare was confined to her room for the rest of the day but she didn't mind. Her face was beginning to swell from the blows she'd received first from Vanweldt, and now Eduard, and there was nothing she could do about it or the dull ache that accompanied it. She passed the time by recalling the memories she'd stored up during her days on the island: the feast, the drums, doing errands with Anna, the sunsets, and all the times and the ways she and Dominic had made love. Those memories alone could have sustained her for months or more. The remembered feel of his kiss and his hands; the earth-shattering feel of the little death, and the way

he held her when they finally sought sleep evoked a
bittersweet smile, because she was not in his arms.
Her thoughts then moved to her children. She wondered if they were safe with Dominic, or still with
their owners. She hoped it was the former because
she had no idea what might be awaiting her should
she have to return to Savannah to try and free them
again.

The heat of the day had finally waned and her
stomach reminded her she hadn't eaten since that
morning. She supposed not feeding her was Eduard's way of flaunting his hold over her, but she
knew it would only be temporary because Dominic
was on his way to take her home.

An hour later, Eduard entered. "Excuse my ne-
glect. I had business to oversee. Would you care for
dinner?"

"Yes." Clare wondered why he was pretending to
be nice. They both knew it was a lie.

"Come with me."

The dining room's table was set formally with
tarnished silver and chipped china. Goblets holding
drinks were at each seat. Nancine was in a chair
at one end of the table. Across the room near the
French doors, Yves stood silent as a statue. Clare
wondered how long it would take for Nancine to
storm from the room now that she had arrived.

But she said instead, "I suppose if I must have you
as a guest, I must, so welcome to our home." She
gestured her to the chair positioned in the middle of
the table. "Please be seated. I must speak to my son

for a moment." She stood and added, "Avail your-self of the wine. Cook will be serving us shortly. Eduard, will you step out with me, please. There's something I wish to discuss."

"Of course, Mother. Clare, if you will excuse us."

She nodded and took her seat. Still surprised but not trusting Nancine's apparent change of heart, Clare picked up her goblet intending to quench her dry throat, but the loud grunt Yves made caused her to look his way. He was at her side in an instant. He took the goblet from her hand, switched it with the one at Eduard's setting, then moved back to the wall just as they reentered the room. Clare was so startled by Yves's actions she was shaking. Had something been wrong with the goblet of wine she'd been given? Then she remembered how Dominic's mother had reportedly died. *Poison.* Heart still racing, she drank a bit of the new wine and then set the vessel down. Calming herself, she gave the now seated Nancine a false smile. Clare then shot a discreet glance Yves's way but he offered no response.

The servants brought in the meal. Over the course of eating, Eduard drank his cup dry. As he stood to replenish it, he swayed and then began to claw at his throat. He fell onto the table, sending dishes tumbling and platters crashing to the floor, as he fought whatever had him in its throes. Awful gasping noises came from his throat. Nancine jumped to her feet and screamed, "No! Oh! No! Eduard! Oh my god!"

Eyes blazing with fury, she screeched at Clare,

"You switched the cups! Whore! It was meant for you, not my son!"

She ran to him. The servants came in, and after looking for a few moments retreated.

"Eduard!" she cried again, but her son was beyond her calls. His tongue, black as leather, had swollen to such large proportions it hung thickly from his mouth. Jerking with spasms, his eyes rolled back unseeingly, he fell from the table to the floor and was still.

Clare didn't remember getting to her feet but she found herself stepping away from the table in horror. That terrible death had been meant for her.

Nancine knelt over Eduard's body and screamed, "No! No!" She began to sob as if her heart had broken. Looking up at the wide-eyed Clare, she launched herself, punching and scratching and screaming like a banshee. Then she was lifted from her feet and thrown across the room. Her body hit the wall hard, then slid down into a broken seated position. The unnatural angle of her neck showed it to be broken.

The terrified Clare looked up at the giant and he put out his large hand. Shaking so much she found it hard to stand, she put her hand in his and let him lead her through the French doors and out to Eduard's carriage. After she got in, he set the horses to a brisk pace and headed for the water.

Once there, he left the carriage, and she followed him to a small wooden building not far from the water's edge. She watched as he brought out a canoe and two oars. A man came riding up and Clare froze. Yves looked up but ignored the man for the moment. Instead he took Clare's hand and guided her into the canoe.

"Oh, it's you, Yves."

It was the overseer Griggs. His eyes went to Clare before he said to Yves, "Guess LeVeq tired of her. Looks like she put up a fairly good fight, though." And he grinned and chuckled while indicating her bruised and battered face.

Yves left Clare sitting in the boat, walked over to the grinning man, and lifted him clear of the ground. Yves turned his broad back, effectively blocking Clare's view. Griggs gave a short strangled sound. His neck had been broken. Yves carried the body to the canoe and put it inside, then pushed the boat into the water. When the tide caught it, he got in and began to row.

When his powerful arms cleared them of the coast, and the water became deep enough, he dropped Griggs's body into it and rowed on.

"May I ask you a question?" Clare asked, still shaking.

He nodded.

"Why can't you speak?"

He opened his mouth and showed her that most of his tongue had been severed.

She was appalled. "I'm so sorry."

He shrugged.

"Did Vanweldt do that to you?"

He nodded.

"Are you helping me to get back at him?"

Again the nod.

"Do you have any idea where we're heading?"

He shook his head negatively and smiled.

She smiled in reply. "I suppose anyplace is better than the one we left. Thank you for alerting me to the poison and for helping me get away." She then told him the story of Nancine poisoning Dominic's mother and added, "I suppose poisoning her own son balances the scales."

He nodded.

"I wish you could tell me your story. How long has Vanweldt owned you?"

He raised one hand and flashed five fingers twice.

"Ten years?"

His eyes said yes.

"If we could somehow make our way back to Liberté, you would be able to live free there." And she would be grateful to him for the rest of her days. "It's very beautiful."

He gave her no response, but she wondered how long he'd wanted to be free of Vanweldt. She decided probably since the day his tongue had been cut out. She couldn't imagine the pain he must have endured and how angry and helpless he must have felt. "Thank you again. I owe you my life." And quite possibly the life of her child.

The sun would be setting in another few hours and bringing with it nightfall. As he continued to row, she didn't want to think about how dangerous it might be on the open seas in such a small vessel at night. Instead, she prayed Dominic would find them.

He looked at her and used his hand to mimic talking.

"You want me to talk?"

He nodded.

"To pass the time?"

Again, he nodded.

So she told him her story and how she'd been captured, and about her children and her life in Savannah. She also told him of her love for Dominic and how it felt to be free. "You'd like it," she told him, and he smiled in reply.

She told him of her love for sunsets also. "Back home, I was always too busy to see them. Until I met Dominic I had no idea how beautiful they were."

Suddenly he stopped rowing and turned his head and looked out over the ocean.

"What's wrong?"

For a moment he offered no response, then he pointed north. She looked out but saw nothing at first, and then a few moments later a far-off ship slowly came into view. "Is it Vanweldt?"

Eduard had mentioned that Sylvie and the slaver would be returning. Clare didn't have the long-range viewing all sailors seemed to have, so she couldn't determine if the ship was friend or foe.

"Can you tell?" she asked tensely. She tried not to think about what recapture might mean for both of them, but the horrific ramifications filled her anyway.

The ship drew closer, still too distant to see its flag, but then he smiled and pointed to her and then to his heart. Confused, she mulled over his actions.

Peering at him in an effort to glean his meaning, she touched her own heart and then her eyes went wide. "Is it Dominic? Is it the *Marie*!"

The smile in his eyes said yes, and all the pent-up fear and emotion drained away and she cried tears filled with love and joy.

Chapter 16

The lookout in the nest yelled, "Captain! There's a canoe up ahead. Two people."

Dominic grabbed his glass and scanned the sea. The small boat was still a ways off, but the *Marie* was close enough for him to make out the man and the woman. The sight of Clare put a sheen of tears in his eyes. "It's Clare!"

The crew cheered as one. Dominic had no idea why she was with what appeared to be Vanweldt's Yves, but it didn't matter. His Clare was within sight and would soon be held next to his heart. Dominic swept the sea for ships. "Do you see any sails!" he called up.

"Nothing but open water, sir."

Gaspar appeared by his side. He used his own glass to sweep the sea. "I see no sails anywhere, either, but Yves is never without Vanweldt close by. Do you think this might be a trap?"

"Not unless Vanweldt has a ship that can rise from the depths like Poseidon."

"If Yves is holding her hostage I hope he's ready for a seat in hell."

"I hope so, too, but just in case this is not as benign as it appears . . . Battle stations!" he shouted, and his men rushed to their positions.

All Dominic could think about was holding her, kissing her, and being near her again. He'd been in agony since the moment Dot relayed the details of her abduction. Now, in a few minutes they'd be reunited, and he thanked all the gods from both of his parents for her safe return.

As the familiar ship came alongside, Clare wept. Seeing the *Marie* was akin to seeing home. Looking up, she saw the man who'd stolen her heart. "Dominic!"

"Good evening, *petite*!"

"Yves rescued me, so please don't shoot him!"

He laughed. "Thanks for the warning. Yves, I am in your debt. Do you wish to come aboard?"

Yves nodded.

The rope ladder came over the side and the giant guided the canoe closer, then grabbed hold of the net and held it while Clare made her slow climb. She was two-thirds of the way up when Dominic reached down and hauled her up and into his arms. He paid no attention to Yves as he climbed the rope to the deck.

"I'm so glad you are safe," he whispered hoarsely.

"It's so good to be in your arms. So good." He was holding her so tightly she just knew her spine was cracking but she didn't care.

"Are you hurt?" But before she could respond, he saw the bruises and swelling on her face. "Who did this!" he demanded.

"We'll talk of it later. Right now just hold me, please. They were planning to sell me and the baby."

Placing a kiss against the top of her hair he did so, and felt himself on the brink of exploding from the intensity of his love for her. Vanweldt wanted to steal this, extinguish this. If he and Eduard had been successful in their heinous plan it would have torn out his heart, but she was safe and sheltered in his arms. "I'm never letting you out of my sight ever again," he husked out emotionally.

Their tender reunion was such that every eye of every crewman held a tear.

Looking down into the bruised but still beautiful face, Dominic told her softly, "I've a surprise for you." And he beckoned to someone behind her. She took a moment to give watery smiles to Gaspar and James Early and the rest of the men who'd left their homes and families to come to her rescue. She said to them, "Thank you. I've no idea how to repay you or if I ever can."

When Ben walked up, she went silent and stared. Her hand went to her mouth and the tears gushed. "Benjamin?" she whispered. "Oh my word. Benjamin!"

Grabbing her son whose height topped hers by a good five inches, she held him as tight as she'd held Dominic. She rocked him and no doubt embarrassed him but he held her just as tightly. "How did you get here?" she asked, awed at how tall he'd grown since she saw him last. "Where's your sister?"

"I'm a member of the crew, Mama. Sarah's on the island."

Clare turned to Dominic and Gaspar and the words wouldn't come. Through her tears she said with a choked laugh, "I can't seem to stop weeping. Oh, Dominic, Gaspar, all of you, thank you." She embraced Dominic again. "My children. Thank you."

"You're welcome." Her emotion moved him. Being able to free her children was yet another way to prove how much he loved her. "I don't mind if you weep for all eternity as long as you do it in my arms."

Ben interrupted them. "Mama, I must get back to my post."

She smiled. "I know, dear. You go on. We'll talk much longer later."

He bowed and departed.

Dominic turned to Yves and said genuinely, "Thank you for helping her. If you wish to become a member of the crew you are welcomed."

The giant nodded, but Dominic couldn't tell if the nod was an acknowledgment of the thank-you or a nod of agreement to join the crew. He decided to deal with that later. "Come, let's go to my cabin, and Clare can tell us what has happened, and then we go kill my brother and Vanweldt."

"Your brother's dead."

Dominic stopped.

"Nancine poisoned him."

Surprise filled his face.

"Come," Clare said, "I'll explain."

Once everyone was settled, Clare told her story, beginning with her being sold and abducted on the streets of Charleston and ending with Eduard's poisoning and her escape with Yves.

"So the fates cheated me out of sending them to hell," Dominic growled.

"Does it really matter who sent them?" Gaspar asked. "We're simply pleased they were sent."

Dominic smiled. "I suppose you are correct."

"Maybe the fates will give us Vanweldt as a boon instead," James added.

"And let's not forget the duplicitous Sylvie," Dominic added. He'd never committed violence against a woman but Sylvie made him want to break that code. "Vanweldt was due to return to Martinique sometime today?" he asked Clare.

"According to Eduard, yes."

Dominic held no grief for the man who'd lived life as Eduard LeVeq. In fact, he thought hell too pleasant an end for the evil souls of Eduard and the treacherous Nancine, but he found it highly ironic that her poison had killed her own flesh and blood.

"So do we go home, or do we try and catch Vanweldt?" Gaspar asked, bringing Dominic back to the conversation at hand.

Dominic looked to Clare and she said, "I'd prefer we go home so that I can see my Sarah, but I don't wish to have Vanweldt's shadow looming over our future."

He agreed, but he had a question. "Where does Yves stand?"

Clare's eyes sought the man who'd saved her

life. "Vanweldt cut out his tongue. There is no love there." But she asked him, "Do you stand with the crew of the *Marie*?"

He nodded. Raising his hands, he slowly mimicked breaking something in half.

Gaspar said, "I believe we have our answer."

"Then let's go hunting." Still moved by Clare's presence, he told the men, "I'll meet you above deck in a moment."

They exited, and when the door closed, Dominic and Clare were alone. Words were unnecessary. She moved into his arms and let herself be wrapped in his love and held against his strong beating heart. "I knew you would find me," she voiced, basking in the glory of being with him again. "I had no doubts, ever."

The love he felt for her had no bounds. "I'm so glad you are here, and it pains me that I can't make Eduard pay for harming you."

"He earned his reward. Violet as well." She thought about Dot. "Did Dot make it back to Savannah?"

"Yes. She came straight to the dock to find me. She's on the island with Sarah."

That good news added to the joy of knowing Sarah and Ben were safe. "Thank you for rescuing them, but how was it accomplished? I don't remember describing them to you."

So he told her.

She leaned back and looked up. "You threatened the Hamptons with guns?"

"Had no time for niceties. Had to find you." He

then told her about seeing Sarah sweeping the porch and tripping over Ben at the docks.

"So you knew what they looked like?"

"I did. Ben has your eyes, and when he gazed up at me, my heart stopped."

"He's grown so much." She reached up and placed her palm against his cheek. "You're a very resourceful man, Captain."

"I'm just selfish. I wanted my love back."

She rose up on her toes and kissed him. "Thank you for loving me this much."

"You're welcome, *petite*."

"Will you kill Vanweldt?"

"He stole you, Clare. He hurt you and he'd hurt you again given the opportunity. Surely you're not going to plead his case."

She shook her head. "I just don't want you to have his blood on your hands."

"Rather his blood on mine, than yours on his. There's no other way."

"I know."

He gave her a solemn kiss on the brow. "When we get home, I'm going to draw you a bath and fill it with every flower on the island."

In response to the promise she hugged him tight and said against his heart, "Then hunt quickly and well."

Above deck, Dominic gave his decision to the crew and they cheered lustily. As a slaver, Vanweldt was a threat to them, their families, and their friends, and they all wanted his presence swept from the seas forever.

With Clare safely tucked below in his cabin, the anger Dominic had been holding in was given full sail. Antigua was north, so he instructed Esteban to turn the ship in that direction and they waited tensely for the lookout to spot their prey. The sun was just beginning to sink to the horizon, which meant they had less than an hour of light left. Dominic prayed they'd catch Vanweldt before nightfall, otherwise he might be able to sail past them unnoticed in the dark.

"Sail!" the lookout called out.

Dominic grabbed up his glass. The ship he focused on was a smaller craft, and because Dominic had no idea what type of vessel Vanweldt might be captaining, he handed the glass off to Yves. The big man took a long look. An evil smile curled his lips. He nodded and handed it back.

"It's him!" Dominic shouted to the crew. "Everyone to the ready!"

As men scrambled to their assigned duty stations, the deck became a beehive of activity. Dominic didn't bother yanking down the French flag flying high on the mast. Vanweldt knew the *Marie* on sight, and Dominic hoped that sight was enough to make the Dutchman soil his breeches.

"He's turning about, Captain!" the lookout cried. "Must've recognized us."

"Give me all the sail you can. We want to catch him before the sun sets."

Because Vanweldt's ship was smaller, depending on the skill level of the crew and the wind, she had the potential to be faster. At the moment, though, the lack of a good wind put the *Marie* at a disadvantage. "Keep him in sight!"

If Dominic were in Vanweldt's position he'd look for someplace to hide until dark. He assumed the Dutchman knew the waters well, but so did Dominic. There were twenty or so islands stretched like a curved strand of pearls from the Virgin Islands to Tobago and they offered many coves and channels. Some of the coves were wide and held waters deep enough to support a ship the size and weight of the *Marie*, others did not. Were he Vanweldt, he'd be searching for one of the latter, but only if the hidey-hole held an alternate route back out to sea, otherwise Dominic and the crew could simply drop anchor and wait. Dominic had stocked his ship with supplies enough for thirty days. Since the Dutchman had been taking only a short trip between islands, he'd probably not laid in a large supply of provisions. He would be ill-prepared for a siege.

Finally being able to confront him filled Dominic with a deadly satisfaction. That the Dutchman had attempted to carve out his heart by taking Clare and possibly her unborn child meant he'd be given no quarter.

For the next quarter of an hour, the lookout kept them abreast of the position of their prey. The ship remained on a northerly course but began hugging the island coastlines as if Vanweldt was indeed looking for a place to put in and hide. Suddenly the wind picked up. As the sails on the *Marie*'s three masts rose and filled until they resembled sheets billowing in the breeze, the men all roared their appreciation for the blessing from the sea.

While the *Marie* continued to cut her way purposefully through the azure blue water, Dominic took a quick trip below decks to see if Gaspar and the weapons crews were in need of anything. He also wished to discreetly look in on Ben.

"He's doing well," Gaspar informed him after taking Dominic aside. "He's got that fear in his eyes of course—we all had it going into our first battle—but he's managing. Richmond and I both will look out for him."

Dominic nodded and continued on. He went next to his cabin to see about Clare. Opening the door he found her curled up in his bed asleep. He savored the sight of her safe and sound, and just for a moment let his icy cold purpose be warmed by swells of relief and love. He'd had no real measure of the depths of his feelings until she was taken. The arrogance in him ensured he would have found her even if it had taken decades. The man in him who cared for her more than any pirate treasure embraced that arrogance because he refused to contemplate a life void of the sound of her voice or the beauty of her smile.

He wanted to stand and watch her until the stars fell into the sea, but he had to go. Leaving her to her dreams, he soundlessly closed the door and departed.

Back up on deck, he turned his glass on Vanweldt and knew he'd been right. The Dutchman did

know the area because he appeared to be heading
for the tiny island of Diablo. Too small for the Europeans to claim and too mountainous to clear and
cultivate, even by slave labor, Diablo was one of the
few uninhabited places left in the Caribbean. Dominic pulled down his glass and called to Esteban to
adjust course. A look over the side showed a large
pod of dolphins racing the ship. The sight of the
sleek gray bodies rising and falling so rhythmically
against the surface of the sea usually put a smile
on Dominic's face, but not this time. If anything
they seemed as purposefully focused upon catching
Vanweldt as he.

The *Marie* reached Diablo twenty minutes
behind Vanweldt. They could see his small ship anchored near the coast. Because of the shallowness
of the water, the *Marie* took up a position farther
out and dropped anchor. Dominic didn't want to
risk beaching her or having the hull breached by the
submerged rocks.

Vanweldt's ship sent off the first cannon volley
but the balls fell yards short. A quick scan through
Dominic's glass showed only ten guns. With the
wealth of weaponry at the *Marie*'s disposal, this
fight wasn't going to be anywhere near an even
battle, but Dominic hadn't run him to ground to be
honorable. "Blow her out of the water!"

The *Marie*'s cannons roared and death hurtled
across the distance. The first two blasts blew the
masts apart and the next shattered the deck. The
third, focusing on the waterline, exploded against
the hull. The cannons belched again, treating

the enemy ship to another round of mayhem and misery. Through his glass Dominic saw fires burning and thick smoke curling up against the red sky of sunset. There were dead men lying on the decks, while others scrambled off the vessel and ran through the surf to seek shelter on the island.

"Longboats!" Dominic yelled.

The boats were slashed free and crashed down onto the surface of the water. Leaving behind enough men to protect the ship if need be, Dominic, his officers, and two large complements of well-armed crewmen hastily climbed down the ladders to the boats. Yves was among them. Dominic was still unsure about the mute's true motives, but sensed his true colors would be shown soon enough, and he planned to be ready.

The two boats rowed their way over to the crippled listing ship now fully engulfed in flames. As they neared, acrid smoke burned their eyes and filled their noses. Soon they were passing bodies floating facedown in the water. Men on board could be heard screaming from within the inferno. A token round of small arms fire greeted the arrival of Dominic and his men but it was paid no mind.

More of Vanweldt's crew jumped from the burning ship into the sea to escape the flames. Dominic helped pull one into the boat, and he collapsed in the longboat's well.

"Where's your captain?"

The man's face was black from smoke and he coughed, then rasped angrily, "The bastard left us as soon as we dropped anchor. Told us to fight or we wouldn't be paid. He and the woman ran inland."

James made his way to the man and offered what assistance he could while the oarsmen rowed on.

They reached the beach just as dusk rolled in. In a few more moments it would be so dark they'd be unable to see a hand in front of their faces. Once everyone was out of the boats, they lit some of the torches they'd brought along and stuck them in the sand. At one time Diablo had been an active volcano according to the Caribbean lore, and the land was pocked with hard rock, and caves, both above and below the waterline. In theory if Vanweldt found a decent place to hole up it might take a week or more to flush him out, but Dominic was prepared for however long the quest took.

The boat Vanweldt had captained slowly began to slip beneath the surface. All who'd been able to escape had done so. The few crewmen not so lucky rode the battered ship to the bottom.

After watching it disappear, Dominic turned to his crew. "Let's fan out and use what light we have left to search the immediate area. If you find anything send up two shots. Yves, with me."

So in small groups they set out away from the beach. They rounded up a few of the survivors. The men were bound hand and foot and made to sit on the beach under guard. As night fell and full darkness took hold, it became apparent that the search would have to be called off. Neither the moonlight nor the torches they carried cast enough illumination for them to see, and the landscape with its crags and uneven terrain was treacherous. Dominic wanted no broken limbs or injuries from falls, so vocalizing the wild turkey call they used on a mission such as this, he signaled everyone back to the beach.

It was decided that some of the search party would return to the ship to secure the prisoners and to bring back supplies while the main forces remained behind to set up a makeshift camp on the beach. The frustrated Dominic wanted to find Vanweldt there and then, but there was nothing that could be done until sunrise. The night crew stationed on the *Marie* would know to keep their eyes open to make certain Vanweldt didn't some-how slink away. A similar night watch would be set up on the beach.

Dominic and Gaspar took the first shift while the others made themselves as comfortable as they could on the sand beneath the stars.

Back on the *Marie*, Clare anxiously watched James and the Cherokee Julian climb aboard. They said they'd returned to turn over the men they'd caught and to gather supplies.

Seeing her, James walked over and filled her in on the latest happenings.

She looked out over the black water. "So Vanweldt and Sylvie are still on the island somewhere?"

"Somewhere. We'll be better able to search once the sun comes up."

That surprised and disappointed her. "I'd hoped they'd be found quickly."

"It doesn't matter. They'll be found eventually."

"Thank you for letting me know what's happened."

He nodded and left her to see to his tasks.

Clare wanted this all to be over so she and everyone else could return to their families. Although she agreed that Vanweldt had to be punished, her puritan raising continued to bedevil her about Dominic shedding his blood. There was nothing for it, however. If the slaver wasn't stopped he could come back to haunt them again and again.

Ben appeared at her side.

"How are you, son?"

"Well, and you?"

"Anxious."

"The captain will set everything right."

She allowed herself a small smile. "You're pretty confident for only having known him such a short while."

"I am. He's someone I'd like to emulate."

"Then you have chosen well. He's a fine man. We'll pray that he finds Vanweldt soon and we can sail for home." She then asked, "Your sister is well?"

"Yes. It will be odd, the three of us living together as one."

"But in a nice way."

He nodded. "We don't know each other very well, do we?"

"No, darling, we don't. You were four years old and your sister had just turned two when the Sullivans took you from me. We have a lot of catching up to do, but I believe we will do well as a family."

"I do, too. I was scared when the captain and the men came to the Hamptons to get us. I didn't know where they were taking us or why."

"Did Dominic explain why?"

"Yes, but not until after we were on the sloop. I like the sea, Mama. I think I might want to be a captain someday."

"That's fine, but you'll have to go to school as well."

"Will you teach me and Sarah how to read?"

"Yes, Ben, and anything else you may wish to learn."

"I'd like that. Sarah will, too, I'm thinking."

Clare's heart was full. She still found it hard to believe he was there with her.

"Do you think it will take the captain long to find the people he's after?"

"I hope not. I'm anxious to get back to our new home and start our new lives."

"So am I."

He turned and looked up into her face. "Does your face hurt?"

"A bit, but seeing you and knowing I'll be seeing Sarah soon makes me not mind it so much."

He nodded as if that made sense to him. "I have to return to my station. Richmond allowed me up to get some air and I don't wish to be late getting back. I'll see you again soon."

"Thank you for your help with my rescue."

He gave her a kiss on the cheek and disappeared into the torch-lit darkness.

After finishing his shift, Dominic didn't remember falling asleep but he must have because when he opened his eyes, it was dawn. He felt no more rested than he had been yesterday and couldn't remember the last time he'd had a full night of uninterrupted sleep. The weariness in him seemed to be steeped into his bones, but he set it aside as best he could because of what he had to do.

As everyone else came awake they shivered in the cool gray air. The fire they'd slept around had burned throughout the night, but by now it was little more than embers. Their breakfast consisted of hardtack and mugs of cold tea. No one complained about the meager fare, however, because they knew that just as soon as they tracked down Vanweldt they'd be going home to yet another feast and celebration. With that in mind, a skeleton crew was left on the beach to keep watch while Dominic and the others went hunting.

After an hour of combing the interior they found footprints in the sand on the other side of the island. Unlike the side they'd landed on yesterday, with its wide plain of sand and grasses, here only a thin strip of sand stood between the sheer dark face of the old volcano and the crashing surf of the Caribbean.

"They look fresh," Gaspar said to Dominic. There were two sets. One was a flat-soled boot print large enough to have been made by a man. The other was smaller, made by a woman's slipper with a small heel.

Dominic took a moment to scan the rocky landscape above the beach. He doubted their prey had had time to move up there. It looked to be a hard climb, too, but the prints said they'd been there and were probably near. The island's small size gave the searchers an advantage. Unless Vanweldt and Sylvie sprouted wings to fly, they'd be found soon. "Spread out and keep your eyes open. Vanweldt will undoubtedly shoot us in the back without hesitation."

Gaspar added, "Remember, if you find anything, sound two shots. I want them found before midday. Otherwise the sun's going to cook us."

They set out in small groups. Some climbed, while the rest stuck to the area fronting the beach. All followed the directions of the tracks.

After thirty minutes, the thin strip of beach disappeared, and Gaspar, Dominic, and Yves found themselves walking in the surf. The farther they walked, the higher the water climbed up their boots.

Dominic shouted above the noise of the surf, "Would they have come this far?"

Gaspar answered, "Sylvie wouldn't want to, that's for sure. By here, her gown is soaked to her knees, she's tired, wet—maybe even lost a shoe, if not two."

Dominic stopped and looked around. "Maybe we should turn and go back. I don't see any places of refuge. Do you?"

Gaspar shook his head. "No."

And then, Dominic saw a flash. "Get down!"

The three men dove into the surf an eye blink ahead of musket fire. They didn't know its origin because they were too busy trying to not be hit.

Dominic cursed.

Another crack was heard and the ball whizzed by them to die with a sizzle in the surf.

In the silence that followed, they jumped to their

feet and ran farther out into the surf until they were effectively out of range.

Dominic cracked. "That was fun."

Gaspar grinned and withdrew a small spyglass from his pocket. Searching the rock face he saw nothing. Only after moving away from the face and looking farther up the beach did he see the small outcrop of rocks. He handed the glass to Dominic and said, "See that outcrop of rocks? Do you think he's hiding behind it?"

Dominic searched the area silently for a few moments. "Yes. Ah, there's Sylvie, dirty face. Now she's gone. He must have forced her back down."

He handed off the glass to Yves, who looked for a moment before passing it back to Gaspar.

The other members of the *Marie*'s search party were coming down the beach at a run.

"They must have heard the shots," Dominic said.

"So what do we do about Vanweldt?" Gaspar asked.

"We go and get him."

When the others joined them, it took Dominic only a moment to outline his plan. They would assault Vanweldt's position in much the same way they assaulted enemy boats—en masse and screaming for blood.

On Dominic's signal, the thirty-five revenge-seeking men thundered towards their target. In the face of such overwhelming odds, Dominic didn't think Vanweldt would be able to defend himself for long.

And he was right.

Vanweldt came out from behind the rocks. Limping into view on an injured leg, he was struggling to keep his hands in the air. Sylvie, looking as though she'd been drowned and brought back to life, showed herself as well. Fear pulsed in her eyes.

Dominic and his men slowed to a walk.

As they approached, Vanweldt offered a pain-filled, self-deprecating smile. "My leg's broken. Guess I'll have to surrender." Upon noticing Yves standing with the *Marie*'s crew, his eyes widened. "What are you doing with them?"

"He was kind enough to return Clare to us."

"What?" The exclamation caused him pain. Wincing, he grabbed his leg. "Is your doctor with you, LeVeq? I need his assistance." He seemed to have forgotten his interest in Yves for the moment.

"I'll have James see to you when we're done, providing there's enough of you left."

The Dutchman went still.

Sylvie let out a soft, terrified moan.

Dominic skewered her with a stare.

"Dom, please," she begged. "Please. I'll do anything. I'll service every man on your ship. I didn't know they were going to sell her. Don't hurt me."

"Silence!"

She cringed and cried softly.

Dominic wanted to rip her in half; instead he turned his attention back to Vanweldt. "You put your hands on the woman I love. You hurt and terrified her. Now, we fight."

Vanweldt's eyes went wide. "My leg's broken."

"Then this shouldn't take much time. Toss him a sword."

Three swords landed at his feet. He looked up into Dominic's deadly eyes. "You'll kill me."

"Yes."

"But—"

"Please don't say it isn't fair. It wasn't fair for you to do what you did to Clare or the children you captured and sent to the bottom in barrels. Pick up the sword, slaver, or I will geld you and leave you to bleed to death, right where you stand."

Vanweldt's leg couldn't hold his full weight, so he had trouble picking up the sword and even more getting himself into position. Sweat poured down his face. Whether it was from pain, the heat, or sheer fear, Dominic didn't care. Rapier in hand, he lunged, and the fight began.

Dominic dominated from the first crossing of swords. Vanweldt tried but couldn't move quickly enough on his broken leg to evade Dominic's strikes, nor could he advance himself offensively to strike back with any power. As a result, Dominic sliced him like bread. The first slash went across his right cheek, and before he could react, a second quick slice opened the opposite side of his face. Furious, he wiped his fingers over the cuts, studied the blood for a moment, and hate blazed in his eyes. He lunged, but Dominic had no problem parrying the attack. The air sang with the clashing of blade on blade. The Dutchman's weak defense offered opening after opening, allowing Dominic to torment him one nick at a time; on his face again, the sides of his throat, his ribs and thighs. Under normal circumstances, the onlookers would have been cheering, but this was not sport, this was revenge, so they watched in grim silence.

As Vanweldt moved slower and slower, the ringing from the blade grew duller. Vanweldt grabbed the last of his strength and went on the offense, only to have Dominic respond with a slash that sliced through his arm to the bone.

Vanweldt screamed and dropped the sword in one motion. He fell to his knees. "No more. Please, I beg of you."

"Get up!" Dominic seethed with fury. "Get up!"

Vanweldt raised his head. Blood poured from the wounds on his face and down his chin. The hand covering the gash in his arm was awash in it. "Please!"

Dominic slammed his sword back into the scabbard. Clare hadn't wanted him to have Vanweldt's blood on his hands and he loved her enough to honor that. He planned to turn the slaver over to the British authorities in Jamaica. "Take him to the ship."

He glanced over at the crying, horrified Sylvie. He wasn't sure what her fate would be yet. "Her, too."

Certain his orders would be carried out, he walked back into the surf and strode off for the beach.

Dominic didn't want to be anywhere near Sylvie for fear of what he might do to her, so he and a large number of the men were in the first longboat to return to the *Marie*.

He'd just climbed back on board when the lookout shouted, "Something's happening over there, sir!"

Dominic grabbed up a nearby glass and turned it on the island. On the beach, one of his men, Jacobs was jumping up and down and frantically waving his arms as if trying to signal the ship. No one else was in sight. "Do you see the quartermaster?" Dominic called up.

"No, sir. I don't see anyone but Jacobs."

Dominic sighed. He felt the fates were conspiring again to keep him from Clare, but as if he were being thrown a bone, she walked up.

"Is it over?"

"Apparently not. Gaspar and the prisoners have apparently vanished."

"What?"

"I'm going back."

"You've blood all over you."

He nodded. "I'll return shortly." He took a moment to steal a kiss, then went over the side.

Jacobs was waiting for them.

"What happened?" Dominic asked.

"Not sure, sir. Gaspar and Yves stopped a minute because the lady said she needed a pee and he told us to go on ahead and they'd meet us here. When they didn't show up, some of the men went to look for them. We found the quartermaster. Someone hit him over the head with a big rock, but the giant and the prisoners are gone."

"Where's Gaspar now?"

"Other side of those rocks over there. Doc Early was patching him up."

"Thanks, Jacob. Fine job."

"Thank you, sir. I'll keep watch here until you get back."

James was putting a bandage on Gaspar's head when Dominic and the men with him walked up.

"Is he okay?"

"Except for this coconut-sized knot on his head, he's fine."

Gaspar groused, "I can answer for myself. I'm not mute."

"Was it a gift from Vanweldt?"

"No. He was too injured. Had to be Sylvie or the giant. We sent the men out to search."

Dominic sighed again. He was just about to ask where Gaspar had been when this all took place but was interrupted by Washington Julian.

"You should come see this."

"Did you find them?"

His face was grim. "Yes."

They followed the Cherokee a short distance, then all stopped short as they took in the grisly sight just a few feet away. The severed heads of Vanweldt and Sylvie were mounted on tree limbs stabbed into the earth. A few of the crewmen in the search party retched in response and even Dominic's stomach roiled. Back during the late seventeenth and early eighteenth centuries, during the golden age of piracy, the authorities often displayed the heads of pirates in this way as a warning to other pirates to repent.

Dominic and Gaspar moved closer.

"Yves?" Dominic asked, looking around the area before viewing the gruesome handiwork again.

"Possibly," Gaspar replied, taking a walk around the horrific display.

Sylvie's head of tangled hair made her look like the Medusa. Her eyes were wide with surprise as if she couldn't believe her fate.

On the other hand, Vanweldt's eyes appeared to be filled with terror, even in death. A short stout stick had been stuck between his teeth, propping the mouth open. The lower half of his face and chin, and what remained of his neck were covered with drying and congealed blood. A closer look showed that his tongue had been cut out. Dominic's stomach lurched again.

Gaspar gave an awed whistle. "I'm glad the big man was on our side."

Dominic could only agree. "I wonder where he is?"

For the next little while, they called to him from various points on the island, but received no answer. In the end, they gave up. Yves either didn't wish to be found or had lost his life after the beheadings somehow. No one knew, so they packed up and rowed back to the *Marie*.

After Dominic and the men boarded, he told the crew and Clare of Vanweldt's and Sylvie's grim fate. When he finished and the stunned crew returned to their posts, Clare looked out from the rail at the island and shivered thinking about the grisly scene. "Do you think Yves is over there still alive?"

He shrugged. "No way of knowing, *petite*."

She shook her head all the while, wondering. "I still don't understand why he helped me escape Martinique."

"Maybe he'd already decided he was going to kill Vanweldt and simply chose to take you with him. The fact that Yves gave your poisoned cup to Eduard says a lot to me."

"It does to me as well. Had Nancine drunk the poison, Eduard would have still been alive, making our escape next to impossible."

"Nancine's fatal mistake was in thinking like a slave owner and placing the poison in your cup while Yves was in the room."

Clare nodded. "Because he couldn't speak and because to her he was nothing more than a dull-witted slave who knew his place. To her, he may as well have been a piece of the furniture."

"She didn't think he'd take any actions to oppose her and she was wrong."

"I'm glad she was."

He looked down at the face he planned to wake up and see every morning for the rest of his life. "Are you ready to sail home?"

"Aye."

"Esteban! Take us home!"

"Aye!" the pilot shouted in reply.

As the anchor was raised and the sails caught the wind, Dominic used his glass to do a final scan of the island before they lost sight of it. Suddenly there on a hilltop he saw Yves watching the *Marie* move away. As if he knew Dominic was viewing him, he stayed stationary for a few long moments before he turned his broad body and walked away. Dominic drew down the glass and gave him a silent nod of farewell.

Chapter 17

The sail home took less than six hours, and they neared Liberté just past midday. They were welcomed back by the sounds of happy drums and celebrating. On the crowded beach Clare could see the frantically waving Sarah and Dot standing beside the beaming Anna. The sight of them was so moving she wanted to dive off the side and swim the remaining distance in order to hasten the reunion arrival. For Clare, the *Marie* couldn't reach the dock fast enough. It finally did, and when she walked down the plank holding on to Dominic's arm, the residents roared for her as if she were queen.

Sarah received the first hug, and only after Clare was completely convinced her daughter was indeed real and in her arms did she move to embrace Dot, Anna, Lucinda, Dani, and the rest of the friends she'd made on her short earlier stay. Now, however, like them, she was going to be a permanent resident, and again her heart brimmed with elation and joy.

As she and the children, Dominic, and Dot clambered into the wagon, Anna said, "Captain, there are two solicitors from London awaiting you up at the house."

Seeing the surprise on his weary face, she continued, "They arrived this morning on the ferry from Jamaica. They say they've come to discuss the duke's estate."

He and Clare shared a look. According to the tale told to him by his cousin Gabe, Eduard had been disqualified as heir, but Dominic was too tired at the moment to even begin to speculate on what that meant to the estate and to any claims he might personally have. He was too exhausted to do anything other than wait and hear what the men had to say.

"Mama, have you ever eaten alligator?"

"Yes, and it's very good. Why?"

"Anna says we are having a feast tomorrow and that the men are going to cook an alligator."

Alligator meat had been one of the new foods Clare had been introduced to while on the island. "There will be many new experiences for us here, Sarah."

Sarah didn't appear certain that eating alligator would be a good one but Clare simply smiled. She noticed that Ben spent the entire ride silently watching Dominic as if fascinated by his captain's every move, and she enjoyed that as well.

When they reached the house, Dominic excused himself to go and speak with the solicitors. Anna and Dot headed to the kitchen to prepare something for everyone to eat, while Clare and her children went up to Dominic's room so she could begin re-connecting with them.

The children took a wide-eyed look around the expansive quarters and for a moment could only stare.

"It's awfully large, isn't it?"

Ben asked, "Is our new father wealthy, Mama?"

She shrugged and smiled. "I suppose you could say that."

Sarah boasted, "I have a large room, too, Ben, and it has a big beautiful bed that I can sleep in."

Neither child had ever been given the luxury of a bed. Clare asked, "Ben, did the captain assign you a room when you were here last?"

"No. There was no time."

As he continued to view the room and its contents, she promised, "There will be one for you, too. We'll just have to wait and see which one he and Anna think is best."

Ben then asked, "Are we truly free?"

"Yes, darling. From this day forward we belong only to ourselves. No one can sell us or trade us for a horse, or do anything to separate us against our will ever again."

"And we'll live here?"

"Yes."

After a moment of mulling that over, he met her eyes and smiled. "That makes me feel good inside."

"Me, too," Sarah piped up.

Clare drew them into her arms, the happiest mother in the world.

* * *

Dominic walked into his study and nodded to the well-dressed men seated in the chairs. "My apologies for keeping you waiting, and for my attire." He'd taken a moment to splash some water on his dirty face but his shirt and breeches were still grimy from the night spent sleeping on the beach.

"We heard you were at sea on a dire mission. Did everything turn out well?"

"It did."

Dominic knew the men. They were his father's solicitors and friends—Messrs. Lacy and Preen.

Anna slipped into the room silently to leave a platter of fruit, meat, and bread for them to enjoy along with a pitcher of sangria and some cups. She quietly withdrew.

"You are here about my father's estate?" he asked, taking a seat behind the desk.

"Yes. We've notified Eduard and his mother that a true version of your late father's last will and testament has been filed in the London and Paris courts, but we've yet to hear from them or their representatives."

"And you won't."

In response to their curious faces, Dominic proceeded to tell them why.

"Poisoned, you say?" Lacy asked. He was the older of the two, but his bright blue eyes were sharp with life and intelligence.

Dominic nodded.

"Your mother's been avenged."

"I guess one could say that, yes."

"One can. Antoine left you everything contrary to what you were told by them. This makes you an extremely wealthy man, Mr. LeVeq."

Preen added, "And nullifies any legal ramifications hanging over your head for saving your fathers' workers from the auction block since in reality they were your workers."

"Which means you may come out of hiding and take your rightful place as heir. A letter from your mother's sister alerted us to your presence here. It's a paradise. Wouldn't mind coming down here to escape the nasty English winter."

"Consider yourselves welcome at any time. As far as the estate, I know I'll be elated once I'm rested, but at the moment, I need sleep."

They smiled. "All that's required is your signature on a few documents and we'll be off."

Moments later when all the papers had been properly signed, blotted, and seals placed upon them, the men stood, offered their congratulations, and said their farewells. Anna would be driving them back to the ferry owned by the Julians for the late afternoon run to Jamaica.

Upstairs, Dominic entered his bedroom and was greeted by the sounds of voices and laughter coming from the verandah. Smiling, he walked in quietly, hoping not to disturb them so he could silently savor their happiness without them knowing he was there. Clare was speaking to them about going to school, learning to fish and swim, and being able to play with the other children on the island.

As the children questioned her about various

things, he stood listening for a few moments longer, then joined them.

Sarah noticed him first and offered up a shy smile. He was struck again by her strong resemblance to her mother.

Clare asked, "Have you concluded your business with the solicitors?"

"Yes, and it went very well. We'll speak of it later. Right now, we need to find Ben a bedroom and I know the perfect one."

They followed Dominic around to the other side of the house and into a large bedroom not far from Sarah's.

Ben glanced around the large space and its dark wood furnishings and verandah, then turned his eyes to his captain. "This is for me?"

"Yes."

Clare's heart swelled, and she met Dominic's eyes. He smiled back.

Ben walked over and touched his hand to one of the posts of the large net-draped bed. "But this is too fine."

"A fine room for a fine young man. Will it do, or would you like another?"

"I'm honored, sir. I'll take this one."

Clare was so moved, tears stung her eyes.

"Then it is yours."

Sarah asked, "Mama, why are you crying?"

"Because I'm happy, Sarah. Very happy." She turned to her son. "If you'd like to wash up and sleep awhile, you may. You and the captain look exhausted."

"So do you, Mama," her son replied.

Dominic took in the tiredness in her eyes, but the bruises on her face continued to tug at his heart, and he wished he'd been able to prevent her from being hurt.

"I'm fine," she said. "I slept on the *Marie*. So Dominic and Ben to bed. Sarah and I will see you both later."

Downstairs, Clare sought out Dot. Clare gave her a strong hug. "Thank you so much for helping me."

"You were always kind to me, Miss Clare. I had to help. Thank you for my freedom."

"I want you to be a member of our family, if that is acceptable."

The young woman grinned. "Very acceptable."

Sarah said with a laugh, "I have a sister."

"Yes, you do," Dot said. "Anna said once we are all settled, I may go and speak with Miss Odessa about attending school. Do you think I am too old to begin learning?"

"Of course not. I think schooling is a sound idea."

"May I go, too?" Sarah asked.

"Yes."

That evening, as Clare stood out on the verandah and looked out at the sunset, she turned to Dominic and said, "It's good to be home."

He fit himself against her back, wrapped his arms loosely around her waist, and placed a solemn kiss on the scented column of her neck. "Yes, it is.

Thanks for allowing me a few hours of uninterrupted sleep."

"You earned your rest, and besides, you'll be needing your strength."

"True, but you sound as if you have something in mind."

"I do, and it's my turn to be selfish. You owe me quite a bit of loving, Dominic LeVeq."

"Oh really?" he asked with a grin. "You do realize that now that we have the children in the house you'll have to be less—vocal?"

"Then maybe we should go back up to the waterfall where I can't be heard," she tossed back saucily.

He chuckled. "I propose we get married first."

"When?"

"Tomorrow during the feast."

"I can't wait that long."

He threw back his head and laughed. "I see the scandalous Clare Sullivan has returned."

"Because she knows what she has been missing."

He turned her to face him, eased her against him, and hugged her tight. "Heaven knows I've missed making love to you, too." His voice turned serious. "Are we really having a babe?"

She could hear his heartbeat. "I'll know soon, but if the answer is no, we'll have all the time in the world now to practice making another." As a captive, Clare had refused to dream of things that would never be, like giving birth to a child who was free, but if the Ancestors were kind, the dream would be fulfilled. "I love you, Dominic."

"I love you, too, Clare."

So they were married that following evening. All the island residents gathered on the torch-lit beach. Inside the circle of rocks, Esteban, the island's only other true captain, would preside over the proceedings. Gaspar, who was very pleased, stood behind Dominic as his second, while Dot and Sarah, each holding a bouquet of tropical blooms, represented Clare.

As Tait began to play "Ode to Clare" on his violin and the beautiful notes filled the night, a solemn Ben escorted his mother down to the beach to where everyone waited. After leaving her beside Dominic, he took up a position next to Gaspar.

Mimicking Dominic's teasing words on the evening Gaspar and Suzette were married, Esteban asked Clare, "Are you certain you wish to do this, Clare?"

She turned her smile on Dominic standing beside her in the sputtering torchlight and nodded. "Yes, I am."

"Then let us begin." In a clear, strong voice he asked, "Do you, Clare, take Dominic LeVeq to be your spouse and heart's mate, in fair winds and in storm, in times of plenty and times of want, until the end of your days?"

"I do."

He turned to Dominic. "Do you, Dominic, take Clare Sullivan to be your spouse and heart's mate, and treasure her above all others in fair winds and foul, in times of plenty and those of want, until Poseidon takes you home?"

"I do."

"Then let these words bind your hearts and your lives forever. Kiss your bride, Captain."

The crowd cheered and Dominic gave Clare her first kiss as his wife.

Afterwards, the happy Dominic told everyone, "We have one more thing to take care of. Would Ben, Dot, and Sarah please step forward."

The confused trio complied. Clare was confused, too, as she had no idea what he planned to do or to say.

Dominic raised his voice and said, "Let the world know that I, Dominic LeVeq, claim these three children as my own. I pledge my protection and my love to them for as long as I draw breath."

Clare started to cry.

The children all looked surprised at the public declaration, especially Dot. He then took a moment to give each of them a strong hug, and Clare cried more tears.

When that was done, Tait began sawing away on a lively tune and the drummers joined in. Clare and Dominic and their children stood for a short while to accept the congratulations and well wishes of those in attendance, then everyone trooped back up the hill for the feast and more music and dancing.

After the meal and the celebration began in earnest, Clare saw Esteban talking with Odessa and leaned over and pointed out the two to Dominic. "Do you think they will ever reconcile?"

"Only if he grows up inside."

"Anna told me Sarah found the missing ring in the grass yesterday. She gave it back to him this morning."

"Once he figures out one love is better than playing the field, I hope Odessa is still waiting. If not, he may miss out on what I already know."

"And that is?"

"Only love can make you free."

"Very well said."

"I think so, too."

"Speaking of love . . ."

He grinned. "We can't leave until the morning. Too dangerous to try and drive up there in the middle of the night."

She pouted.

He laughed. "You'll be screaming soon enough, Mrs. LeVeq."

So the next morning, after leaving the children in the care of Anna, the newlyweds made the trek up to the waterfall. Once there, they played in the water and made love, again and again and again. And although Clare was very vocal in her responses, no one heard her but the stars in the midnight sky.

Author's Note

I hope you enjoyed *Captured*. It is the third book featuring the House of LeVeq, and could be called a prequel in that it chronicles the founding of the New Orleans clan my readers and I have come to love. To answer the oft posed question as to whether Dominic is the fabled "Old Pirate" mentioned in the other LeVeq books, *Through the Storm* and *Winds of the Storm*, he is not. That person is Esteban da Silva, Dominic's friend and the pilot of the *Marie*.

The *Marie*, its captain and crew are loosely based on the famous pirate ship *Whydah*. Its captain was a White man in his late twenties from the colonial northeast, who went by the name of Samuel *Black Sam* Bellamy. According to historians, over a third of his crew members were men of color, including fugitive slaves, Native Americans, and free Blacks. In fact, the *Whydah* was a slave ship when Bellamy first attacked it and claimed it as his own. When he targeted other slavers he often offered the captive Africans on board the opportunity to join his crew. In April 1717, the *Whydah* went down in a violent storm off the coast of Cape Cod. Of the 146 crew-men on board, including an eleven-year-old boy, only two survived, a Welshman named Thomas Davis, who was subsequently tried for piracy, ac-quitted, and released, and John Julian, a half-blood Native American, also tried for piracy, but found guilty and sold into slavery—some reports say, *back* into slavery.

Although the career of Bellamy and his crew lasted only a year, they succeeded in taking down 53 ships, and all that plunder was inside the *Why-dah*'s hold when it sank off Cape Cod. For over two hundred years the exact resting place of the wreck and its legendary treasure was searched for but never found, until 1984, when treasure hunter Barry Clifford located the ship's remains on the ocean floor, near Wellfleet, Massachusetts. Since the discovery, he and his team of divers have recov-ered over 100,00 items, including the bell, assorted cannons, an ornate pistol, gold coins, and the leg bone of the eleven-year-old sailor mentioned earlier. As I write this, some of the artifacts are touring the country in an exhibit sponsored by *National Geo-graphic* titled: *Real Pirates: The Untold Story of the Whydah—From Slave Ship to Pirate Ship*. You can read more about this fascinating exhibit, tour dates, and locations via the *National Geographic* website. Make sure you check it out when it comes to a city near you.

I've been wanting to do a story set during the American Revolution for some time because very little is known about the contributions made by people of African descent to the fight that freed the colonies from the crown. An estimated five thousand men of color fought on the side of the rebels. According to historian Benjamin Quarles, Negro soldiers served in the minutemen companies of Massachusetts in the early weeks of the war, in state militia of Northern colonies, and in Continental forces. At Yorktown, Baron Von Closen, an aide to General Rochambeau noted that three-quarters of the Rhode Island regiment consisted of Negroes, and when they passed in review, the men were the most neatly dressed, the best under arms, and the most precise in their maneuvers. Recently, in Savannah, Georgia, a monument was erected in honor of the Haitians who fought on the side of the Americans, so the next time you are in that historic city, please seek it out.

In writing *Captured*, I barely scratched the surface of this "lost" piece of American history, but it is my intent to do more books set in this period, in the near future. To help you get a head start on the research, here are some of the sources I used to tell the story of Dominic and Clare.

Bolster, W. Jeffrey. *Black Jacks: African American Seamen in the Age of Sail*. Cambridge: Harvard University Press, 1997.

Cordingly, David. *Under the Black Flag: The Romance and the Reality of Life Among the Pirates*. New York: Random House, 1995.

Lanning, Michael Lee. *African Americans in the Revolutionary War.* New York: Citadel Press, 2005.

Quarles, Benjamin. *The Negro in the American Revolution.* Chapel Hill: University of North Carolina Press, 1961.

Thomas, Hugh. *The Slave Trade. The Story of the Atlantic Slave Trade: 1440–1870.* New York: Simon & Schuster, 1997.

Webster, Donovan. "Pirates of the *Whydah*." *National Geographic Magazine.* V. 195, no. 5. May 1999.

In closing, I'd like to thank my readers for their continued support. It's been fifteen years since the publication of my first historical, *Night Song.* I loved you then and I love you even more now. Be blessed and keep reading.

B.

JQ 0609

AVON

978-0-06-143438-9

978-0-06-164836-6

978-0-06-164837-3

978-0-06-146852-0

978-0-06-173383-3

978-0-06-154778-2

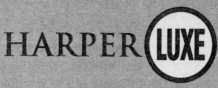

*Unforgettable, enthralling love stories,
sparkling with passion and adventure
from Romance's bestselling authors*